Eri

MW00944340

UNICORN BAIT

S.A. HUNTER

Other books by S.A. Hunter:

The sequel to Unicorn Bait ~
Dragon Prey *(coming in 2014)*

The Scary Mary Series ~
Scary Mary
Stalking Shadows
Broken Spirits

Cover design by Karri Klawiter
artbykarri.com

ISBN: 1494346575
ISBN-13: 978-1494346577

DEDICATION

To my mother, who always turned a blind eye when I stole
her romance novels.

CHAPTER ONE

"I always thought unicorns were magical and special. They were like horse angels. When I was a little girl, I wanted them to be real."—Naomi Taylor

Naomi stood in the center of the living room, though no one would know that was the purpose of the space. All the furniture was gone. The space was full of cardboard boxes with labels written in thick black marker. The labels said things like: clothes, dishes, books, knickknacks. Naomi's brother was stacking boxes to prepare to take them outside.

"We shouldn't just get rid of his stuff in a yard sale," Naomi said, experiencing a sense of betrayal on behalf of her late grandfather.

Her mother had asked them to come over to help set up, and Naomi had willingly agreed, knowing something had to be done with Grandpa's stuff, but now, being faced with the reality of selling everything twisted her heart. He'd loved all his stuff, and yes, there was a lot of it, but

1

each piece of clutter had been a beloved part of him.

Bobby, Naomi's younger brother, stood patiently waiting, holding a packed box to take outside. It was labeled "Sweaters." "A yard sale would've suited him. Someone will come today, see a little treasure where we see junk, and take it home to love, just like Grandpa did when he bought it at a yard sale. Anyway, you do not have room in your apartment."

"I know." She sighed and knelt down to open a box. Chipped plastic dishes with pale flowers painted on them were nestled inside. "His old 'china'!"

"No," Bobby said. His tone was clear. She was not taking it home.

"Someone should keep these."

"They aren't worth anything. They're cheap and cracked. Anyway, you don't have pretend tea parties anymore. At least, I hope not."

Naomi smiled as she gently picked up a saucer to examine. She remembered sitting at a small kitchen table with teddy bears seated around it, and Grandpa Harry and she clinking empty cups in a toast with pinkies in the air. She sighed and set the saucer back in the box. She knew that if she took the dishes, they would just stay in the box, be put in an already overcrowded closet, and never see the light of day again. Hopefully someone would buy them, give them a good home, and maybe let a little girl play with them.

"I want to go through the boxes first and make sure we're not selling anything that we may want to keep."

Bobby looked like he wanted to argue, but he just set down the box that he was holding and took the box of dishes instead. He left her to take it down to the front yard. Naomi began digging through more boxes.

She thought the footsteps she heard coming up the front steps belonged to Bobby returning for another box, but it was her mother who stuck her head in.

"What's taking so long?" her mother asked. She saw her answer. Naomi sat in the middle of the floor with crumpled newspaper and partially unpacked boxes all around her.

"No," her mother said the same way that Bobby had said earlier.

"But, Mom, I want to keep something."

Her mother looked at her with wry amusement. "Fine, but you can only keep three things. The rest has to go. Your father and I are already keeping a lot of stuff that your grandfather treasured. You can keep three mementos."

Naomi nodded. She knew her mother was just trying to keep her from weighing herself down with memories, but she wanted to keep a few reminders. Three would do.

Bobby came and took boxes as she was done with them. So many things were stamped with memories. Naomi didn't know what to choose. She finally settled on an old overcoat that Grandpa Harry had worn for years and had the smell of his cologne still on it. She wouldn't wear it, but it would always be in her coat closet so that she could rub her face against it and smell him for years to come. Next, she decided on his "fancy" cuff links. They were small garnets. She remembered him wearing them when she graduated from college. He had been so proud of her that day.

The third and final piece was difficult to choose. She took longer and longer with each box. She began to wonder if she would find her third memento. Finally, after digging through tens of boxes, she uncovered one that looked as though it had been packed by Grandpa Harry himself. The cardboard was discolored and weak. There were no black sharpie letters to indicate what was inside.

"Do you know what this is?" she asked Bobby, who stood leaning against the doorway.

"No." He came to stand beside her.

She opened the box carefully and peered inside. It

looked to be assorted knick knacks. She began to unpack them to see the items better.

"Oh, gross," she blurted, catching sight of the first item. She dropped it and wiped her hands on her jeans. The first item appeared to be a shrunken head.

"Cool." Bobby picked it up to peer at it. He turned it over and looked at it. "I don't think it's real," he said.

"Are you sure?" Naomi asked suspiciously. It looked real enough to her.

"Well, the 'Made in China' stamp sort of indicates it's not. It looks pretty real though," he said. He slipped the macabre item into his pocket. It seems Bobby had found himself a memento. Naomi shuddered and looked warily back into the box.

A necklace of animal teeth came next. Both siblings passed on it. The box contained snake skins, bird feathers, crystals, and at the bottom of the box, there was a glass case.

"I wonder what this is?" Naomi lifted it out. They both peered at it. The glass case was long and narrow and resting inside it appeared to be a bone.

"There's a slip of paper taped to the bottom," Bobby said. He plucked it off. The note was yellowed and brittle. He unfolded it and read carefully, "'*A unicorn horn, for Naomi's twenty-fifth birthday.*'"

"A unicorn horn?"

"Probably a carved piece of bone made to look like a unicorn horn."

"Do you think Grandpa really believed it?"

"No." He showed her the note. "Unicorn" had quotation marks around it.

She smiled at the glass case. It would certainly have been a unique gift. This was her third memento, the gift he meant to give her.

She felt an ache in her chest then. It was so like her grandfather to think of the dearest things to do or give to his family. A unicorn horn for a woman who had recently reached adulthood but still felt like a little girl sometimes. He had known that the innocence and fantasy would have appealed to her.

"You can take the rest of the boxes. I'm not looking through any more," she said.

"Are you sure?"

She nodded and took her three things out to her car. She couldn't look through his belongings any further. It was becoming too painful. She asked her mother if she could go home. She couldn't handle peddling Grandpa's belongings. She knew she'd been no help so far with the yard sale, but she couldn't bring herself to assist. She missed Grandpa Harry too much to hawk his personal possessions to complete strangers. Her mother gave her a hug and a pat on the back. She understood. It was why Naomi's father wasn't there either. He could accept letting everything go, but he couldn't help with the actual letting go.

At home, the coat went in Naomi's hall closet, the cuff links went in her jewelry box, and the unicorn horn was to go on her coffee table right after she washed the dust off of the glass case. She opened the top of the case and lifted the horn out. It certainly looked "authentic." The horn was about eighteen inches long and tapered to a point. She set it aside and filled the sink with water. After she'd cleaned the case up, she'd have a nice relaxing day at home. She'd planned to go through her mail, do the crossword, and maybe watch a little television. Yes, just a nice, relaxing, normal day.

Standing before her kitchen sink as it filled with water, Naomi smiled down at the unicorn horn, a little misty-eyed. She wished her grandfather had gotten the chance to give it to her as he'd intended, instead of her finding it while helping to clean out his place. Where he could've gotten it was beyond her, but then again, he'd always loved visiting junk shops and flea markets, picking up this and that as it struck his fancy.

Once the sink was full, she put the case in the soapy water to gently wash off the grime. She glanced over at the horn on her kitchen counter and chuckled. It might well be the oddest thing to ever grace her countertop. She'd been fascinated by unicorns like every young girl before her. She'd collected little figurines and had treasured them. The notion of owning a horn, even if it were a facsimile, gave her a little thrill and made her feel young and magical. She was too old to believe in unicorns anymore, but the idea was lovely, and it certainly *looked* authentic. She wondered what it was made of. She rinsed off the glass case and placed it in the drying rack. She shook off her hands and picked up the horn to wash it next.

It didn't feel plastic. It appeared to actually be some sort of bone. Naomi hoped it wasn't ivory. The horn was milky white, and spiraled to a point, which, on closer inspection, looked rather sharp. She put her fingertip to it to test, and promptly pricked herself. She jerked her hand back and put the wounded digit to her mouth. A drop of blood hung from the tip of the horn. Before she could wipe it off, the horn absorbed it.

There was a bright flash that startled Naomi and caused her to drop the horn. It broke in two on her kitchen's linoleum floor.

But Naomi wasn't there to pick it up.

It felt like an invisible trap door opened up beneath Naomi, but her feet stayed firmly planted on the ground. She blinked and swayed from the sudden vertigo. She rubbed her forehead in discomfort. She bent down to pick up the unicorn horn and yelped when her fingers encountered a hard packed floor rather than tile. She looked around her in panic and saw her kitchen was gone. In its place was a room with rough white walls. There were two broken benches and an overturned table. She didn't have a chance to look around more because the strange building's thatch roof was on fire.

She covered her mouth, but she was already coughing as she dashed from the single room building. She ran a couple of yards out and stopped. She bent over to gulp down some clean air. She didn't understand where she was or how she'd gotten there. She had no memory of leaving her apartment. She was sure she'd been in her kitchen a moment ago. She looked at her fingers and saw that they were still pruney. So how the devil had she gotten there? And where in Hell was she?

Her confusion was cut short and replaced by panic again when she was grabbed by her hair and wrenched upright.

A man with a smoke-stained face and greasy hair pulled her nose-to-nose with him. "Well, aren't you pretty," he said through piss yellow teeth.

Naomi reacted on instinct. She twisted in the man's grasp and clawed at his hand. Her nails gouged his skin. "Let go, asshole!" she demanded.

The repulsive man hissed and shoved her away. She landed on her backside and almost went head over heels. She scrambled to get up, but the man moved in and shoved a bloody sword into her face.

Sword? Her brain blinked at the choice of weapon, but pragmatism made her glad it wasn't a gun. She could outrun a sword, but not a bullet. The repulsive man had his other hand tucked against his stomach. She could see the edges of the angry scratches she'd given him.

"Gonna make you pay for that!" he snarled.

"Who are you? Where am I?" she demanded.

"The name's Hammond. And you're in a lot of trouble, lass. You're gonna wish you'd been sweet to ol'

Hammond when I'm done with you."

Naomi didn't agree. She thought she'd regret not going for his eyes. She began to inch back and gathered herself to spring up and run.

Hammond noticed her movements and moved in closer with the sword. "No need to go anywhere. We can have fun right here."

She went cross-eyed focusing on the bobbing sword point inches from her nose. Her stomach twisted at the way he said "fun." She highly doubted his definition of fun synched with hers. She was proved right when he began loosening his belt.

Naomi had never been a violent person. Sure, she'd been in her share of schoolyard scraps, but those were far behind her. She didn't even carry pepper spray. But she'd made a vow to herself long ago. It was something every woman considered at one point or another, and that was what she would do if a man attacked her and tried to rape her. And Naomi had sworn to herself that she would fight. She would not be a victim.

Her hand closed over a fistful of dirt. She wasn't going to let this gap-toothed, Ren Fest reject touch her. She waited until his belt was undone, and his trousers fell to his ankles. She couldn't help noting the tiny Tootsie Roll bobbing so proudly between his legs. He leered down at her as he grabbed his minuscule member with his free hand and waggled it at her. She smirked back at him and threw the handful of grit in his face. She hit him square across the eyes. He dropped his penis to wipe his face, but unfortunately, he didn't drop the sword. He blindly swung out. She barely ducked it.

"You goddamn stinking whore. I'll skewer you!"

She took off while Hammond struggled to pull his pants back up. She quickly made it to a street and raced down it. She scanned for help or someplace to hide, but every building she passed had all of their doors and windows boarded up. She also came across more men fighting with swords. She skirted around them and kept her eyes averted. She could see red in her peripheral vision, but she would not let herself turn to confirm. The screams were bad enough. She was definitely no longer in Atlanta. She doubted she was even in Georgia.

She was peering around a corner to gauge the safety of going down a new thoroughfare when someone grabbed her hair again from behind. Hammond jerked her back against him. She clawed again at his hand, but instead of letting her go this time, he raised his sword. She froze when the blade touched her throat.

When making that oath to herself, she'd shied away from really thinking about bodily harm. It was one thing to swear to fight, but it was another thing to consider dying; she had to consider that now. The sword was very sharp against her throat. She was scared to struggle in case it cut her.

"Now, are you going to be a good girl or a dead girl?" he asked.

Her eyes swiveled as far as they could to look back into his bloodshot eyes. She couldn't help it—her teeth began to chatter. She couldn't bring herself to consider either option.

"How about a good woman? The world could always use more of them," said a woman from behind them.

Hammond lowered his sword as he tried to twist around to see the newcomer, but before he could fully turn, a loud crack sounded, and he went limp. The sword fell, and he released Naomi's hair. She whirled around to find him crumbled to the ground before a pair of granny boots. Her eyes traveled up over a long brown skirt and white peasant blouse to arrive at a wrinkled face with a pair of steely blue eyes peering at her.

The old woman hefted up the frying pan to consider it. "And I don't even like to cook."

Naomi giggled with a touch of hysteria at the old woman holding the frying pan, AKA her savior. She smacked her hands over her mouth to hold in her panicked mirth.

"Are you okay, lass?"

She nodded, still covering her mouth.

The old woman looked down at the sword. "You gonna pick that up?"

Naomi thought about shaking her head. The sword had dried blood on it. But she could hear distant, angry male shouts, indicating more Hammonds in the area. She picked it up. With the sword in her hands, her panic dropped a few degrees. She took a deep breath and asked the skillet-wielding woman, "Do you know anyplace we can go that's safe?"

The old woman nodded. She grabbed the sleeve of Naomi's sweatshirt and pulled her down the street. "Why didn't you leave with the others?" her savior asked.

"What?" Naomi stumbled as she struggled to manage the sword and fall in step with the old woman.

The old woman stopped to peek around a corner. "Damn it, they've probably blocked every road," she muttered. Naomi took a quick peek too. There was a barricade blocking the street. A couple of men stood sentry at it.

"Where am I? I just want to go home."

"You can't go home. You have to escape, but every way is most likely blocked."

"Where am I? What's going on?"

The old woman turned to her with narrowed eyes. "What do you mean, 'What's going on'? The town's being pillaged by Tavik and his horde! If you don't get out of here, you'll become a spoil of war. I've managed to get all the other women and children out. Where have you been?"

"I just got here. One minute I was in my kitchen, and then I was in some burning building. I don't know how I got here. Or where here is."

The old woman's eyebrows rose. "You arrived by magic?"

Taking her comment as sarcasm and finding that offensive—Because hey, she'd just been attacked!—Naomi threw up her hands, wagging the sword in the air. "Yeah, it was magic. Abracadabra! Poof! I'm here. Where is here?"

"So you're a witch?" the old woman asked.

Naomi's arms dropped back to her sides. "What?"

"You're a witch?"

Naomi began to think that the old woman hadn't been joking about the magic. "No, I'm not a witch."

"Did a witch send you?" Naomi really didn't like how seriously the old woman was interrogating her about this.

"No, and there's no such thing as magic or witches."

The old woman crossed her arms and drew back to coolly look down her nose at her. "Then how did you get here?"

"I don't know."

Agatha shrugged. "Then it could've been magic."

"There's no such thing!" Naomi exclaimed, exasperated that she had to even state this.

Agatha was unperturbed. "Then how did you get here?" she asked coolly.

Seeing how this could keep going for quite some time and the sound of fighting men creeping closer, Naomi capitulated. "All right! If it makes you happy, it might've been magic."

"Believe me, dear, I am not happy about any of this. You are in grave danger."

She slumped. "How are we going to get out of this?"

The old woman cupped her chin and appeared to go into deep thought. Naomi waited tensely. They should probably be moving. The old woman's eyes would lift slowly up every few seconds and then quickly fall back to the ground with a muttered, "No, that won't work."

After a few minutes, the old woman shook her head. "I don't know, but I promise I'll do everything I can to help you."

For some reason, Naomi felt like she really meant it. This old woman may have been crazy, but a determined crazy person could accomplish surprising things sometimes. Naomi stuck out her hand. "Thanks. My name's Naomi."

The old woman's eyes snapped to her. "What?"

"Um, Naomi. I was named after my maternal grandmother. What's your—"

The old woman grabbed a fistful of Naomi's sweatshirt and started dragging her down a lane.

"Where are we going?" Naomi asked, trying to keep her pilfered sword from banging into everything as the old woman pulled her along.

The old woman pointed up the slope. "To the castle," she told her.

What formed in Naomi's imagination when she heard the term "castle" was the Disney trademark. What was on top of the hill was a cluster of stumpy stone towers with a wall around it. It didn't appear to be on fire at least.

"Do you think we'll be safe there?"

"Yes, I know someone."

"So they'll be able to hide us or get us to safety?"

"Don't worry. I have a plan."

She had a plan now? How about sharing? "So what's the plan?"

"Don't worry about it."

Nervously, Naomi asked, "Does it involve witches and magic?" Because if it did, Naomi was going to start working on a plan B.

"Not yet."

Naomi wasn't sure how to take that. She decided to stick to safer topics. "So what's your name?"

"Agatha."

"And where are we?"

"Harold's Pass." That didn't tell Naomi anything.

"How far is that from Atlanta?"

The old woman shrugged her shoulders. "I don't know where in Terratu that is."

"Terratu?"

The woman looked at her slightly askance. "Yes, Terratu. The land," she made a sweeping motion with her arm.

The name meant nothing to her. Naomi wished she paid more attention in geography class. She tried again to get her bearings. "What's near here?"

"The Akron Mountains, the road to Ravant."

"What?"

"Do you really not know how you came here?"

Naomi started thinking about what she could remember. There'd been so many immediate things to worry about, mainly Hammond, that she hadn't had a chance to really think. Here she was on a footpath headed to a castle, dragging a sword with someone else's blood on it, with no clue how she got into this mess or how she was going to get out of it.

"No, I really have no idea."

"Well, I think it's safe to assume that your luck is atrocious."

Naomi couldn't argue with that.

When they reached the castle, they had to skirt past more fighting men in the courtyard. The two women slunk through a large pair of wooden doors into an enormous room. There were people talking loudly and running everywhere. It sounded like they were looking for someone. Agatha stuck to the wall and led the way to a staircase. After several twists and turns, they ducked into a bedroom and closed the door behind them. The furniture was large and adorned with ornate scroll work. It looked like someone important slept there.

"Whose room is this?" Naomi asked, not for a second thinking it was Agatha's.

"Does it matter? We're safe for now." The old woman went over to an upright bureau and began rummaging through it. Naomi leaned against the wall. She hoped someone would show up soon to help them. She couldn't wait to get back home.

"Here, put this on." Agatha took the sword and pushed a gown into her hands.

Naomi took it but was befuddled by order. "Why?"

"For a disguise! You need to look like one of us."

Naomi's confusion lifted. That made pretty good sense. She did stick out in her jeans and sweatshirt. She quickly stripped off her clothes and threw on the gown.

"How do I look?" she asked.

Agatha nodded with approval. "Like a lady."

"Is that good?"

There was pounding at the door. Naomi jumped and looked wildly around for something to protect herself. "Where's the sword?"

Agatha shook her head. "You won't need it."

"What's the plan? What should we say to them?"

"'No, ack, don't, let go!' That sort of thing."

"What?"

Before she could demand further explanation, the door burst open, and a group of men with swords streamed in. One turned back and shouted into the corridor, "Alert the others, we've found her!"

Naomi didn't like the sound of that. "Found who? Wait! What's going on?"

They grabbed her by both arms and began to drag her from the room. The men pushed Agatha back.

"Don't fear, Lady Naomi. Everything will be all right!" Agatha shouted.

"What! Wait!"

The men hauled Naomi out. She kicked and yelled, but the men didn't let her go. She only knew one thing. Agatha had set her up. That just went to show, never trust crazy old women. They'll give you up to medieval throwbacks every time.

The men took Naomi back into the large hall where now there were more men, but thankfully no fighting. The men hauling her muscled their way through the others until they reached the dais at the end of the hall.

One man broke off and stepped forward. He knelt on one knee and announced, "Sir, we've secured the Lord's lady. The castle is yours."

She looked up at the dais to see who the soldier was speaking to, and gaped. The man, who stood above her, had on some sort of full helmet. The helmet was made of a dark metal and covered his face completely. There were two long rectangular holes for his eyes and small holes punched out over the lower half for breathing. He had on full armor which had splashes of red still wet on it. In one hand, he gripped a massive sword. It was wet with red, too. All he needed was a severed head in his other hand to complete the picture. When he turned toward her, she felt the weight of his gaze like a shroud. She hoped it wasn't her head that was supposed to complete the picture.

She gulped and said, "I really think there's been a mistake."

CHAPTER TWO

The horn of the unicorn is called an alicorn.

The helmeted man stepped down from the dais and approached her. Naomi strained back in a feeble attempt to keep away from him, but the soldiers held her firmly in place and would not give her even a quarter of an inch. The masked man came to stand in front of her. He was not tall. He had to be about five foot seven. Instead of looking up to quiver in fear, she looked directly into the dark eye-holes where she saw not a glint of humanity reflected back to her. Just black pits.

"Do you know who I am?" he asked. His voice was deep and a bit scratchy. The voice matched the helmet too well.

She shook her head. She could feel tears creeping out of the corners of her eyes. This was just too unreal. What the hell was happening to her? Where was Agatha? How was she going to get out of this?

"I am Lord Tavik. I have taken your husband's land, castle, and by right of conquest, you are mine as well."

"Who the hell do you think I am?" Naomi blurted out.

"Lady Naomi, I offer you a choice. You can die here today or become my bride. Which do you choose?"

Naomi shook her head wildly. "Wait, wait, wait. You've got me confused with someone else. My name is Naomi, but I'm Naomi Taylor from the United States. An old woman named Agatha brought me here. This is all just one huge mistake. I don't even know where I am or anything." He had to believe her. Why wasn't anyone stepping forward to tell him that she wasn't this Lady Naomi? She looked around the hall, but from what she could see, all of the men stood at attention for Lord Tavik. They were his men. Where were the castle's inhabitants? Her eyes dropped to the dripping sword. It was her silent answer. She felt sick.

"An old woman named Agatha?" the masked man repeated.

She bobbed her head.

"What is your choice?"

She boggled at him. "I'm not Lady Naomi!"

He stepped closer and raised his sword. "You will choose."

"Between marrying you and dying?"

He nodded.

She couldn't believe the question.

"I will give you until the preparations are complete to decide. Take her back to her room," he told the men holding her.

They pulled her out of the room. The trip back to the room was another blur. She barely kept her feet under her. Her brain was still sputtering over the situation. None of this made any sense, and she seemed to be powerless to stop any of it.

The soldiers thrust her back into the room she'd been

in when they found her, locking the door behind her. Agatha was no longer there. She was alone, didn't know where she was, who these people were, or what was going to happen to her. She began to worry that she was in a very bad situation.

There was a piece of folded paper on the bed. She picked it up and read,

Naomi,

I am sorry for abandoning you, but this is the safest place for you. If Tavik takes you as his bride, you shouldn't come to harm as long as you go along with whatever he wants. I'll try to contact you once you're settled in his castle. Do not fear, I will help you.

Sincerely,
Agatha

P.S. You should tear up this letter and throw it out the window. Tavik does not like me and would take it very ill if he knew you were acquainted with me.

Naomi read the postscript three times. Each time she read it, it got funnier. She tore up the letter, still giggling over the fact that she was doomed. She wandered to the narrow window and threw out the bits of paper.

Watching the paper float away, she looked down. She was several stories up. Below was a medieval courtyard. Men ran around shouting at each other and carrying bundles. She guessed that's what pillaging looked like. A lot of shouting, running, and carrying. *And grabbing, can't forget grabbing,* she thought as she rubbed her bruised arms and neck.

When she lifted her eyes to the sky, she gasped and stumbled back. She rubbed her eyes to clear her vision and looked back into the bright day sky. Her vision was still mistaken. She must have something in her eyes. She rubbed them until they watered and became irritated, but something had to be wrong with them. She must have bumped her head and was now seeing double, because she could not be seeing two moons, never mind the two moons were not identical and looked nothing like the Earth's moon. Her vision was definitely messed up, that's why she saw one ruddy-red moon, and another moon that was a lopsided, pale yellow oval. There had to be something wrong with her eyes because if this were real, her situation became effectively much, much worse.

What in the world had she gotten herself into? *What world indeed?* her mind repeated with an unhinged twitter. She paced away from the window as her brain tried to push away the idea, but when she turned to pace back, she was facing the window with a view of the two moons.

The very idea was impossible, improbable, impracticable, impermissible, and any other words that began with "im" that meant that this *could not be happening*. She could not have somehow gone to another planet. Maybe her apartment had *imploded*, she was in a coma, and her *imagination* was creating all of this. She pinched herself to test her theory. She felt the pinch, but she refused to accept the tactile evidence.

She looked back up into the sky and placed her fingers around the view of the ruddy moon and closed her fingers, pinching it, but when she moved her hand, the lopsided moon still hung in the sky. *This couldn't be real*, she kept repeating to herself. None of this could be real.

There was a soft tap at the door. She wrenched her eyes from the sky. The door was gently pushed open partway, and a stout, middle-aged woman wearing an apron looked around its edge at her. She gave Naomi an unsure smile. Naomi blinked back at her. Seeming to take her blank expression as welcome, the woman opened the door fully and carried in a large tray. She took it to a small table, and Naomi crept over to her. She silently implored the unknown woman to turn and fix all her problems. This was just a big joke, right? She was about to be told she was on hidden camera? That had to be it, but no TV-show host popped out of the wardrobe. The woman pulled out a chair and held it for her. Naomi took a seat and waited for everything to be explained.

The woman placed a plate before her with fruit and cheese on it. The fruit was normal: grapes and peach slices. This had to be Earth, then. Some alien planet wouldn't have the same fruit or people. Everyone looked human, except for the guy in the mask. He probably had tentacles or something, but everyone else looked like someone she could meet on the street, except for their clothes. The Amish dressed more modernly than these people. The silent woman poured something into a cup and set it down by the plate. The fermented smell of wine wafted out.

She didn't touch the food or wine. She felt too unsettled to keep anything down. She swallowed and hunched forward. In a near whisper, she asked, "Please, help me."

The woman's eyes flicked to her for a second. The tension around the unknown woman's eyes showed pity was there. Maybe she could help her? Maybe not solve all her problems, but maybe help her in some small way...

"Look, my name's Naomi, but I'm not a Lady with a capital *L*. My name's Naomi Taylor, and I shouldn't be here. I don't know what happened, but I'm here by accident. Please help me."

The woman continued to putter with the tray. "You can weave whatever tales you like. You will not be freed."

Her frustration made Naomi spring up. "But I'm not her! I don't know where I am. I don't know how I got here, and I just want to go home!"

The serving woman turned away to leave the table.

Naomi grabbed her arm. "There has to be someone here who knew this Lady Naomi? Find them and bring them. They'll tell you I'm not her!"

"Any servant still in the castle will, of course, agree with you and claim you aren't Lady Naomi to assist you in an escape. It's not going to happen, girl." She removed Naomi's hand and walked over to the wardrobe. She opened it and began going through the gowns inside.

Naomi flopped back into the chair. Everyone was insane. There was no help on the horizon, and she was alone. She pressed the back of her hand to her mouth to hold back her sobs. Her brain was a maelstrom of confusion and anxiety. Questions flashed in her mind like lightning, but there was no answering thunder.

"Milady, you should eat. You'll need all the strength you can muster for the upcoming event."

Naomi blinked dumbly at her again. The woman indicated the fruit and wine before her. She glanced at the plate. She wanted to hurl it at the wall. She wanted to break stuff and scream. She turned her eyes away and found her gaze unconsciously turning to the window. The two moons were still there, and it felt like they were mocking her, asking her if she really think she could understand any of this, that any sense could be made of anything. She could almost hear laughter coming down from the sky. She dropped her eyes to the floor. She wished the room didn't have a window.

Taking one last stab at some sort of information, she asked, "What's your name?"

The woman turned from the wardrobe. "My name is Yula. I am a cook for Lord Tavik." She gave a slight curtsy.

"Nice to meet you, Yula. Now where am I?"

Yula looked puzzled and glanced around the room. "Isn't this your chamber?"

Naomi flicked her eyes around the room and turned them back to her. "No, this isn't my room."

"Would you like to be moved to your room?"

She slumped in her chair. "I don't live in this castle.

I'm not who you think I am. I'm a US citizen."

Yula shook her head. "You can lie all you want. It won't change anything, but it would make Lord Tavik angry, and he isn't someone to make angry."

"You mean the scary guy in the mask?"

Yula nodded. "Yes, the 'scary guy in the mask.' He holds your fate in his hands. I suggest you be careful around him."

"Was he serious about the marriage thing? I mean, why marry me? How does he know I'm Lady Naomi? What if I'm not her and he marries me, and the real Lady Naomi pops up? What then?"

"You better pray another Lady Naomi doesn't 'pop up.'"

"But it's possible, since I'm not her. The real Lady Naomi could be somewhere hiding in the castle right now."

"If it's proven—" and Yula stressed the "if"—"that you're not Lady Naomi, then you will be executed."

Naomi sat back in shock. Well, that answered that question. She stared at the floor as she chewed on her thumbnail trying to think of something to do to help herself. She was stuck on another planet, and her only hope, a crazy old woman with a frying pan, had disappeared. She remembered Agatha's letter with a grimace. She'd already ruined her chances with her big mouth. The wedding was probably off, but hey, the execution was still on. She could feel the maniacal giggles creeping up again.

She slowly raised her eyes when she saw Yula had come to stand in front of her. The servant didn't seem mean. She'd been fairly nice to Naomi, really, as far jailers went.

"Is there anything else I can get for you, milady?"

"Yes, a way out of here," she mumbled against her thumb.

Yula absently nodded her head, not as though she

would help Naomi escape but only to acknowledge that she had spoken. "I will be happy to fetch anything you need."

"You can't keep me here," she said, but her voice didn't hold any conviction; it held despair.

All of this is ridiculous, she reasoned. She could not be on another planet. How had she arrived here if she were? Her eyes turned back to the window to look at the two moons. Only one thing came to mind. Though she could not believe she was pursuing this, she asked, "What do you know about unicorn horns?"

The cook looked at her in surprise. "Unicorns are rare and wondrous beasts. Their horns can heal the sick and purify water. They are very brave and wild. Only someone of unbroken virtue may approach the beasts."

"Do you know anything else about their horns? What can they do?"

"What is your interest in unicorn horns?"

She lowered her eyes. "I think one brought me here."

"Do you still have it?"

She shook her head. "I dropped it."

Yula sighed. "That is tragic."

"Could I get another unicorn horn?"

"I couldn't say. I've never considered it."

"Where would I find one?" Naomi knew her hope that they were stocked in the corner store was a sick delusion, but she still held out hope.

The other woman shrugged her shoulders. "I have no idea."

Well, there went that avenue of hope. Time to change the subject. Naomi cast about for ideas and only one thing outside of escape interested her. After all, he might or might not be her future husband. "What does Lord Tavik look like?"

"No one knows. He wears the helm at all times. Anyone who has dared to try to remove it did not live to regret it."

"Why won't he let others see his face?"

Yula shrugged again.

Naomi dropped her head and slumped. "God, I hope I'm dreaming."

Yula reached out and pinched her hard on the arm, making Naomi yelp.

"You're not dreaming," the older woman said.

Naomi glared at her and rubbed her bruised arm. "Fine, this is all real, but none of it makes any sense! When I say I'm not from here, I mean not from this planet. My planet is Earth. We have only one moon, and we don't have unicorns or scary guys in metal masks."

The cook began to bustle around the room again. "It sounds nice, but you're here now, and the day is growing old, and I have to get you ready for the ceremony. And you will be ready, no matter where you think you're from. None of it matters now. Accept it."

Naomi was surprised by Yula's sudden harshness. "What's wrong?"

"Just accept your lot. It'll be easier if you do. Now slip this on." She held out a long simple gown of white. Naomi took it to feel the fabric. The action of taking another gown in this room made her cautious.

There was a tap at the door. Yula went to answer it. She stepped outside and left Naomi alone. Naomi went back to the window to stare at the two moons. The gown, most likely her wedding dress, hung from her hands. She shifted the fabric until her right hand was free. She brought the tip of her finger to her face. Faintly, she could see a red prick. She rubbed her thumb against the tiny wound. That little pinprick was how she got here.

She could hear Yula on the other side of the door. She was speaking to someone, and the other voice sounded familiar. The voice was deep and a bit scratchy, and it didn't sound happy.

The door flew open, and Tavik strode in. Yula followed at his heels. Naomi jumped back. The white gown slipped from her hands to puddle at her feet. She wondered if she should pick it up, but then reasoned it didn't matter. From the looks of her visitor's stance, she probably wouldn't need it.

"How do you know Agatha?" he demanded.

She flinched at his accusative tone and edged away. "She tricked me into coming here and putting on a gown."

"Tricked you how?"

She picked at a seam of a sleeve. "I was being attacked by this soldier, and she knocked him out with a frying pan. She told me to follow her to a safe place, and that's how I ended up here. She gave me the gown to put on, saying it would be a disguise, and not really thinking, I did what she said."

"You expect me to believe that?"

Her head jerked up. She stared into the eye holes of his mask. "I don't know what you'll believe. All I know is what happened."

He stood silently, staring at her; at least it felt like he was staring at her. She couldn't tell for certain due to the mask. She began to fidget in earnest.

"If you're not Lady Naomi, where is she?"

She plucked at her sleeves. She really wished she were in her sweatshirt and jeans. She felt like an idiot arguing in the gown: her "disguise." She wondered what had happened to her clothes. Had Agatha taken them? Or had the soldiers destroyed them?

"I don't know. I'd never heard of her until everyone assumed I was her. I'm not her."

"You look like her."

Her eyes shot to him. "What?"

He snorted. "Yes, Lady Naomi," he drawled.

"I'm not her!" She stamped her foot in frustration.

Tavik crossed his arms. This didn't seem to bother him

at all. He didn't care. He'd kill her or marry her. Whichever. Why didn't this matter to him? Wouldn't he care if he were about to get married? Oh man, what was marriage like here? Were women no better than indentured servants? How many wives did he have?

"Have you made your choice?" he asked.

Her hands clenched into fists. "Choice?" she echoed.

"Between death and marriage."

"But I'm not Lady Naomi!" She knew this argument wasn't getting her anywhere, and the thought made her sick.

"The preparations are almost complete."

She turned her eyes to Yula, but the serving woman was not going to help her. She was standing by with the damned wedding gown ready to dress her.

"What can I do to make you believe me?" Naomi pleaded.

"Nothing," he said.

"You're going to kill me if I don't marry you?"

"Yes."

"Why?"

"To cement my victory. You must either die or be taken by me."

His use of the word "taken" made Naomi's stomach churn.

"This doesn't make any sense. Why does this Lady Naomi matter? You've clearly won. Just let me go."

"Because I wasn't able to catch the coward Lord Gerald before he fled. I must now find another symbolic way to claim this hold. My only other options are I take the lord's lady or kill her."

"If I weren't here, what would you do? Would you grab some poor girl off the street and call her Lady Naomi?"

He didn't reply.

"Milady, just do as you're told. It'll go better for you,"

Yula said.

"But I'm not her," she repeated.

"You're either her or the poor girl off the street I call Lady Naomi and then kill. It's your choice."

Naomi froze. She didn't really like either option, and it was her big mouth that had put that second, even less appealing option on the table.

"What if we compromise?" she asked.

"What?" Tavik demanded.

Yula stared at her in disbelief.

"I'll marry you if we agree on one thing."

"What's that?"

"No sex."

Yula dropped the wedding gown.

Naomi really hoped she hadn't just pissed him off so bad that he beheaded her on the spot. She stared at him and waited. Without comment, he grabbed her arm and pulled her out of the room. Yula scrambled to gather the wedding gown and followed at his heels.

Naomi tried to stop him or at least slow him down, but her slippers slid along the stone floor.

"What are you doing? Let go of me!"

"Lord Tavik, she's not properly dressed!"

He ignored both of them and continued to drag Naomi down the corridor toward the hall. She struggled as best she could. She kicked out at his feet to trip him up and pried at his fingers. All she seemed to do was annoy him.

He stopped and turned to her.

"So I guess you're just going to kill me. Is that it? Well, I hope you rot in Hell!"

Without a word, Tavik picked her up and put her over his shoulder.

"Now wait a minute!"

He again began striding down the corridor. Her weight didn't seem to faze him at all.

"Put me down!"

He still ignored her. She tried to kick him, but he wrapped his other arm over her legs and pinned them to his chest. With her legs pinned, she dug her elbows into his shoulder blades. She hoped it was bothering him, but he didn't shift her or do anything to indicate discomfort. When they entered the hall, all the soldiers fell silent. She frantically looked around the room for someone to help her, but all eyes were on Tavik.

"Someone tell him I'm not Lady Naomi, please!"

No one spoke up.

Tavik stepped onto the dais and finally put her down. Three men in robes were there beside a lit brazier. They had the dour expressions of officiating priests. Tavik held her upper arms in a viselike grip. She quickly understood why as she watched one of the priests pull a branding rod out of the brazier. The brand glowed red. It was a shaped like a large dour *T*. The priest stepped toward her. Her eyes widened.

"What the hell? This is how you people get married?"

Tavik jerked her close to him and growled, "You will wear my brand so all will know you belong to me."

"That's sick. Let me go!"

He shook her roughly. "You will do this." His voice was harsh.

Her eyes couldn't leave the priest who stood waiting with the rod. Tavik suddenly let her go, and she stumbled back.

She looked around the room at the crowd of impassive soldiers. "No, this is insanity. You people are barbarians. I will not do this!"

"You will do this, or you will die."

"And if I let you do this, what happens next? What else are you going to do to me? There are worse things than death!"

He reached out and jerked her to him again. She looked up into his grisly helm. When she was this close, she could just make out his eyes. They were blue.

"I promise you that this will be the worst that you will suffer. After this, you will have my protection. You will be my wife."

His assurances made her laugh. His wife! Oh yes, everything would be lovely if she'd just marry this guy. It was better than death!

"Just do this, Naomi, please," he whispered.

The plea surprised her. She stopped resisting to think a moment. She averted her eyes from the priest and the glowing branding iron. Could she go along with this? Did she have a choice?

"What about the deal?" she whispered.

Tavik's grasp tightened on her arm, and he pulled her forward. She tried to stop him, but he was like a moving mountain. Her feet slid across the dais. He handed her over to two of the priests, who each took an arm. They held onto her with stony faces.

This was not happening. She was not here. "No," she kept saying over and over, but no one was listening to her.

The head priest handed Tavik the branding iron. Her eyes widened.

"No, please no, don't do this!"

He showed no indication that he was listening to her. She really began to panic when the priests ripped open the back of her dress.

"Stop! What are you doing?" she cried out.

No one was listening to her. The priests tightened their holds on her arms. Tavik stood before her with the red branding iron. The priests began to turn her around. She struggled to stop them. She shook her head over and over.

"Wait, please. Don't do this!" she begged. She craned her neck around desperately to see Tavik. The priests' hands dug into her arms to keep her from turning back. She watched in horror as Tavik lifted his arm and leveled the branding iron at her back.

"Hold her completely still," he said.

The priests held her tight. She couldn't move an inch. She didn't have a chance.

When the iron touched her back, she screamed. She had never been hurt this badly in her life. She had never broken a bone or cut herself so severely as to need stitches. This was the absolute worst physical experience ever. The pain was so intense she saw large black spots. Only the priests' wooden arms kept her from collapsing.

Everything was leeching gray. She tried not to think about the new smell in the air that made her want to retch. Dimly, she was aware of being moved around. An arm went around her waist and another under her knees that lifted her up. She looked up into the grisly helm of Lord Tavik.

"You bastard," she whispered and passed out.

CHAPTER THREE

Unicorns mate for life.

Naomi resurfaced from unconsciousness unwillingly. She was lying on her stomach. She didn't know how long she'd been out, but it didn't feel like long enough. Her back ached and still felt like it was on fire. The actual brand shot pain out in a steady throb.

From her right, she heard Tavik ask, "Why hasn't she awakened yet?"

Yula's voice came from her other side. "She'll be fine. She's just had a few too many shocks is all. She needs rest."

Naomi couldn't stop the sigh that escaped her lips when she felt a cool balm spread across the branding mark. There was no hiding her consciousness now. She let out a low groan and tried to sit up. She quickly regretted that and hissed in pain.

"Lie still," Yula ordered.

She let herself collapse back on the bed. "My day can't get any worse, can it?" She turned her head, and through her curtain of hair, looked at Tavik sitting by her bedside. "Oh, my mistake. The day isn't even half over, and I bet you've got all sorts of wedding day festivities lined up. What's next—thumb screws or Chinese water torture?"

He leaned forward. "Remember the deal you proposed?"

She nodded.

"I accepted."

Her eyes widened.

"Then why didn't you say so?"

He rose and left without answer. He'd accepted her deal. What did that mean? He wouldn't have sex with her, but what else might he do to her?

She turned and looked at Yula. The other woman was carefully dipping a cloth into a basin of water. Her eyes never leaving her task.

"What do you make of that?" Naomi asked.

Yula shook her head. "The affairs of man and wife should remain between man and wife."

"You really think we're man and wife? More like man and cattle. That's the only thing we brand where I'm from."

That evening, Naomi stood at the window in a light trance, staring at the two moons. The brand was bandaged, and she'd changed into another dress. Yula had been her constant companion. They hadn't said much to each other, but if she hadn't been there, Naomi would've jumped out that window.

Yula could rouse her if she spoke to her, but if silent, Naomi's gaze would float back to the night sky without focus. Yula had expressed worry that her dazed behavior was due to her injury, but Naomi had assured her that she was fine. She'd told her that she just had a lot on her mind, but that had been a lie.

She did not have "a lot" on her mind. All she could think about was how she'd get home, and she had no idea. She didn't understand how she'd arrived there, so couldn't fathom how to reverse it. She wanted to go home. She wanted her one bedroom apartment back. She wanted to return to her bank teller job. She wanted her family. She quickly veered away from thoughts of her family in fear of tears. It wouldn't do to break down. She didn't want to distress Yula. She turned her mind back to thinking about how she would get home, and her mind went blank again.

Yula gathered her mending and stood. Naomi's eyes barely glanced in her direction at the woman's movement.

"I am retiring now. Lord Tavik should be with you shortly. Is there anything I can do for you before I leave?"

"I guess Lord Tavik has to stay here for appearance's sake, huh?"

She nodded her head. She didn't look comfortable.

"What is it, Yula?"

She averted her eyes, but straightened her shoulders. "You asked for my thoughts earlier, and I wasn't sure what to say, and I'm still not sure, but I will say this: Lord Tavik is not exactly a cruel lord, but he's a lord and used to getting whatever he wants, and this agreement of yours— I'm not sure how much weight it has. I mean, what reason does he have to keep it? Not that I am questioning my lord's word, but…"

"Stop worrying, Yula. I think he'll keep his word. He didn't have to agree to get me to the altar." Naomi rubbed her bruised biceps as silent testament.

"But why would he agree to not bed you? It makes no sense."

"Does he have a mistress or someone he sees regularly?"

Yula shook her head. "No one that I know of. I've

never seen him take up with any woman, actually."

Naomi sighed and turned back to the window. Their speculation didn't seem to be getting them anywhere. "Well, we'll just have to wait and see."

"I'll keep an ear out for you. Call me if you need anything." Naomi wondered if what the older woman meant was *"Scream if you need more bandages."*

After Yula let herself out and locked the door behind her, Naomi stayed at the window. She was obsessed with the moons. Their alienness inspired revulsion, but she couldn't stop staring at them. She'd decided that the red one looked like a giant, angry potato while the yellow one looked like a hard-boiled egg. They must torment the hungry. She wasn't hungry. She wasn't cold. In fact, after the "wedding"—she couldn't help curling her lip at having to call an act of physical harm and extreme terror a wedding—she'd had a quiet day. She'd taken a nap for most of the afternoon, and when she'd woken, she'd eaten a thick stew. It had been quite tasty, and Yula had been very pleased when she'd complimented it. No one else had come to the room, and the activity outside had quieted.

Fed up finally by the Laurel and Hardy moons, she turned away from the window and went to the hearth. How was she supposed to get home? Who could possibly help her? Her mind went blank again at the questions, and she slipped a little further into desolation. She picked up a fire poker and began jabbing the red embers, stirring up sparks. She didn't know what she was doing, but she needed something to do. When she heard the door unlock, she jabbed the poker harder into the embers. That would be her husband. Her lip curled again.

"It's not good to stir a fire too much," Tavik said from the doorway.

She straightened from the fireplace and watched smoke waft off the poker. It suddenly reminded her of the branding iron. She wanted to drop it, but the thought of Tavik picking up another piece of burning hot metal near her was terrifying. She turned to face him with it shaking minutely in her hand. The first thing she noticed, and would probably continue to notice for some time, was that he had the helm on. For some reason, she began to think about others who regularly wore masks: robbers, serial killers, rapists, monsters, vigilantes, opera singers. She really doubted he sang or protected innocent people in the night, but she wasn't sure of anything else.

"Is something wrong?" he asked.

The question jerked a laugh out of her. "Wrong? What could be wrong?"

Her grip tightened on the fire poker as he crossed the room, but he went past the bed to take a seat at the small table. He relaxed in the chair with his legs crossed and one arm resting on the table. Her hand started to ache from the fire poker.

"I think we have much to discuss," he said.

She cocked her head to the side. "Discuss what?"

He shrugged his broad shoulders and slumped back in his chair. "We could begin with your claim that you are not Lady Naomi. Do you still hold to that?"

She nodded.

"But your name is Naomi."

She nodded again. She understood fully now why Agatha had stopped in her tracks when she'd given her name. The plan had probably begun to form then.

"You say you were brought here by trickery."

She nodded one more time.

"And the witch's name was Agatha."

Tired of glumly nodding, she ventured, "It seems like you know her."

"Yes, and if I find out that you are in collusion with her, your punishment will be absolute."

"Believe me, I only met her today." Absolute? She hefted the poker up, forgetting about the ache.

"Tell me your story."

She raised her eyebrows at the request, surprised he

was willing to listen. "I'm not from here. Terratu I mean. I'm from a very faraway place. I don't know how I got here. I was attacked by a soldier, and Agatha helped me fight him off. She brought me here and put me in a gown. I trusted her because she helped me with Hammond, and there was no one else to turn to. Then all of this happened."

"How do you think you came here?"

As ridiculous as it seemed to her, she was sure it was the unicorn horn, but she wasn't about to tell him that. "I don't know."

"But Agatha brought you to the castle."

"Led me here like a stupid, sacrificial lamb."

"Why do you think she did that?"

She shrugged. "She said she'd gotten all the women and children away safely already, but that all the ways were blocked now. I guess she was lying. She sure didn't get me away or safe."

"My men think you are the Lady Naomi. You will let them continue to think that. If you try to escape, you will be punished. If Agatha tries to contact you, I want to know about it immediately. I don't think she is done with you. And I have unfinished business with her."

"Why do you want everyone to think I'm this Lady Naomi?"

"Because this is over if I have her. I can return to my fortress victorious, and everything settles down for a while."

"What about the real Lady Naomi? What if she turns up?"

"If she has any sense, she'll go very far away and change her name. She knows what will happen if I find her."

She didn't have any reply to that.

"Do you have any other questions?" he asked.

"Like what?"

"If you are new to this land, you must have questions."

Her brow knitted. "I don't know if I want to know anything more about this place. Everything I've learned so far has been rather unpleasant."

Tavik crossed his arms. "That is probably true, but do you want to be taken by surprise again?"

She caught his drift. "All right, what exactly am I supposed to do as your wife, other than what we agreed to exempt me from?"

He chuckled at the not so subtle reminder of their agreement. "Other than that, you are supposed to follow any order that I give you and tend to me."

Her eyes narrowed. "Well, that is very vague and blanketing. How am I supposed to 'tend' to you?"

Tavik raised a hand to rub one of his shoulders. He tilted his head and thought a moment. "You tend to me by looking after my home, being available to entertain guests, and a massage would not be out of the ordinary."

"A massage?" she said flatly.

He nodded. "Yes. One now would be nice."

Her jaw dropped. She could not believe him. He motioned her over. Taking the fire poker with her, she hesitantly stepped across the room.

"Naomi," he said. He held out his hand. He wanted the fire poker. She looked at it in indecision. She didn't really think attacking him with it would do her any good, but having it as an option was nice. Maybe that was why he kept the helm on. She doubted she'd be able to make a dent in it. She reluctantly handed over the fire poker. He set it on the floor.

She took position at his back. He dropped his head and waited. She nervously cracked her knuckles and rubbed her hands together to stall for a few seconds, but soon her hands were loose and ready, and if she took much longer, he was likely to say something. She put her hands on his shoulders and began to knead the muscles.

The only person that she could recall ever giving shoulder massages to was her father. The thought of him made her hands still for a moment. She hadn't spoken to him for a week, and now she was stuck here. She wondered if he and the rest of her family knew she was gone yet and what they thought. The worry they'd experience would be awful. She hated the thought that they were searching for her right now and fearing for her safety.

"My shoulders are still knotted."

She jumped slightly at the sudden interruption of her thoughts, which made the tears that had gathered spill. She began working the muscles again and cried silently. It was all right. No one could see her.

She kneaded Tavik's shoulders as instructed. There was a large scar on one of them. She worked her thumb into it and heard him sigh at the action. Her father had encouraged her to become a masseuse. He said her hands were magic on his shoulders. She'd always laughed it off. She couldn't imagine giving strangers massages. It'd seemed too personal. She wondered if she'd ever see her dad again. Mom had invited her to come by for dinner after the yard sale, but she'd bowed out, wanting some alone time. She wished she had said yes. The idea that she wouldn't ever again sit around the dining room table with them hit her like a physical blow.

A tear hit Tavik's neck. Before she could wipe it away, he reached back and brushed his hand over the spot. He brought his hand to his face and looked at the moisture smeared across his fingers. A sniffle escaped her. He twisted round to look at her. Another tear slipped down her cheek. She lifted her hand and wiped it off.

"What's wrong?" he asked.

A sardonic smile twisted her lips. "You keep asking that, and the answer is still everything."

He waved for her to sit in the other chair. When she sat, she hunched over and let her hair fall forward. *Keep it together*, she told herself. It wouldn't do to completely lose it. Blubbering was not going to endear her to him, but she really wanted to cry. She scrubbed her face and pushed back her hair to face him again. He still sat in his chair with his mask pointed at her. It was like sitting with an executioner. They were another sort that kept their faces covered.

"Do you really have to wear that thing?"

His back stiffened slightly, but he merely nodded. She slumped at his response. She folded her arms across her stomach.

"I wish I were home," she said. She smirked to herself and clicked her heels together three times while whispering for each click, "There's no place like home."

When she looked back over at Tavik, she couldn't help the shudder that ran through her. He just sat there! No fidgeting. No shrugging. Nothing. With the helm on, he was faceless. Emotionless. She was miserable, and he just sat across from her. No comfort. No consolation. No connection. She'd feel better if she were alone.

"It has been a long day. You should get some sleep," he said.

She nodded and sighed. "Maybe I'll dream of something nice."

He didn't respond. She cast her eyes to the bed and then back to him. "Are you taking the bed?"

"I am the lord," he replied. She snorted. Yeah, he was the lord, but he wasn't a gentleman. She curled herself into the chair. She knew that she wouldn't be very comfortable, but other than the floor, there was nowhere else for her.

He did retrieve a heavy blanket from the chest for her, but as she reached to take it, he drew the blanket back before she could grasp it. "I am going to douse the fire and blow out all the candles. You are not to spark any light within this chamber. I sleep lightly, so do not think you will be able to accomplish anything without my knowing. If you attempt anything, I will kill you. Are we understood?"

She blinked up at him. He was serious. He would kill

her. She nodded jerkily. He gave her the blanket. She wrapped it around herself tightly, but the shivers that went through her were not caused by a physical chill. He went around the room extinguishing the lights. She'd closed her eyes before he was done. Exhaustion was tugging at her, and her creeping sense of hopelessness leeched away any wariness she might still harbor.

Naomi's sleep was muddled with half-formed dreams and nightmares. She struggled up to consciousness, but it took her a few blinks before she realized she was awake. She couldn't see anything. She flailed out a hand to turn on a light but met only emptiness. She scrunched her brow in frustration. She was still half asleep when she lurched up out of the chair. The blanket made her stumble and grumble. She kicked the blanket loose and cast it aside. She raised both hands before her as she tried to find her way. She wanted to turn on a light. She knew there was a light switch on the other side of the living room. She went toward it only to bump into a mysterious bed, and the hand that wrapped around her arm made her yelp.

"I did not figure you for such a fool, Naomi. I thought you'd wait a full week before attempting this."

"Let go of me!" She blindly swung at her assailant. She hit his shoulder.

He released her arm, and she fell back onto her backside with a jolt. "Help! Police!" she screamed.

A spark of light blinded her as Tavik lit a bedside candle. He had on the helm. The candlelight danced over the metal and made it look demonic. Seeing it snapped Naomi into the present. She wasn't in her apartment, and she had just struck the true owner of the room, the one who had vowed to kill her if she tried anything, and he'd been serious. He'd gone to bed with his sword, and it was pointed at her now.

"Oh God," she breathed. This wasn't a dream or a nightmare. It was very, very real.

A sharp rapping on the door made both of their heads

snap to it. Tavik cursed vehemently as he went to answer it. He swung the door open and filled the door frame with his body. Naomi could just make out Yula on the other side.

The woman cowered on the other side in a long gown and lace sleeping cap. "Is everything all right, my lord? I thought I heard a scream."

"Everything is fine. Naomi received a fright."

"A fright from what?" Yula persisted as she caught sight of Naomi still sprawled on the floor.

"A fright from me. Will that be all, Yula?"

The older woman's eyes shot to Naomi again. Lord knew what she thought. She wanted the servant to stay but knew it was pointless. She was as powerless as Naomi.

"Does my lord need anything?"

"No, you may return to your quarters. Please do not trouble yourself with any further noises you hear from this room."

The color drained from Yula's face. "Noises, my lord?"

"Good night." He closed the door on her horrified face. He turned back to Naomi.

Feeling very vulnerable on the floor, Naomi got to her feet. If she was going to die, she wanted to be standing.

"Tell me, what did you think you were doing?" he demanded.

She swallowed nervously as her eyes darted around. This was bad, and she didn't see a way out. Tavik leaned back against the door, the only exit in the room other than the chimney.

She considered the chimney for a moment but discarded the idea when she imagined herself getting stuck. He would probably light a fire rather than pull her out.

"What does Agatha want you to do?" he asked.

Her eyes flew to him at the question. What was the deal between him and Agatha? She was just some old woman. Sure, she was pretty damned feisty, but he was the big bad warrior. What did he have to fear from her frying pan?

"I told you. She tricked me."

He straightened from the door and took a step toward her. "I will spare you if you simply tell me."

Her eyes fell to the sword, and she began to shake at the reverse threat. She had no answer to his question, not even a possible lie. He was going to kill her. She crumbled to the floor and wrapped herself into a tight ball. So much for dying standing up.

"Naomi," he said.

She lifted her head from her tightly wound arms. Her face was wet with tears again. "I don't know anything. When I woke up, I thought I was home. I swear I wasn't trying to get the drop on you. I was confused."

He knelt down in front of her. "How am I supposed to believe you?" he asked.

Her face twisted in frustration and fear. "I don't know," she choked and buried her face again against her arms. He rose back to his feet and sat down on the bed.

She shivered as the cold stone floor leeched away all her warmth, but she was not going to move. Her nails dug into her arms where she clasped them. She was as good as dead. She wanted to laugh. She never stood a chance. She would have happily left him alone, but she had forgotten everything in her sleep. She had been practically sleepwalking when he'd caught her.

"Naomi." She didn't raise her head. Her thoughts were spiraling down a dark mental drain.

"Naomi," he repeated a little louder.

She finally looked up at him cautiously. She was sniffling, with tears dribbling out of her eyes.

"I must be sure you will not try something like that again."

She didn't respond but continued to stare at him.

"I need assurance you will not do that again."

"I promise I won't. I swear," she said, but her voice was small. It held no conviction. She had promised before but look where that had gotten her. It seemed pointless.

"I need more assurance than that."

He rose from the bed and went to the chest on the far wall. He flipped it opened and reached inside. She watched him as he drew out sheets and began ripping them into long strips. She knew where this was headed, and she knew protesting would be useless. He came and stood over her.

"Get in the bed."

She cowered at the request. She had assumed he would tie her to the chair or just tie her up and leave her on the floor.

"What?"

He indicated the strips of cloth. "It will be easiest to tie you to the bed."

"Can't we do something else?"

"Get in the bed."

She got on the bed with a sad rueful laugh. She looked at him and shook her head. "It hasn't even been twenty-four hours and you're already breaking the deal. I knew it was too good to be true."

"Lie down."

She did as she was told and stretched out on her back. Her body shook with shivers. He stood at the foot of the bed and took her ankles in his hands. Her shivers increased. Her teeth began to chatter. Silently, Tavik coiled the cloth strips around her legs and lashed them to the bed post.

She knew she should protest, but she was done. There was no more fight left in her. She'd been broken. Being tied up was better than dead. *And anyway, this was the perfect honeymoon to go with the wedding.* The sarcasm helped calm her some. She shook her head to herself and closed her eyes as her "husband" tied her arms. He did not tie her cuttingly tight. She could still flex her arms and legs a little. She could twist some, but not enough to free herself.

When she was completely restrained, he once again doused all the light in the room. She waited tensely for him to come back to the bed. Instead of feeling his weight disrupt the other side, she heard him sit in the chair that she had been sleeping in earlier. Her eyebrows rose at this, but she didn't comment. She was tied to a bed. The situation was seriously screwed up. Just because he wasn't going to force himself on her didn't mean she should be grateful to him.

She wondered if her situation could get anymore surreal. As she drifted off to sleep, she heard a soft snore come from the other side of the room. A small smirk crept onto her face. Of course, he snored. She went to sleep with the hope that the next day would be more sensible and possibly nicer.

"Naomi, wake up."

She groaned and tried to turn away, but her hands were above her head and she couldn't seem to move them. She had a similar dilemma with her feet. She cracked open one eye to discover what her predicament was and found a demon staring down at her.

"Oh shit!" She tried to jerk away, but with her limbs still secured, she couldn't go anywhere.

"Wake up," the demon ordered again. She blinked and realized that it was Tavik. She scowled at the masked man and jerked her arms and legs in annoyance.

"I'm awake. You can untie me."

He straightened and crossed his arms.

"What?" she demanded.

"Do you work for Agatha?"

"No, I don't. Please, untie me." She really wanted out of that bed immediately. She wanted her freedom.

"Are you in collusion with anyone else against me?"

"Who? I just got here! Please untie me."

"And you're not Lady Naomi?"

"How come you don't know what this lady looks like? I mean, if she was potentially going to be your wife, wouldn't you check her out beforehand? While you answer, you can untie me."

He still made no move to her bonds. "It wasn't

necessary to see her beforehand. If I saw her and found her unsuitable, I would have disposed of her." Well, that was a cheerful thought to start the day. If he hadn't thought Naomi was cute enough, he would've just gutted her instead of forcing her to the altar.

Her voice cracked when she made her request again. "Please, untie me."

For a second, she thought he would still refuse, but he finally reached out and undid the knots at her wrists. She lowered her arms and rubbed them. Her hands were numb from poor circulation. Tavik moved down to her ankles and undid those knots as well, but he held her ankles lightly after untying them.

"I promised I would not harm you."

"Why not? I'm not really your Lady Naomi. What does my welfare matter?"

"Because I keep my promises."

He said that seriously. She didn't understand why he'd keep promises to her since she was powerless in this whole mess, and he seemed not to trust her an inch, but she nodded her head to show she accepted his statement. He removed his hands from her feet. She swung her legs over the side to the bed and sat up. She watched him warily. She had no idea what was expected of her now. Tavik, on the other hand, seemed content to ignore her for the moment. He turned away and stretched. He had on a loose shirt and a pair of baggy pants. When he lifted his arms, his shirt rode up, and she got a glimpse of his lower back. It was smooth and well-muscled. She could tell from the soft cloth of his sleep pants that he had a nice firm ass, as well. The back of him was a very pleasant sight, and she didn't feel bad for ogling him. She deserved a tiny moment of pleasure after all the shit she'd been through recently. When he was finished with his stretch, his arms flopped down, and he scratched his ass. *And thus endeth our Diet Coke moment,* Naomi thought with a quiet snort.

There was a tap at the door. Tavik opened it to let in

Yula with a tray of food. Yula shot Naomi a worried look. She smiled to reassure the servant. Yula set the tray on the small table and put out one plate and one set of utensils. Naomi got up but hung back at the side of the bed. Was the plate for her or Tavik? Tavik sat down in the chair without the plate. She came over and sat across from him.

She ate a small spoonful of what tasted like oatmeal. Tavik lounged across from her. Eating breakfast with a masked man was certainly strange. But then again, doing anything with a masked man was strange.

"Yula, please keep Naomi company today while we travel."

"Yes, milord."

They were leaving? "Where are we going?" Naomi asked.

"Home," Tavik said.

She was annoyed by the vague answer. Before she could ask for more details, he rose. "Make sure you are ready when the caravan leaves."

Yula nodded. Naomi held her tongue. Once he was out of the room, she turned to Yula. She needed information. Any information. "Humor me?" she asked.

Yula tilted her head in confusion.

"I'm going to ask you questions. Just answer them, please? Don't try to tell me that I know the answers because I'm Lady Naomi, okay?"

Yula nodded her head.

"Where are we going?"

"Lord Tavik told you."

"Lord Tavik didn't tell me anything. You know where we're going. Please tell me."

"We're returning to the heart of Lord Tavik's domain."

"Why aren't we staying here?"

Yula shrugged. "He never stays in his conquered lands. He sets up a man to oversee the area and collect his taxes and then leaves."

"So this is all about money? That's why he does this?"

Yula didn't immediately respond. She looked down at her hands. "Lord Tavik's reasons are his own. Money is one reason, but there are others."

"What are they?"

Yula shook her head. "That is our lord's business, not ours. We need to get ready."

"How far away is Tavik's castle?"

"A full day's journey. And he'll want to leave as early as possible. We don't want to be out after dark."

"Why's that?"

Yula shook her head. "Please, milady, finish your breakfast. I have packing to do."

Naomi heard the stress in Yula's voice and focused on her meal.

Yula was putting the blanket Tavik had used back into the trunk when she said tentatively, "You seem well, considering, milady."

Naomi had finished her sort of oatmeal and was trying to help Yula, though the cook seemed determined for her not to do anything. "Yes. Tavik kept the deal."

"I feared the worst when I heard you scream."

"Honestly, I did, too. Thank you for coming to check on me. That was very brave of you."

Yula ducked her head, seemingly embarrassed by the compliment. "I'm glad it turned out all right. It's good that Lord Tavik likes you."

"You think he likes me? He tied me to the bed. He threatened me with his sword. What does he do to people he doesn't like?"

"Kill them."

That hadn't been a flippant answer. Yula was serious. Naomi's body went cold. *Ask a stupid question, get terrible answer*, she thought to herself and had to quietly agree that it was a good thing that Tavik liked her.

CHAPTER FOUR

A group of unicorns is called a blessing.

Naomi sat hunched beside Yula in a covered wagon. They'd been packed in like any other supply. There'd been no carriages left at the castle, though Naomi wasn't sure if a carriage would've been any better to ride in. She was sitting on two pillows, but she already had butt bruises, and they were still in their first hour of travel. She was sorely (har, har) missing modern suspension. It was going to be a long day. She closed her eyes and tried to sleep.

Yula shook her awake a couple of hours later. The wagon had stopped. "Tavik wants to speak to you." She pointed outside. Naomi rubbed her eyes and climbed down from the wagon.

Tavik waited outside on his horse. He leaned down and offered his hand. Naomi blinked owlishly up at the hand.

Her brain was having trouble computing the gesture. Though she may have napped, she was more tired than before. It was hard work sleeping in a jostling wagon.

"Ride with me so that I can tell you what is expected of you when we reach my home."

She shied away from the outstretched hand. "I don't know how to ride."

"You don't have to."

"Can't I talk to you from the wagon?"

He continued to hold out his hand. She reluctantly grasped his arm in both hands, and he pulled her up. She had a moment of panic as she tried to figure out how she was supposed to sit: sidesaddle, astride, behind him, in front of him? Tavik did the deciding for her by setting her sidesaddle in front of him. Reflexively, she wrapped one arm around his waist and grabbed the pommel with her other. Her legs wound up draped over his thigh. Before she could get her bearings, he nudged the horse into a walk. Her hold tightened around his waist as she tried to keep her seat. One of his hands fell to her thighs, and the other wrapped around her waist to help hold her steady. Her eyes shot to the hand on her thigh and wondered what the hell he thought he was doing. That hand did not appear to be helping her at all. It was warm and heavy. And unwanted.

She tried to get him to remove his hand by twitching her leg, but he only pressed his hand down harder. She quietly huffed in irritation. She decided the quicker she got this talk over with, the sooner she could get back to the wagon. "So what's expected of me at your castle?"

"You will be the lady of the castle, but do not think that gives you control of my household. The servants and guards know that even though I am gone, I will be back, and I will be displeased if things are not the way that I left them." Tavik was turning his head side-to-side, scanning the road. His helm had to limit his field of vision. He probably couldn't see her unless he purposely bent his head to her. The realization actually relaxed her a little. She openly stared at him, knowing he couldn't tell.

Naomi frowned. "So what are you going to do? Throw a drop cloth over me when you go away? What can I do while you're gone?"

"You may do what you want with the gardens. I will tell the gardeners to listen to you. You can sew, of course. Start a tapestry to gift me. Oversee the maids. Go for walks outside the castle with guards."

Naomi's stomach turned as she listened to him rattle off his list. She was not a feminazi but neither was she a fifties housewife. She couldn't do anything with thread except tangle it; she made plastic flowers wilt; the idea of ordering women around to do menial tasks repelled her; and going for walks would be tortuous because she had the feeling that if she started walking away from the castle, she wouldn't want to turn back.

"Um, none that really appeals to me."

"Then what would you like to do?"

She said the first thing that came to her. "Learn how to ride."

Tavik chuckled and patted her thigh. Her leg jumped under his touch. She clenched her hands in silent frustration. The bastard was fully aware of the awkwardness of their situation and was having fun with it, and she couldn't retaliate in fear he'd dump her off the saddle.

"I will tell the stable master to see to it personally. He will probably be the only one with enough patience to handle you."

Naomi was a little stung by his assessment. "And what makes you think I'll be such a terrible student? I pick up things very quickly."

His hand settled more firmly on her thigh, and she stiffened in reaction. "Because horseback riding is not something you can be told how to do and then do. Your mind can't just order your body to do it. Your body has to

50

accept it. Like right now, if another man were holding you, he would have lost his grasp by now, and you would be on the ground a quarter mile back."

"So how should I be sitting, then?" she asked as she shifted self-consciously.

"First loosen your body. You have to let yourself move with the horse."

She tried to do as instructed. She loosened her grasp gradually from around his waist and flexed her back a little to relax. She let her claw-like hold on the pommel lessen. Her hand had begun to cramp anyway. She was grateful when he removed his hand from her thigh and placed it on his own hip. She tried to let her body flow with the horse but kept flinching when it took anything resembling a jarring step.

"I feel like I don't have any control," she said.

"Here, take the reins," he offered.

She looked at him to make sure he knew what he was doing, but with that stupid helm on, she couldn't tell. She took the reins and clenched them in her lap with both hands. She jolted in alarm when the steed stamped his feet in displeasure.

"I didn't tug on them or anything," she protested as the horse continued to be finicky.

"Yes, but Victor can feel how stiffly you hold the reins, not giving him any leeway. He can't even shake his head to throw off a fly."

She gave the reins some slack to allow the horse a little more freedom while Tavik soothed him with gentle words. The steed settled down.

"Sorry," she mumbled.

He patted her thigh where it settled once again. "You're learning."

She scowled at the return of the hand. "I'll be learning to ride on my own, right? This stable master won't be sitting on the horse with me every lesson, will he?"

Tavik threw his head back and laughed. "No, I don't

think his wife would approve of that."

She was comforted slightly by his answer. And his laugh emboldened her to ask, "So at your castle, what are the sleeping arrangements going to be? Am I going to be tied to a chair or could I just be locked in a room?"

"You'll have your own room."

She perked up at this. Funny how certain things that would have been horrible a few days before now were reassuring. Her own cell. How marvelous.

They rode in silence for a while longer. Naomi began to wonder when he would let her return to the wagon. He didn't seem inclined to. She tried to put the time to good use and practice her balance like instructed, but she knew that her odd seat would not be something she would often have to use. She hoped the stable master would let her ride astride and not sidesaddle. Tavik's hand remained on her thigh.

They'd been alternating between small fields and forest all day as they rode. They'd just entered a wooded area again. It was several degrees cooler in the shade. The caravan was comprised of a long line of wagons with riders flanking either side. All the men were armed and wore light armor. Yula had explained to her that the horsemen would accompany the loot wagons while the foot soldiers would make their way at a slower pace after them. She'd wondered if Hammond was among the foot soldiers and hoped it took them a very long time to catch up.

She found herself yawning again, and the involuntary stretch had her almost falling off the horse. Tavik's strong arm around her waist kept her from falling over, but she felt that it was definitely time to end this little experience.

"You know, I'm sure we'd both be more comfortable if I got back into the wagon."

He chuckled. "I thought you wanted to learn how to ride."

"I'm not learning anything."

His hand rubbed her thigh. "You're becoming more

comfortable. It's a start."

She frowned down at her thigh. No, she was learning how to ignore his hand.

A man from the front of the line was riding back to them. "Milord, I need to speak to you." He brought his horse alongside theirs.

"What is it?" Tavik said.

The man's eyes darted to Naomi.

"Speak."

"Umbrek tracks," he said in a hushed tone.

The term didn't mean anything to Naomi. She turned between the two men for an explanation, but Tavik's attention was focused on the soldier.

"How old?"

"A few days, sir. They may have left the area, but I can't be sure."

Tavik nodded. "Alert the others. Tighten the line. Have swords ready. I'll go to the front once Lady Naomi is safely back in her wagon."

The man saluted and rode ahead.

"Umbreks?"

"You don't know of them?"

"No, but I take it they're bad news?"

His hand tightened on her thigh. "The worst news. Listen to Yula and stay in the wagon. Do you understand?"

She nodded. He slowed Victor and flagged the wagon. She slipped off the horse and climbed back in.

"Yula, do you know what umbreks are?"

The other woman's eyes widened. "Have they been spotted?"

"Um, they found some tracks. Tavik's taking precautions."

"Oh sweet Calax, look after us in these risky times," Yula said as she made what looked like a religious hand gesture. She covered her face with her hands, then turned her palms outward to the sky. Naomi was curious about

53

that, but she still wanted the scoop on umbreks.

"What are umbreks?"

"Foul demons."

Naomi didn't like the sound of that. "What do they look like?"

"They stand like men on two legs, but their legs bend in the reverse. Their arms are short with nasty razor claws. Their mouths are crowded with fangs. They rip men apart and eat them. Woe to the lonely traveler who finds himself in their woods."

"But we'll be all right. We're with a bunch of soldiers and horses. These umbreks wouldn't attack us."

Yula hugged her shawl closer. "I have heard of large, robust villages decimated by them. Bits of small children littered the ground. The grass painted red."

Naomi's heart lurched at the description. She found herself hugging her arms to herself, too. "These umbreks can be killed, though, right?"

"Yes, but they do not die easily."

Naomi peered out the back of the wagon, and the world looked a lot darker and colder. She suddenly wished she was still up in Tavik's lap. His horse was fast, and he had a large sword. She would have gladly let him rub her thigh. She didn't consider herself weak or cowardly for the wish, just extremely practical, and hiding behind large men with weapons in the face of danger was extremely practical. Okay, maybe she was a fraidy-cat, but bravery and stupidity gladly went hand-in-hand into battle while scared and intelligent ran the other way.

"Don't worry yourself, milady. Lord Tavik will not let those devils get us. He is brave and strong."

Naomi's mouth twisted into a sardonic smile at Yula's assurance echoing her mantra.

All chatter had ceased throughout the caravan. All eyes darted into the woods as ears strained for sounds of umbreks. They were going at a faster trot. The road was not really built for it. Naomi bounced in her seat.

Everyone's tension had gripped her, too. She didn't know what they were afraid of, but she knew it had to be bad.

A strange whooping sound drifted to them through the woods. The caravan let out a collective gasp in response. Naomi didn't need to ask. It had to mean umbreks. The wagon drivers whipped their horses to go faster. The whooping grew closer very quickly. Umbreks must be fast.

Naomi peeked out of the front of the wagon. The driver, whose name was Dennis, was lashing the horses with a snarl on his lips. A form leaped out of the forest. She watched it soar through the air over the road. Yula had not said the fiends could fly.

"Miss, get back inside," Dennis said as he snapped the reins. The horses didn't need much incentive. They were hauling the wagon as fast as they could. They were as frightened as the humans.

But Naomi couldn't duck back in because she was getting her first good look at an umbrek. It was everything Yula had said, but the old woman had left out one key thing.

"They're kangaroos!" Naomi exclaimed.

"What? Miss, please get back inside," Dennis begged as he tried to keep some semblance of control over the horses.

Naomi wasn't listing to Dennis. She couldn't stop looking at the umbreks. They were a lot like kangaroos—but the Halloween version. They were bigger, had mouths of fangs, long sharp talons on their paws, their coats were striped tan and dark brown. They were evil kangaroos. Naomi's jaw worked back and forth as she took in the lunacy and the horror. She wasn't sure whether to fall over laughing or fall down screaming. She was pulled back by a sharp tug from Yula.

"Do you want to be torn apart and stuffed into their pouches?"

Naomi's jaw continued to work. Her head was stuck on one thing, and it was all she could say: "Evil kangaroos."

"What?" Yula asked.

"Your world has evil kangaroos. This place is so messed up that even your kangaroos are scary. What else is out there? Brain-eating koala bears? Eviscerating deer? Poison-spitting bunny rabbits?"

"Do I need to slap you?"

"No."

"Then shut up."

Naomi's jaw jutted out. She wanted to argue the lunacy of evil kangaroos with Yula, but the wagon hit a bad bump, and they both fell down. She crawled to the back of the wagon to see what was going on. The soldiers were falling back as they engaged the umbreks. Tavik was easily recognizable on his large black charger.

She watched as an umbrek rushed Tavik. He stabbed at it but only pierced it shallowly. The thing leaned back on its tail and lifted its feet to kick Victor. The horse was hit but not fully due to Tavik's long swipe that slashed the umbrek's legs. It fell back into an ungainly heap. Tavik wheeled Victor around and sliced the thing's throat.

Another soldier was not as quick to slice and stab. An umbrek kicked, and the horse fell with his rider pinned underneath. Before the horse could stand back up, the umbrek was upon them. She quickly averted her eyes before she could see anything go into its pouch.

The wagons raced down the road, leaving more and more soldiers behind. Not all the umbreks, though, were left behind. Several were following them. They leapt and crashed a wagon. Its contents spilled across the roadway. It hadn't been the last wagon either, but the third to last. The second to last wagon tried to plow through the wreckage but lost a wheel and floundered while the very last was able to bypass both. They were down to eight wagons now. Naomi hoped the drivers of those two wagons were able to defend themselves.

The umbreks continued to pursue the fleeing wagons. If they hadn't been trying to kill them, Naomi would've

56

been amazed by them. They were stronger and faster than Earth's kangaroos. They didn't hop. They pounced. They could jump twenty feet into the air and span about twenty feet.

Umbreks fell upon the last wagon and smashed it. The horses screamed as they were jerked down with the wreckage. Naomi watched the beasts fall upon the helpless driver and horses. Now her wagon was the last in line.

"Get out of the way, milady!" Naomi turned to find Yula hefting one of the trunks that had been stored with them. She moved to the side, and Yula threw the thing out.

"We need to lighten the load," Yula told her. She turned back to grab another chest.

"Wait!"

Yula cast a dark look at her. "None of these things will do us any good if we're dead."

Naomi nodded but threw open the chest and began to rifle through it. "Yes, but let's put them to good use as we get rid of them." She hefted a candelabrum and threw it out the back at a pursuing umbrek. It shied to the side to dodge and lost a little momentum.

Yula quickly got the idea. While she dug through the chests for useful throwing items, Naomi threw as hard and as far as she could, and thanks to summertime softball, she wasn't a lightweight. The other wagons caught on to what she was doing and soon shoes, cups, plates, spoons, combs, and even bars of soap were whizzing through the air. None of the umbreks were killed, but some had black eyes and a couple landed on the discarded objects and got twisted ankles, forcing them to fall back. Soon though, their wagon was completely empty except for the driver and the two women. The umbreks quickly regained the distance lost.

"Crap!" Naomi said in frustration. Now what were they supposed to do?

"It was a good effort," Yula said.

Naomi wheeled around on the older woman. "We are not giving up."

Yula looked around the now empty wagon. "We don't have anything else to throw at them."

"We can't be that far from the castle."

"The horses can't keep up this pace; they'll start to falter."

"If you think we're done, then why don't you jump out the back? It'll lighten the load!"

Yula's back stiffened. "Girl, accept the—"

An umbrek crashed into their wagon, breaking it in two. Luckily the women were in the front of the wagon and not the back when the umbrek crashed through. Naomi barely had a second to loop her arm about the front wagon bow of the bonnet and grab Yula's arm. The back half tumbled away. As the front half now dragged on the road, Yula curled her legs up to keep them from dragging across the ground.

"Lady Naomi!" Dennis shouted.

"Don't you dare slow down!"

"I don't think I could if I wanted to. The horses are running wild. Thank the gods the road's straight. Where's Mistress Yula?"

"I'm still here, Dennis."

Dennis turned and leaned back. His eyes widened when he saw Naomi holding onto the wagon bow and Yula. He reached and got a hand under Naomi's arm. She thought her arm would be pulled off as he dragged her onto his bench. They both helped Yula up. The driver's bench wasn't wide enough for all three of them. Naomi feared one of them would be bumped off.

"Ma'am, we have to leap onto the horses and cut what's left of the wagon loose."

She looked at the two horses galloping in front of them. "I don't know how to ride."

"Well, learn quickly," Yula snapped. She suddenly did a full body leap and landed diagonally on a horse. She clutched the harness to keep her balance. She turned herself around and got her legs to straddle the back. Naomi couldn't believe Yula just done that.

"Your turn, miss," Dennis said, taking her arm. She stared at the back of the draft horse in fear.

"Jump, milady!" Yula shouted back at her.

"Please, miss, the wagon is coming apart."

"Oh, God." She bunched her leg muscles and leaped toward the other horse's back. She crashed onto the heaving horse. Her hands scrambled to find something to hold onto. She'd actually landed better than Yula and only had to spread her legs and swing them down over the horse's flanks.

"Dennis, hurry!" Naomi called.

She didn't know what to do. The horse was running wild like he'd said. She wrapped one hand around a harness strap and tangled the other in the horse's mane. Dennis climbed onto the wagon tongue and unhooked the chains. He held onto Yula's horse, and as the wagon tongue fell away, he pulled his body onto that horse's back.

"Dennis!" Naomi screamed. She'd thought he would come up with her. She couldn't control the horse at all.

"Just hold on, milady!" he shouted once he had gotten himself straightened out and up behind Yula. She stared at the pair on the other horse with wide eyes until the umbreks caught her attention again.

Most of them had stopped pursuit, except two that were still hot on their heels—or hooves, rather. Without the weight of the wagon, the horses picked up a bit of speed, but they were not out of the woods yet, quite literally.

They raced through the forest, but the umbreks were relentless. Naomi couldn't believe how tireless they were, but unfortunately, the horses were tiring. With alarm, she saw that the horse carrying Yula and Dennis was falling behind. Her heart wrenched with the realization that this was why Dennis had picked the other horse. It was to give her the best chance of escape.

"No!" she screamed as she watched her horse steadily outpace them.

CHAPTER FIVE

Unicorns are fierce creatures and have been known to kill dragons.

Naomi watched helplessly as she continued to pull ahead of the other horse carrying Yula and Dennis. She couldn't turn the draft horse back, stop it, or even slow it down. All she could hope to do was not get knocked off by a low-hanging tree branch.

An umbrek caught up with Yula and Dennis and reached out to swipe at their horse. They dodged the swipe, but just barely.

Naomi was so concerned with the two behind her that when an arrow whizzed past and hit the umbrek, she jerked around so hard she almost fell off her horse. Racing toward them was a group of armed men.

"You three keep going! We'll take care of these monsters," one soldier shouted.

Naomi whooped like a maniac as her horse raced through the armed men. Reinforcements! When she looked ahead, she saw the silhouette of towers through the trees. They had reached the castle.

The horses slowed the closer they got to the main gate for the castle. Foamy sweat covered them, and they breathed in heaving gasps. They were spent. It was at a walk that they entered.

The castle was in utter pandemonium. People were running everywhere. More soldiers were mounting up and racing out. It reminded Naomi too much of her first moments in the town of Harold's Pass for comfort. She kept a close eye on Yula. She didn't want to lose the only person she knew.

"Miss, are you all right?" a man asked.

"Oh, I might be in decade or two," she replied.

The man flashed a grin at her and helped her down. She wobbled a minute as she relearned to use her legs. A large man with a bushy beard stormed up to her.

"Were you with the last wagon?"

When she nodded, he pushed her toward the main building. "Go to the hall. The women will tend to you." She balked. She didn't want to go anywhere without Yula, who was marching over. At the man's touch, a murderous look entered the cook's eyes.

"Are you well, milady? I do hope you won't let this awful reception be your first impression of your new home." She shot a dirty look at the gruff man.

Naomi was quite taken aback by Yula's demeanor. She didn't want to give a bad first impression either, and demanding niceties during an emergency seemed like the making of a terrible first impression.

"I'm fine, Yula. I'm so glad the soldiers met us. It was such a relief." She said this to the man to show him that she wasn't upset with him, but he'd already jumped away from her and was looking everywhere but at them. If an umbrek were to jump between them at the moment, Naomi thought the man would've been relieved.

"Let's go inside. I'm sure the men will keep you

apprised of your husband's—*Lord Tavik's*—status." Yula said this more to the man than to her.

Naomi smiled weakly at the man to soften Yula's combative tone, but he was still avoiding their eyes. "Um, what's your name?" she asked, hoping to get on a little better footing with him.

In response, the man got down on one knee and bowed his head. "My name is Boris. I am Lord Tavik's steward. Please allow me to welcome you to Castle Tavik. If it pleases the lady, there are refreshments and attendants waiting in the hall. I hope my gruff manner did not displease you too greatly. I did not realize you were our lord's bride. If there's any way I can make amends, please tell me."

"Um, nice to meet you, Boris. Please, uh, get up. No worries about the reception. It's really crazy right now. I'm sure you have a lot to do. I'll just let you get on with that."

The man slowly rose to his feet. She hoped the smile on her face was comforting, though she was kind of freaking out. He still looked the furthest thing from happy, but she didn't really think all that was due to her. There was an emergency happening at the moment which she was not qualified to help with in any way. She turned to Yula and let her lead the way into the hall, where there were more people shouting and general commotion, though several skidded to a halt to usher them in and scrambled for food and drink. She was starting to realize that she was considered royalty or something. She had no idea how she was supposed to act, but Yula seemed to know how everyone else was supposed to behave and expected it. Naomi was so out of her depth.

They were shown to a side room off the main hall. The main hall was set up like a makeshift triage unit. Wounded soldiers were lying everywhere, with medical people running around frantically trying to help all at once. From her little sanctum, Naomi could hear the wounded's moans and cries. She tried not to listen for fear of noticing when one voice or another would go silent.

A new worry had settled upon her. What would happen if Tavik were killed? Would people expect her to be in charge? Everyone referred to her as their lady. Did that mean she was the inheritor of whatever Tavik had, or was she something to be inherited, and by whom? The dread increased every hour that passed with no news of Tavik.

Yula picked up on her mounting apprehension. "Lord Tavik will be fine, don't worry, milady."

But Naomi did worry. Her worry increased exponentially when Boris came looking for them. He wasn't smiling, which probably wasn't unusual for him, but there was a tightness to his face that made her stiffen. She stood up to meet him, but she didn't know what to do. She looked around her. Should she sit back down? It was better to be sitting when one received bad news. Why was she standing? She looked back at the chair. It meant nothing to her. What was she doing? Boris came to stand before her. She turned to leave because standing and sitting both seemed like stupid ideas, but she had to do something. Yula's hand on her arm stopped her escape. She hadn't seen the cook come over to her.

"I just want to stretch my legs."

"It will be all right, milady."

She shook her head and tried to move away. Yula wrapped her arms around her.

The noises outside had quieted. Boris stood silently as if waiting. She wondered what he saw. Did he see a scared noblewoman or a scared normal woman? Did they look different? What was she supposed to be doing? Why was she there? Why wasn't the man saying anything?

"What is it?"

"Lord Tavik's horse has returned."

She didn't understand. "And?"

"The horse was riderless. The steed is badly injured. We fear Lord Tavik—"

Naomi's brain decided at that moment that she really

didn't want to hear another word and shut down.

When she next opened her eyes, it was to find Yula hovering over her. "What happened?"

"You fainted."

"Oh, I need to stop doing that." Naomi heaved herself into a sitting position.

She had been put in a bed. A candle flickered on the night table. The room was large and filled with dark wood furniture. Over the hearth, a shield and a pair of swords hung. She realized that she'd been placed in Tavik's room. No one had known to not do that. It felt like she was someplace she wasn't supposed to be. She was trespassing on a dead man's sanctum.

"Would you like something to drink?"

She nodded, and Yula turned to pour her some water. "Have the soldiers returned?"

She saw Yula's back stiffen. "They have."

"And Tavik?"

She turned back around and handed her a cup. Her mouth was set in a grim line. No verbal answer needed. Naomi sipped the water while keeping a close eye on her. "What happens now?"

"Tavik will return."

"Victor came back without him."

"Yes, but we must have hope."

"But if he doesn't return…"

"Do not worry."

"Fat chance. What's going to happen?"

"We must have hope."

Naomi set the cup down and lay back against the headboard. She already hoped for so many things: a way home, a unicorn, an escape. She wasn't sure if she had room to hope for Tavik as well. Yula helped her prepare for bed and exited with a gentle call of good night.

Naomi slipped into unconsciousness, hoping for pleasant dreams to distract her from all the badness that had been her life for the past couple of days—and she did dream. She was out in a meadow in the moonlight, but the moon wasn't the brightest thing out; it was the unicorn racing toward her. She watched in disbelief as he galloped toward her. He was beautiful. The horn glowed golden, and his mane and coat shimmered like snow on a bright day. His hooves thundered as he pounded the earth, kicking up large clumps behind him. She reached out her arms to grab him, knowing he was her salvation. She strained to catch him as he ran past, but her fingers didn't even graze his flank. He wheeled around and began racing back toward her. She tried to catch hold of him again, but he slipped by her a second time. She felt desperation. She had to catch the unicorn. The magical beast turned again and ran at her, and she missed again. They played this game several more times before the unicorn got tired and didn't turn around again but continued to gallop away. She screamed for him to come back, but he grew steadily smaller.

She sat up in bed with a gasp. Her arms were reaching out as her desperation carried over to the waking world.

"Naomi?"

She jumped and looked for the source of the voice. The room was dark, but she could make out the shape of a man, and she knew the voice.

"I thought you were dead."

Tavik let out a low chuckle. "Sorry to disappoint you."

She frowned but brushed off his comment. "Are you hurt?"

"I'm fine."

She couldn't tell if he had the mask on but decided not to ask. "But Victor came back all cut up. How did you get away from the umbreks?"

"I didn't get away. I killed them."

"Oh."

She looked away feeling uncomfortable. She didn't know how to react. Violence had never been a part of her world. Before she'd come here, she'd never been in a fight or had her life threatened. This was Tavik's world. He probably found it all old hat: kill some monsters, burn a town, and come home for a relaxing nap. With a start, she remembered she was in his bed and that he probably wanted it back. She moved to get up.

"What are you doing?"

"Getting up. You should rest."

"Don't bother. I'll sleep elsewhere."

"But this is your room."

She heard Tavik sigh. "I'm tired, Naomi. I don't want to argue."

"Then stop arguing and do what I say," she said with a mixture of frustration and humor. She climbed off the bed and folded the blankets back.

"Naomi," he said with a warning tone.

"You slept in a chair last night. You rode all day and fought umbreks. You need to rest in a proper bed tonight."

"Where will you sleep?"

She'd been avoiding that question because really she had no idea. She didn't know where Yula's room was, or else she'd go bunk with her. She hunched her shoulders. "If you'll sleep in the bed, you can tie me to a chair."

"What were you dreaming about?"

She was startled by the change of subject. She wasn't sure if telling him the truth was wise, but she couldn't think of a lie. "I was dreaming about unicorns."

"It didn't seem to be a pleasant dream."

"I was trying to catch one and couldn't."

He walked over to the bed and sat. She could tell by the shape of his head that he had the helm still on. He kicked off his boots. "You might as well sleep here as well," he said.

"What about my own room?"

His shoulders slumped. "I will see to it tomorrow."

Naomi realized she was being a bit prudish. He was obviously bone tired. She could see that by how slowly he moved. Anyway, she could sleep above the covers and scream like a banshee if he did anything. She wasn't sure if that would do any good, but she could scream really loud. Even if no one came, he should at least get a headache. She walked around to the other side of the bed. She watched him lay his head back without removing the helm.

"You're going to sleep in that thing?"

"Yes," he replied without inflection. She scrunched her eyebrows together at that but didn't comment. She slipped under the top blanket, leaving the rest underneath her. Tavik sighed, and she could feel his body go limp as he fell asleep. She didn't think she would get back to sleep, but she was wrong.

The next morning, she woke to a very odd sensation. It didn't feel bad, but considering it'd been six months since she'd broken up with her last boyfriend, and there'd been a very dry spell—a veritable drought, actually—waking up to an arm draped over her waist made her pause for a moment, and wonder did she really want to wake up? Either this was a dream, or a nasty hangover was waiting in the eaves for her. But as anyone knew, thinking about waking up defeated the purpose.

Naomi reluctantly cracked open one eye. She was lying on her side facing the arm's owner. Being the second morning that she'd woken to the grim visage of Tavik's helm, it didn't startle her as bad this time. The masked lord didn't appear to be awake yet. She could hear soft snores. She wondered what time it was. Dim light streamed in through a narrow window. She wanted to get up and look through it but not wake her bed partner. She figured he needed the rest.

She rolled over to her stomach. Tavik's hand shifted to lay heavily on her back. If she could just ease out from under his arm, she'd be out of this odd predicament. She grasped the side of the bed and began pulling herself to the edge. Tavik's arm tensed. She thought he was waking up and prepared to apologize for disturbing him. To her chagrin, his arm stretched out, curled around her waist, and drew her back to him. Her head was now nestled under his chin, her arms flush against his chest. In alarm, she felt him lift a leg and throw it over hers. She was now completely pinned against him. Her only consolation was that there were a layer of blankets separating them. She scowled at the turn of events. She still didn't want to wake him, but he'd made it impossible by becoming Mr. Grabby.

A quiet knock sounded at the door. She craned her head around to look and contemplated whether to call the person in. Whoever it was knocked again. She felt Tavik tense. His arm tightened around her, and his head turned toward her.

"Good morning," he said. His voice had a trace of confusion.

"Hi, do you mind letting me go so I can see who's at the door?"

He removed his arm and leg. If she could have seen his face, she thought she might find a blush on it. The thought that he could find their situation a little awkward made her smile. She crossed the room and opened the door to let Yula inside.

"Lord Tavik, I am very glad to see you," Yula said.

He nodded. He'd sat up on the side of the bed. Naomi wondered about breakfast. Yula didn't carry a tray.

"Milady, if you'll follow me, I will show you to your chamber."

Naomi cocked an eyebrow at Tavik. Her chamber?

He nodded and waved her out. "Enjoy your morning."

She couldn't stop the smile that stretched across her face. He was keeping his promise. "You should get more sleep."

He shook his head. "I'm awake now, and the work won't fade away. Go with Yula. I'll see you later."

She nodded and fumbled a curtsy in her nightgown. She thought she heard a derisive snort come from behind

69

the mask but didn't pay it any attention. She had a chamber to get to.

Yula led her down a series of twisting hallways. She didn't think she could retrace her steps even with bread crumbs. They arrived at the end of one and stopped. Yula swept the door open. Naomi ventured into it in wonderment. Light streamed in from many windows, flowers were everywhere, making the room smell wonderful, and off to the side, steaming the air around it, sat something that made her weak in the knees. It was a bathtub full of soapy water. She turned to Yula, and she knew an ear-to-ear smile split her face.

"Would my lady like to bathe?" Yula asked with a teasing smile.

"More than like. I'd marry that tub and have its children." She began stripping off her clothes. She normally would've felt some inhibition around anyone while getting naked, but she felt so grimy and gross, and Yula had dressed her before, and she was another woman. And Naomi just did not care. She was taking a bath!

She hummed while soaking in the bath. She had her head laid back, and her arms draped over the sides. She knew she was well past pruney but couldn't bring herself to leave the warm scented water. Yula coughed politely from behind her, and she tilted her head back to look at her. She had an armful of towels ready for her.

"Can't I stay in here all week?"

"If my ladyship wishes to, she may, though I imagine Lord Tavik would be disappointed that you didn't venture further than the bath your first day in his castle."

She grinned at the idea. It would perturb him. She could imagine meeting him this way now: bubbles spilling out of the tub, her hair loosely pinned up, perfumed soap scenting the air, flowers everywhere and pretty candles— oh, and kittens tumbling over each other, while little song birds twittered from gilded cages, and he'd stand across from her decked out in armor and weapons with his helm covering his face, caked with mud, or maybe drying blood. He would tell her he was going out to slaughter, maim, and pillage all in his path, and she would raise a bubble-clad arm and wave good-bye and tell him to have fun killing lots of people and bring her back any chocolate that he might find.

Her brow scrunched when she mentally stepped back from her daydream. While the frilliness was fun and laughable, Tavik's side of the image was all too real. He would go back out and do what he said in her fantasy. Why he felt the need to commit senseless violence, she didn't know, but she couldn't just wave good-bye flippantly, though what else she could do eluded her. It wasn't like she could stop him, and her main objective had to be to get home. She needed to find a unicorn or find some other way.

She shook her head and raised herself up. She certainly wasn't going to accomplish anything while lounging in the tub.

Yula helped her out and began drying her. She was getting used to being tended to. "Will you want to meet with the housekeeper, milady?"

"Does she have stuff she wants to tell me?"

"No, miss, but don't you have things you wish to tell her?"

Naomi remembered Tavik saying she could order around the household help if she liked. She had not liked. "No, but I guess I should invite her over for, like, tea or something so we can meet."

"Of course, milady. I'll arrange it."

Once she was dressed and had breakfast, Yula slipped out to meet with the housekeeper. Naomi nibbled on the remains of her breakfast, worrying over how she could possibly make headway in her unicorn hunt. It had to be her prime concern. She needed information. She wondered if Tavik had anything resembling a library in the castle. He didn't seem the bookish type, but she had to get information somehow.

A spot of movement on the floor caught her attention. A small light brown mouse had darted out from under the bed. Her first reaction was to figure out how to kill it, but the only ways she knew were bought in supermarkets. She kept an eye on the mouse, figuring she liked better knowing where it was than not. She looked at the cup she had drunk out of and wondered if she could catch it under it. The mouse was near the wardrobe. She knew if she lunged for it now, it would run under there, and she would lose it. She had a few pieces of bread left. She tore up the bread and flicked a couple pieces to the floor in the direction of the mouse. She saw his nose twitch. She kept very still and waited. The mouse didn't move. She turned her head away but tracked him out of the corner of her eye. The mouse remained still for a few moments longer, then very slowly crept to the first piece and gobbled it down. She kept her head turned but kept a firm grip on the cup in her hand. The mouse ventured a little further away from the bed to reach the next crumb. She still kept still. When he was done with that piece, she flicked a couple more onto the floor, but she didn't flick these as far this time. The mouse, growing extremely bold, ran to the next couple of crumbs, and greedily gobbled them up. He was now less than a yard away from her feet. She finally made her move. She jumped from her chair and slammed the wooden cup down over the mouse. Unfortunately, his tail got caught outside the cup, and he let out a pain filled squeak. Then he began to swear.

"Motherfucker! Goddamn you! Are you trying to kill me? Chop it off, why don't you? *Goddamn!*"

CHAPTER SIX

Unicorns speak from the heart, not from the throat.

Naomi looked around the room, then down at the cup. Then back around the room. Then again at the cup.

No. Way.

"Hello?" she said.

The cup answered. "Hello? Is this how you greet all new acquaintances? Trap them, maim them, and then chitchat?"

She looked around the room again to see if there was any explanation other than the ridiculous one before her. She was definitely alone in the room, and the cup was still swearing at her.

"Let me go, bitch! I didn't do anything to you! Let me go, or I'll…I'll…"

"Or you'll what? You're a freaking mouse!" Did she really just say that?

"Yes, but I'm a talking mouse! If I can talk, just think about what else I can do!"

Naomi's sense of humor finally kicked in because really the mouse could talk, but he talked in a mouse voice. It was high-pitched, and he made little sucking and whistling noises through his teeth. Threatening wasn't a tone he was capable of.

She decided at that moment that Terratu was one messed-up world. It had two ugly moons, unicorns, killer kangaroos, and now, talking mice. What could be next, floating trees?

"I'm kind of new to this world. Do all vermin talk?"

There was a gasp from under the cup. "Vermin! I'm not vermin! I'm a respectable mouse, damn you!"

Laughter bubbled up in her throat, but she swallowed it back. "OK, so how come you can talk?"

The cup didn't respond.

"Are you going to answer me, or have I stopped hallucinating?"

Naomi heard some mumbling from under the cup. "I can't hear you," she said in a singsong voice. She was losing it. This place had made her bonkers.

"I was a wizard, but I added powdered aardvark instead of ashes of phoenix to a brew I was making. It exploded, and I woke up like this."

"Do you work for Tavik?"

"That scum lord? Pshaw! Why, if I had the right ingredients, I'd turn that bastard into a duck and then have duck soup for dinner!" Naomi's lips twitched at the mouse's bravado, but a light bulb went off over her head.

"Hey, if you're a wizard, you know stuff, right?"

"If I'm a wizard? I'll have you know, Miss Sadist, that I am one of the most knowledgeable wizards in the land! I know more stuff than you could even comprehend, and you are still killing my tail!"

Naomi tilted the cup a smidgen and watched the little

hairless appendage zip underneath. "What do you know about unicorns?" she asked.

"Tons! I know what they eat, drink, where they sleep, how they mate, where they run! I am the ultimate expert on unicorns."

"Because you're the ultimate expert on everything?"

"Damn right, missy."

Naomi still thought she was having a psychotic break, but she was willing to make it work for her. "All right, if you tell me everything you know about unicorns, I'll make you fat with all the cheese you can eat."

"Can I get wine, too?"

Naomi quirked an eyebrow at the addition. "Yeah, sure. Wine, too."

"Will you let me out from under this cup?"

"Do you promise not to run away and never come back?"

"Do you promise not to kill me, cut off my tail, break any of my bones, snip my whiskers, clip my ears, hit me, squeeze me, kick me, stomp me, or make me spurt blood in any fashion?"

Jeez, he was one paranoid little mouse. She found it adorable. "I promise not to hurt you in any way if you tell me about unicorns and not just promise to. For every bit of cheese and sip of wine I give, you have to tell me something about unicorns."

"Fair enough. Will you lift this damn cup already?"

Naomi lifted the cup, and the mouse looked up at her with twitching whiskers. She stared back, waiting for it to say something to hopefully confirm that she hadn't really been hallucinating. Instead, the mouse turned tail and dashed underneath the bed. She lunged to catch it, but she was too slow for the surprisingly fast mouse.

"Hey, we had a deal!" she cried out.

From under the bed came the reply, "Yes, we do. Stock up on wine and cheese. I know a hell of a lot about unicorns."

"Like what!" she shouted, but the little voice didn't answer. She looked underneath the bed, and she could see a small jagged hole. Her chamber door creaked open.

"Milady, have you lost something?" Yula asked.

Naomi sighed and got up off the floor. "Yeah, my marbles," she grumbled. Had she really made a deal with a talking mouse? When she turned around, she saw Yula's usually placid face was set in an angry scowl.

The cook stepped aside to reveal another woman behind her. "Mrs. Boon is here."

The other woman was round in face and body, but her face did not look like it was naturally inclined to smile. Currently, her face was very rigid and stern. She had her hands clasped in front of her, and they rested on the top of her belly. She had a kerchief covering her hair and a long white apron over her dress. Naomi extended her hand in greeting. The housekeeper looked down upon her outstretched hand and raised an imperious eyebrow. After a second, Naomi realized that the woman was not going to shake her hand. She wasn't sure if she was being snubbed or if people didn't shake hands in Terratu. She hoped it was the latter because otherwise she was somehow on bad terms with the housekeeper, and she had no idea why.

"I hope I'm not taking you away from anything important," Naomi said.

The housekeeper sniffed. "Of course not. Nothing I do is more important than your ladyship's desires."

"Um, okay... Well, it looks like you do a marvelous job. I was hoping, maybe you could spare someone to show me around," Naomi offered, suddenly not wanting to spend the day with this woman.

"Oh, it will be an honor to show you the castle," the housekeeper said. She turned her back and began walking away. Naomi glanced at Yula and saw her shooting daggers at the housekeeper's back.

Naomi quickstepped to catch up with the retreating housekeeper and wondered how she had gotten into this mess.

Naomi sank into the plush chair inside her room with a relieved sigh. She had seen more of the castle than she probably ever wanted to. If she never saw another storeroom, she'd feel blessed. Unfortunately, there was no library in the whole damn place. So the rodent was still her only hope.

Yula slumped into another chair.

"Why does Mrs. Boon hate me?" Naomi finally asked.

"I believe that's my fault. Mrs. Boon and I have long been at odds. She can't accept the fact that Tavik holds me in the same regard as her. I am like his housekeeper when he is away, and since he is away more than here, I interact with him more. Things I do for him on the road are brought back to the castle, and Boon is told to change how she does things and do them like I do. She hates that."

"So you're rival housekeepers."

"I would go so far as to say *warring*."

Naomi smiled at the image of warring housekeepers: Yula and Mrs. Boon facing off with sharpened scrub brushes, steel-plated aprons, and bucket helmets. If anything, it would be a very clean fight. Naomi mentally groaned at her own pun.

Feeling a little bad for the lie she was about to tell, she said, "I could use a snack. Would you get me some wine and cheese?"

Yula nodded and levered herself up. Once she'd left the room, Naomi got down on the floor by the bed.

"Hello, Mr. Mouse. Your cheese and wine are on their way. You may want to come out, come out, wherever you are." Naomi felt like an idiot, but she was an idiot stuck on another planet, and she would take whatever help she could get it.

"What are you doing?"

She jumped and whirled around. She really needed to start locking her door. Tavik stood behind her. He had on leather pants, a chain-mail shirt, and long boots. She thought he looked like a runaway from an S&M movie. "Uh, hi."

He leaned his hip against a table and crossed his arms. She hoped he hadn't heard her calling the mouse. She really didn't want to try explaining that, and she hoped the mouse would be smart enough to keep his trap shut if he appeared now.

He pulled a chair out from the table. "I thought we would lunch together."

She nervously smiled and nodded her head. "That sounds nice. Later this week?"

Yula entered with the wine and cheese. Tavik took the tray from her.

"Naomi and I will have lunch here. Go get us something more substantial from the kitchen."

Yula nodded and left without a word. Naomi took a seat at the table as Tavik poured some wine. She watched the bed for any signs of the mouse. When Tavik set the glass in front of her, she realized she had the only glass. Tavik was not going to be drinking any wine. She took a small sip, not having planned on drinking any of it herself.

"How do you eat without removing the helm?"

"I don't."

Naomi frowned, not knowing how they were going to have lunch, then. Was he just going to watch her eat?

Yula returned with more food. She did set a plate and glass for Tavik. She excused herself, and it was just the two of them again. Tavik went to the door and locked it. When he turned back, he had a long piece of cloth dangling from his hand. Naomi suddenly knew how they were going to have lunch together.

"Why even bother eating with me if it's going to be such a hassle?"

"Maybe I like the company."

"I think you just like tying women up."

Tavik lowered the blindfold over her eyes. She stayed still and let him tie it snugly. He then drew her arms behind the chair and tied her wrists. She'd had bad lunch dates, but none of them compared to this.

Naomi heard him move and take a seat. She assumed he'd removed his mask. She listened to his silverware scrape and his chewing sounds. She hoped the mouse didn't stick his nose out while she was tied up. For one, she would not be able to stop Tavik if he decided to kill the rodent, and two, it was just embarrassing, and she somehow knew the mouse would tease her about it.

"Have you had a chance to tour the castle?"

She frowned at the question. The question was perfectly fine, but being asked to participate in conversation while restrained and blindfolded somehow seemed rude. "Yes, Mrs. Boon showed me around this morning. Your castle is lovely and has an incredible amount of storage space."

He chuckled. "Oh? That is important to some, I suppose. I spoke to Geoff, the stable master. He expects you tomorrow morning to begin your lessons."

Surprised by the reminder of her request, Naomi straightened. "Oh, thank you."

She listened to silverware scrape some more. Hearing all these eating sounds was making her hungry. She shifted uncomfortably in her chair. She hoped Tavik wasn't a slow eater.

When something touched her lips, she snapped her head so far to the side that her neck popped.

"Jumpy," Tavik said.

"What the hell do you think you're doing?"

"It's just a piece of cheese. I thought you were hungry."

"Yeah, but—" She wasn't able to finish her protest with a piece of cheese suddenly in her mouth. *Congratulations, Naomi, you've just been force-fed*, she told herself as she sullenly chewed.

"A feast is being prepared in honor of my return. You will attend."

She nodded, knowing a command when she heard one. She felt something cool and round touch her lips.

"It's a grape," he said.

Deciding to humor the man, she opened her mouth and took the grape. "Yula will help you dress, and you will wear what is put out for you, understand?"

She dutifully nodded.

"A piece of beef," he said, holding a fork with meat to her mouth. She let him feed her the bite. She firmly squelched down the question of whether or not he was using her fork or his, the same way she had squelched her curiosity at whether he'd washed his hands.

"I could feed myself," she grumbled.

"I like this better."

She sat back without a counter. How did you argue about someone else's kink? He placed another grape against her lips. She ate the piece of fruit and quietly fumed. She was being fed like a baby. No, this was worse than a baby. A baby got to see the spoon coming.

"Is there anything you'd like to discuss?" he asked.

She wasn't sure what he was getting at. She'd like to "discuss" his trust issues. She'd like to "discuss" his fascination with bondage. She'd like to "discuss" a lot of things.

"What's your problem with Agatha?" Naomi winced. She wished she'd held onto the question until she could see, because she would've liked to have known if he reacted. The only reaction she got was another piece of cheese being brushed against her lips.

"Agatha and I have long been at odds."

"How are you at odds?" Tavik slipped her another piece of beef.

"She doesn't approve of my decisions."

"What do you mean?"

"I conquer other villages to bring them under my rule. I'm unifying the land. She doesn't like that."

"Are you sure it's the unifying and not the conquering part that she doesn't like?"

"None of them will willingly bow to me."

"Can you blame them? Nobody likes being conquered."

"Agatha has indoctrinated you well."

They were at that again. She sighed and shook her head. "I only met her once. I'm not in cahoots with her. I don't know anything about her except that she finagled me into marrying you."

"Which is a curious thing."

"Why?"

"I'm forbidden from carnally knowing a woman."

"You're a monk?"

Tavik laughed quietly. "I've never considered it, but I guess I am." She let that sink in. "I never wanted a wife," he added.

"But you got me."

"That's right. I got you: the perfect wife. One who does not want to have my child or ever share my bed."

"But that's good, right? Don't need to worry about anything now. Unless… Do you guys practice polygamy?"

Tavik chuckled and fed her another bite of food. "I would have to know what that was to practice it."

"Can you have more than one wife at a time?"

"No, not exactly. A lord can take more than one war bride, but he is only actually married to the last one he took. He can discard any he took before that."

She didn't like the sound of that. She gulped nervously as she considered the implications for herself and all the connotations that "discard" brought to mind. And he would leave again eventually to pillage another castle and possibly take a new wife.

"Oh, here, I should have offered before," Tavik said.

She didn't know what he meant by that as her mind tried to scramble for an idea. She jerked back when unexpectedly a cup was placed to her lips. She felt the wine spill down her front. Tavik cursed softly.

She dropped her head. "Sorry," she said.

"No, it's my fault. You really don't trust me at all."

She wondered how he could expect her to trust him.

She felt a cloth press her chin. The wine had spilled onto her chest. She hoped it didn't stain the gown. It was a pale yellow, and she knew it wouldn't come out of the cloth if it seeped in. She felt Tavik trail the napkin under her chin and over her neck. She probably looked a mess. The napkin moved lower. The gown had a generous scoop. She hadn't thought anything of it when she'd put it on that morning. She'd worn much more revealing things on her nights out, but she had never had a guy pawing her while she was blindfolded. She scolded herself for instantly jumping to conclusions. He had just told her he was a monk! Sure, he was a mass murderer, but he wasn't a lecherous one.

He was still brushing the napkin slowly over her chest. She thought he was doing a very thorough job. She froze when she felt the back of his fingers instead of the napkin touch her skin.

"Tavik?"

His hand disappeared. She took a deep breath in relief. Tavik made a strangled sound. She realized her dress may have pulled somewhat tightly against her chest. What was her monk doing looking at her chest?

"Tavik?"

"Would you like some more wine?" His voice sounded strained.

She simply nodded and held still this time for the cup to meet her lips. He gently tilted the cup for her, and she sipped slowly. She nudged the cup with her mouth to indicate when she was done.

"I will not discard you."

"Sorry?"

"I will not discard you," he repeated. "You are right. You're an even better disguise than my mask to hide what I am."

"Glad I can be of service," she weakly joked. Oh God, she was his beard.

He put his hand on her shoulder. "I know that it has been a hard couple of days, but I want you to know that I appreciate how well you have dealt with everything. An ordinary woman would have pulled her hair out by now and cried herself blind if she had had to go through what you have."

She felt uncomfortable with the praise. She wondered what he would say if he knew she had been keeping herself from going crazy with thoughts of how to ditch him and get back to her home, but then again, was she still sane? She had a meeting scheduled with a talking mouse. "I'm really not that special. Yula has gone through everything I have and more and has stayed strong."

Tavik sighed, and his hand rubbed her shoulder. "Yes, Yula is strong too, but…" He trailed off with another sigh.

"But what?"

Tavik's softened voice was putting her on pins and needles. "I'm not married to Yula."

Her mouth formed a silent O. Wait, their marriage was a sham. What did he care if she was strong and resilient? They were only together because—

Her train of thought was lost when Tavik's lips

covered hers. She froze. Unlike before, her head did not snap away. His kisses began as chaste presses of the lips, and with each press, his mouth opened a fraction more. Naomi's brain was in a tailspin. He was kissing her, and she liked it. Being kissed well was always nice. But they weren't supposed to be kissing! What about his whole monk thing? What about the deal? She was tied up and blindfolded. She shouldn't be okay with this just on principle. Bondage wasn't her kink, dammit!

His tongue inched out and traced the seam of her lips. She liked it. Screw it, she'd had a series of really crappy days, and this was the first day that had been going nicely. She'd had a bath, and met a talking mouse. Kissing would be added to the list of nice things done today. She opened her mouth and returned the kiss. His hand moved up to the back of her neck to cradle her head.

His mouth tasted like the sweet wine they'd been drinking. He wasn't trying to choke her with the kiss or split her lip. No force involved, and he gave equal time. He pulled back and let her explore his mouth. If she weren't tied up and blindfolded, this would go on her top five list of good first kisses. Soon, his lips crept from her mouth to her neck, laying soft kisses down her throat. She sighed in pleasure. She realized as he moved down her throat to the top of her chest that his head was completely bald. She filed that little tidbit of information away. He put his other hand on her breast and gently stroked it. She moaned in appreciation. She couldn't help pulling against the restraints, wanting to participate in the touching. His hand gently stroked her nipple, and it puckered.

"Tavik," she pleaded.

He switched his mouth back to hers. She continued to tug at her restraints. He slipped his hand down her dress to cup her breast. She arched her back and wiggled the restraints. They were beginning to come loose. His other hand left the back of her neck to trail down to pull up the long skirt of her dress to touch her thigh. She was working the cloth loose on her wrists. She would have them free soon she knew.

He left her lips again and returned to her breast. His hand pulled down her dress, and his mouth latched onto her nipple. She cried out in pleasure and victory. She'd worked her hands free. As he suckled, she raised her hands to the sides of his head to press him closer. When she touched him, he jerked away and grabbed her hands. She let out a protesting sound and tried to pull her wrists free.

"Naomi, you shouldn't have done that," he said. His voice was a little breathless.

"Done what?" She tried to tug her hands free or at least tug him back to her. She wanted to go back to the kissing and fondling. He switched his grip on her wrists to one hand. She heard what sounded like the helm being put back on. He released her and stepped away.

"Can I take the blindfold off?"

"Yes."

She pulled it off and tossed it onto the table. "I didn't try to take a peek," she said, a touch grumpily.

"You would have." He'd moved back to the wall and leaned against it with his arms crossed.

She rolled her eyes and looked at the table. She picked up a grape and popped it into her mouth. She was still hungry, but food wasn't going to satisfy her.

"Naomi, put your dress back to rights."

She looked down at herself and found her legs bare with the skirt all bunched up in her lap and one of her breasts spilling out of her top. She sent him a dark look. "I'm not the one who got the dress this way."

"Put your dress back to rights." His voice sounded strained again.

She jerked the top up, and the cloth grazed her nipple harshly. The pain only made her sudden bad temper worse. She threw the dress back over her legs, and crossed her arms like him.

She glowered across the room at him. She saw his throat move as he swallowed. He moved to the door. "I have matters to attend to. Be ready tonight," he said.

She sat there staring at the door after he'd gone. The impact of what had just happened began to creep up on her. She had made out with him. She had almost gotten to third base and may have rounded home if he hadn't gotten skittish. What was she thinking?

"Well, that wasn't much of a rut. You two barely got anywhere," said a high, squeaky voice from behind her.

She swiveled around on her chair and found the mouse standing in the middle of the floor.

"Is there any cheese and wine left?"

She turned back to the table. Three pieces of cheese remained. She picked up the wine canister and found it half full. She poured some of the wine into a saucer and set it down, along with the cheese, on a plate. The mouse scurried forward and began to gorge himself.

"What's your name anyway?" she asked.

The mouse looked up from the saucer. His whiskers dripped with wine. "Mr. Squibbles."

"Squibbles?"

"*Mister* Squibbles."

She smirked but didn't comment on the insistence of the honorific. "So tell me about unicorns, Mr. Squibbles."

"Unicorns are very rare. They have been nearly hunted to extinction by humans."

"For their horns?" she asked.

"Yes, a lot of magic exists in their horns: the power to purify water—not just a bucket but an entire river with one touch—heal mortal wounds, ward off harmful magic, counteract curses and poisons, call lightning."

"Where can I find unicorns?"

Mr. Squibbles had finished the cheese and sucked up all but a few drops of wine from the saucer. "Sorry, you've gotten all you're going to get at this time."

"What? Wait a minute," she protested, but the mouse turned and began to waddle back toward the bed.

"Get more wine and cheese," he said, and disappeared underneath the bed.

CHAPTER SEVEN

For fun, unicorns chase frogs.

Naomi fidgeted in the chair as Yula arranged her hair. She'd pulled it up and fastened it with small bejeweled combs and hair pins. Naomi knew the hairdo was going to give her a headache after a couple of hours, but Yula was so determined to make her look like a fairy-tale princess that Naomi kept her reservations to herself. She had the feeling that Yula was using her to prove something to Mrs. Boon.

Naomi was wearing a long shimmering red gown that was light on her back. The outer material was gauzy and iridescent while the lining was smooth and soft. Thank goodness the dress was light, because the jewelry was not. Heavy bejeweled earrings strained each earlobe. A long necklace with a ruby the size of a baby's fist hung from her throat. Gold bracelets dangled on both her wrists, and several glittering rings were on her fingers. She'd just barely convinced Yula to nix the tiara. Tavik may have said to wear everything presented to her, but she thought he couldn't possibly notice the absence.

Earlier in the evening, she'd gotten a crash course on etiquette for the feast. When she'd asked for the lesson, Yula had stared at her. She reminded her that she wasn't Lady Naomi. Yula had arranged a place setting on the table and instructed her on the proper utensils to use for each course. She'd also given her tips on how to interact with the guests. They would be affluent farmers and merchants. Naomi had asked if there would be dancing. There would be dancing, but Tavik didn't dance and thus she would not be expected to. She'd experienced no small amount of relief at this tidbit of information. As the guests of honor, they would watch the dancing for a while and be the first allowed to leave the festivities. She dimly hoped that Tavik would want to leave as early as possible.

The sun had just begun to set when there was a loud knock at the door. Yula had finally finished dressing her hair, and they had been sitting silently for several minutes. Naomi rose, and Yula hopped to the door and opened it. Tavik stood on the other side in a long red cape, shining boots, black gleaming pants, and a black tunic with gold geometric embroidery upon it. They had been dressed to match. The helm marred the prince-like attire, reminding Naomi that she was not a fairy-tale princess, and Tavik was not her prince charming. But he did look pretty good.

Tavik bowed low to her. "Is my lady ready to meet our guests?" he asked.

In response, she curtsied back and moved to his side. "Let's get this show on the road," she muttered.

She didn't know what to expect when she entered the hall. What greeted her made her hold her breath in surprise. The hall had been transformed. Torches lit the large room from all sides, with candles sparkling on the long tables. Flowery boughs and wreaths hung everywhere, with rich cloth draped on walls, windows, and tables.

While she gaped, the guests in the room had turned to look at them. She became aware of their stares and quickly tried to school her features to a more haughty expression. *I can do this*, she chanted to herself as goose bumps and a cold sweat broke out over her. She hadn't seen a silent cue, but after a moment, the hall broke out into applause, and Tavik raised his hand in acknowledgment of the welcome and nodded at a few of the people closest to them. She nervously smiled. They walked further into the room.

People began stepping forward to greet them. They bowed and murmured how happy they were to see Tavik well and said welcome to his new bride. Tavik greeted the men by name and thanked them for the warm welcome. Naomi nodded politely and smiled shyly. She tried not to make the iron grip she had on Tavik's arm too obvious, but short of a crowbar, he was not going to be leaving her alone with these people anytime that night. She spotted a group of women standing to the side. None of them smiled at her, and she had the feeling that anything they said in relation to her was not flattering. She wasn't going to be making any friends that evening.

She had been minding her p's and q's vigilantly throughout the dinner. She was sitting beside a grandfatherly sort who she happily let monopolize the conversation by telling her all about his grandchildren. He had twelve grandkids, so he had plenty to tell her.

Tavik tended to listen to others and nod and say little to anyone as well. It appeared everyone was having a good time. People were laughing and chatting merrily down the table. She envied their ease. She hoped she wasn't sweating through her gown.

When the feast was over, she glanced at Tavik. He had his chin resting on his hand.

Musicians came into the room carrying their instruments. People began to rise and pair up for the dancing. She wondered how long they would stay to watch. She was ready to go back to her room. The musicians made noises like they were ready to begin and the dancers took their places. She watched the dancing with mild interest. It was not fast or complicated, but knowing the steps beforehand was definitely required if one didn't want to run into someone else or step on another's toes.

Out of the corner of her eye, she saw Tavik wave one of the servants over. He said something low into the manservant's ear and sent him off. She watched the man go to the lead musician and whisper something into his ear. She looked at Tavik with confused curiosity. Had he made a song request? He turned and saw her looking at him. He put his hand over hers where it rested on the table. She gave him a nervous smile and wondered what was next. The current dance was coming to an end.

He rose from his seat, drawing her with him. She rose stiffly. With sickening dread, she realized they were going to the dance floor, not the door. She tried to balk, but he merely put his arm around her and drew her closer.

"Yula said you didn't dance," she hissed.

"Normally, I don't."

"Well, I don't know how."

"What do they teach young ladies in your land?"

"Nothing you'd appreciate," she muttered darkly.

"I will teach you how to dance," he said.

She barely registered his comment before he swung her around and showed her where to place her hands. The music started, and it was different from the first piece. She realized it was like a waltz, and the dancing positions were similar to a waltz as well. His arm went around her while his other raised her hand aloft. Her other hand rested on his shoulder. He began to guide her with gentle pressure. She moved a little woodenly and struggled to relax to make the dancing easier. She felt like she was in the spotlight. Everyone kept their distance as if to better watch them. She knew she wasn't putting on a good show. Not very ladylike at all.

"Dear Calax, Lord Tavik has gotten a common pig wench."

Her back stiffened in response to the overheard comment. She peeked up at Tavik to see if he'd heard the comment as well, but he showed no indication that he had. She tried harder to learn the dance steps, but her nerves and seething resentment of the anonymous insult made her move jerkily.

"The way to vex them is to enjoy yourself," he murmured.

So he had heard the comment. She set her jaw, and she nodded imperceptibly. She renewed her effort to relax and soon had the moves of the dance learned and was able to follow him without trouble.

"You look very lovely tonight," he said, breaking the silence between them again.

She gave him a polite smile in acknowledgment of his compliment. "I think Yula wishes to vex Mrs. Boon by doing her job well," she replied.

He chuckled briefly, and then fell silent again. He tilted his head down to her, and she got the feeling that the light moment had passed before it could be fully enjoyed. Now it was time for something serious. She stared into the dark holes for his eyes. "About this afternoon…" he began, but he trailed off.

She raised an eyebrow as she waited for him to finish his statement. She had a sinking feeling that she was not going to like what he had to say. She had berated herself for what had transpired during lunch, but she didn't exactly want to hear he had found what happened embarrassing or morally questionable.

"I apologize for breaking our agreement," he finally finished.

She blinked at him a moment in surprise. That was right. She had made him swear not to expect any bedroom fun from her, and he had basically taken advantage of her while she was tied up and blindfolded, never mind the fact that she had been a cheering participant.

She dropped her head as the blush crept over her cheeks. She didn't know how to respond to his apology. If she forgave him, he could construe it as an invitation to try to get hot and heavy with her again, and in confusion, she realized that she wasn't entirely opposed to that idea. What to do, she wondered. She worried her bottom lip as she scrambled for a way to reply, but the music stopped before she could formulate a diplomatic response. Tavik didn't prod her for an answer, and for the moment, she assumed that her silence was answer enough. She followed him off the dance floor, but instead of going back to their seats, he took them to the doors. It looked like he was ready for them to leave. Naomi was glad.

They walked from the main hall, up the stairs, and back to her room in silence. He held her bedroom door open for her as she slipped inside. She turned to face him, holding her breath. What now? He bowed his head and closed the door with him still in the hall. She slumped and started to breathe again. As she turned to bed, she shrugged out of her finery and removed her jewelry.

Tavik's silence had unnerved her, but she couldn't blame him for it. She hadn't even managed a thank-you for the apology and merely a shy nod for farewell. Next to her, he had been the chatty one. She fell into bed, happy that the day was finally over. She tried not to dwell on the fact that she had no clue what the next day would bring.

That night, she dreamed the unicorn met her in the great hall. Music began for them to dance. The unicorn bowed low, and she curtsied back, but as they began to move, she remembered that she didn't know how to dance and faltered. The unicorn pranced in step to the music, but she could only stand still and watch as he danced away.

When Yula woke her the next morning, she felt bleary-eyed and grumpy. She became grumpier when Yula told her there was no coffee with breakfast. The other woman didn't even know what coffee was. How was she to survive her adventure without the assistance of caffeine? To further torture herself, she ticked off in her mind other amenities that she didn't have: indoor plumbing, telephones, the Internet, television, and worst of all, no chocolate. She was doomed, and her crabbiness grew.

Yula reminded her gently that she had her first riding lesson that morning. Naomi added another item to her list: no automobiles.

Dressed warmly in a plain gown and shoes, she went down to the stables with Yula to begin her riding lesson. Geoff, the stable master, was waiting with a draft horse.

The stable master had a red face from the sun and an easy grin. She could only muster a grimaced smile to give back to him.

"This, milady, is Stomper. Don't let his size worry you. He's the biggest softie there is. I thought we would start on him, if that's all right with milady."

She lifted her hand to the horse's muzzle in greeting. Stomper sniffed her hand and blew warm breaths of air into it. "Here, give him this. He'll warm to you real quick." Geoff handed her a carrot, which she dutifully offered. Stomper took the carrot happily from her hand, and as he munched it contentedly, she grew bolder and petted the horse's neck. He lowered and stretched it for her and stomped one hoof in enjoyment. She began to warm to the horse.

With Geoff's assistance, she mounted.

"Now, just relax and get your bearings. Go with the horse."

She sat on the back of Stomper as Geoff led the horse around the courtyard. They did several wide circles.

"You're getting the hang of it, milady."

"Oh yes, if you're around to lead him, riding is an absolute breeze."

"You'll be holding the reins soon enough, don't worry. I can see you'll be a fine horsewoman."

"That's not what my husband tells me. He despaired

94

that not even you would have enough patience for me."

Geoff chuckled. "I don't know anything about that, milady. You're doing fine."

She smiled but knew she still had a lot to learn before she would be able to manage a horse on her own, but she hadn't broken anything of hers or the horse, and Geoff was still fine too. All in all, her first lesson was turning out to be a stirring success.

From practically inside her ear, came the comment, "You know, a unicorn will never let you ride him. That will be a sip of wine and a piece of cheese, please."

And with that, Naomi fell off the horse. Well, there went all that success.

Her tumble from the saddle startled Stomper and Geoff. The stable master quickly handed the horse off to a stable boy and went to her side. "Are you all right?"

She winced and took his offered hand. "I think so. A spider startled me. Sorry."

"Nothing to apologize for, milady. How about we call it a day?"

She nodded and hobbled back to her rooms without Yula, having dispatched the woman to get her more wine and cheese.

Once she was back in her room, she looked down at herself and asked an uncomfortable question. "Mr. Squibbles, are you still somewhere on my person?"

"Right here," the mouse said, climbing out from under her hair.

She picked the mouse up off her shoulder and set him down on the table.

"You better not have left any presents up here," she warned, combing her fingers through her hair.

The mouse snorted and began to clean his whiskers.

"I'm not learning how to ride so I can ride a unicorn. I'm learning just to know. Tell me more about unicorns."

The mouse shook his head. "Not until the servant gets back."

Naomi sighed and puttered around the room. She found a thimble and held onto it to use as the mouse's wine cup. She hoped Tavik didn't stop by again for lunch. She wanted to get the mouse stuffed and drunk and learn everything she could about unicorns.

Soon Yula returned with the wine and cheese. Naomi thanked her and said she would be fine on her own for the rest of the morning. She was sore and tired and wished to rest. Yula accepted her statements without suspicion. She departed with a promise to return at midday with lunch. Naomi set up the cheese and wine on the table. Mr. Squibbles scampered forward to begin his feast, but Naomi smacked her hand down between him and his goal.

"I ask the questions, you answer them, and then you get a piece of cheese and a little wine."

Mr. Squibbles' whiskers twitched at her conditions. "Fine, ask your first question."

"Where can I find unicorns?"

"The best place to look is in the northern plateaus. A small herd is supposed to still run in those parts."

Naomi set a piece of cheese and a thimble of wine down before him, which he fell greedily upon.

"How can I catch one?"

"You can go the regular route of hounds and horses, or you can use the traditional method of baiting a trap with a virgin."

She appreciated the offer of two options and decided to be as equally generous and set two pieces of cheese before him for his two pieces of information.

"How does the transportation magic work with the horns?" she asked.

"Unicorns can go wherever they want. They simply think it, and they're there." He gobbled down his new piece of cheese and drank his wine.

"Can a unicorn be told where someone wants to go and take them there?"

Mr. Squibbles sipped from his thimble. It was the

perfect size for his paws. Naomi had to bite the inside of her cheeks to keep from going *aww*. "A unicorn can understand the words of the virgin but no one else."

She dwelt on the fact that all this unicorn lore required a virgin, and she hadn't been one since her high school prom—though she sort of wished she could go back and stop her younger self that night. But she wouldn't have stopped herself with her first boyfriend in college. Happily not a virgin after him. Where could she get a virgin to help her?

Mr. Squibbles politely cleared his throat to gain her attention. Naomi refocused to him, not even fazed anymore by the talking mouse. "May I ask your interest in unicorns?"

"I accidentally got brought here by a unicorn horn, and now I'm stuck. I want to go home, and the only way to do that is to find another horn. I don't want to kill a unicorn or anything. I just want to get home."

"Maybe I know someone who can help," Mr. Squibbles said, punctuating his offer with a hiccup. He'd drunk five thimbles of wine. Naomi wondered if she should start watering down his drinks. "There's a witch in the woods, mad as a hatter but capable of working strong magic. She might be able to help you."

The mad as a hatter comment rang a bell. It was a warning bell. "Do you mean Agatha?" she asked.

"So you've met?"

Naomi wasn't buying it. A talking mouse just happened to scamper into her room, who knew lots about unicorns, and was now recommending help from Agatha? "She sent you, didn't she?"

The mouse rose up on his back legs and swayed unsteadily. "She's not the boss of me! So I made one mistake with an incantation. It was an accident! Rolling r's are difficult with these teeth. Treats me like a common familiar. Fetch this, Squibbles. Don't touch that, Squibbles. I know the difference between mudwort and bloodroot!"

"If you're supposed to help me, what was with all the wine and cheese for information?"

"Because I wanted wine and cheese! Were you going to offer me any otherwise? No, because nobody ever offers proper refreshment to mice. Assume we'll find something for ourselves. You'd have given a laconic cat a saucer of milk or a chatty dog a ham bone, but talking mice always have to forage for ourselves."

"You have issues. Oh God, I have issues. If Tavik finds out that Agatha's trying to help me, he's going to kill me. He does *not* like Agatha."

"The feeling's mutual. Now are you going to make me *earn* the rest of my refreshments or not?"

Naomi pushed the rest of the cheese toward him and poured more wine as she wondered how she was going to sneak away from the castle to see Agatha. The old woman had kept her promise. She turned to ask Mr. Squibbles how they were going to get away but found him passed out in what was left of the wine. She tucked him into her pocket for safekeeping. She sat by the window and thought about possibilities.

Yula came back with lunch and suggested they spend the afternoon in the gardens. They took a basket to pick flowers and put on straw hats to protect them from the afternoon sun. Naomi felt like a young woman in some old Flemish painting. As they cut flowers, Yula told her their names and if they had any special uses other than being pretty.

As Yula sat down to rest and enjoy the sun, Naomi wandered off for a private word with the mouse. She opened her pocket and peered into it. "Mr. Squibbles, are you awake?"

"Oh, my head. Why is the world swaying?"

"You're in my pocket. Don't you dare get sick."

The mouse rolled into a sitting position. He appeared to still be drunk. "You have an unhealthy concern with my bodily functions. You know that?"

"It's because your bodily functions could end up on me. How are we going to leave the castle without anyone noticing?"

"Leaving at night will probably work best. No one will notice you're gone until sunrise, unless Lord Tavik visits you regularly at night?" he asked, and she wasn't sure, but she thought the mouse was leering at her.

"No, he's not supposed to visit me at night."

"Guards?" he asked.

"I haven't noticed. I don't think he has any posted at my door."

"What about the old woman?"

"She sleeps in her own room."

"A nighttime escape it is, then. I know a secret way to get out."

"A secret way?"

"A secret passage between walls. I don't think anyone living knows about it, except mice."

"Where is it?"

"Well, you see, that's the fun part. The entrance is in Tavik's room."

"What!"

CHAPTER EIGHT

Frogs hate unicorns.

Mr. Squibbles flattened his ears and burrowed into Naomi's pocket. He must be suffering a massive hangover. Naomi quickly looked over at Yula to see if she'd heard Naomi's outburst. She had and had risen from the spot where she'd been sitting. Naomi waved to indicate all was well and moved out of eyesight.

She hunched over her pocket and hissed, "Are you insane? Tavik will kill anyone who tries to sneak in."

"That will be problematic, but a nighttime departure is still your best option. If you try to leave during the day, someone will notice you're gone—like your maid."

Naomi paced unhappily. "There has to be another way."

"We could try lots of different ways. We'd have to because none of them would work."

Naomi frowned. "Well, if this is the best plan, how are we supposed to accomplish it?"

"We?" Mr. Squibbles squeaked.

"You know the secret passage, and you know where Agatha lives. Of course, you're going to guide me. That's why she sent."

She held her breath, waiting for Mr. Squibbles' response. He couldn't bail on her. She didn't know if she could escape if she had to face it alone.

Mr. Squibbles appeared to be thinking hard about his answer. He took a long time. Naomi feared she would go blue waiting. "Fine," Mr. Squibbles finally sighed. "I don't suppose you know how to pick locks, do you?"

"No, unfortunately I have always been a fine upstanding citizen."

"We'll have to get a key, then," Mr. Squibbles said, flicking his whiskers.

"We?"

"Sorry, *you* will have to get a key. I suspect only Tavik has the one to his chambers. You'll have to use your feminine charms to distract him and slip it away from him."

"Yes, I'll just do that the next time we're alone together. I'll bat my eyelashes from behind my blindfold and slip my bound hands right into his pocket."

"If you really want to get out of here, you'll figure something out."

Naomi huffed and wondered if there were more helpful talking animals somewhere in the castle, like maybe a hungry cat.

The day was getting late. Yula and Naomi gathered their flowers and went back into the castle. Naomi asked what the plans were for dinner, and Yula said dinner had been arranged to be served in her room. Lord Tavik was to dine with one of his vassals that night and would probably sleep at their home. Naomi was relieved by the news, which meant there was no way for her to act upon her and Mr. Squibbles' nonexistent plan; instead she could spend the night actually trying to formulate one.

Yula sat with her late into the night. Naomi kept to her own thoughts while Yula did some embroidery.

"You are very quiet, milady," Yula said from her seat by the fire.

Naomi looked up from her daze and gave the old woman a wan smile. "I've got a lot on my mind."

"Are you bored?"

She played off the question with a shrug. "It doesn't seem like there's much for me to do here."

Yula nodded and stared at her embroidery. "Once Lord Tavik leaves, you'll find something to do."

"He's leaving? When?" Maybe she wouldn't have to worry about creeping through his room while he slept.

"In a few days, I suppose. He'll be done with all the business that required his attention here. His primary goal for coming back was to get you situated."

"Oh, so he just wanted to dump me here and get back to his wars?"

"A soldiers' camp is no place for a lady."

Naomi snorted. They were no place for anyone.

A frightening thought popped into her head. "Are you leaving with him?"

Yula's mouth thinned for a moment, and she didn't raise her eyes from her work. "Our lord has not said if he will want me to go and tend him. There are plenty of maids in the castle, all of them younger than me. One of them can tend to you."

"But you're who I know! You're who I trust." This was terrible. Naomi had barely gotten a glimpse of these younger maids. Mrs. Boon made sure of that. If Yula left, she'd be alone. Yula's mouth thinned more.

"I have enjoyed tending you, milady, and I would not be averse to staying here to serve you, but it will be Lord

Tavik's decision."

"I'll tell him to let you stay. He can't expect you to go back. If it's no place for me, it can't be a place for you. Let him take Mrs. Boon. She'll probably fit right in with the soldiers, or scare them."

Yula's mouth lifted into a tiny smile. She began gathering her things. "It's late. I'll leave you to rest. And thank you for your kind words."

Naomi went over to her and gave her a hug. "We'll figure something out. I'm not going to let you go easily."

Once Yula was gone, Naomi turned to go to bed. She was a little sore from her riding lesson but felt a good night's sleep would make her as good as new.

"Ready?" asked Mr. Squibbles.

She stopped at the edge of her bed and looked down. Mr. Squibbles crawled out from underneath. "Why are you dressed for bed?" he asked.

"Because I was going to sleep."

"No, you're not. This is the perfect opportunity to get into Tavik's room. I bet he doesn't lock it when he's not there. He doesn't keep any papers or other important things in his room."

"You want to leave tonight?" Naomi asked incredulously.

"We might not get a better chance!"

She looked around her room in apprehension. She hadn't planned on trying anything so soon. She hadn't made any preparations. Like Mr. Squibbles had pointed out, she wasn't even dressed.

"You said so yourself, it's near suicide to try to sneak into his room while he's there. Tonight is our chance," he reminded her.

"Yula just said that he won't be staying much longer. He's planning to return to his troops. We could just wait until he's gone for good."

Mr. Squibbles rose on his hind legs and put his paws on his hips. "Do you really want to wait, or do you want to not do this at all? For someone who wants to find a unicorn to take her away from here, you aren't acting very eager to start."

Naomi stared at the small rodent and knew he was right. If she didn't want to spend another night in this messed-up world, she should leave now, not wait around. She had to consider her life back home. What was happening while she was away? What was her family suffering? With her priorities realigned, she went to her wardrobe and began pulling out clothes.

"What should I bring?"

"I don't know."

"I'll need clothes."

"Okay, bring clothes."

"But what should I bring?"

"You just said. Clothes."

"But what type?"

It was hard to tell, but it looked like the mouse shrugged his shoulders. She supposed clothes would be a non-issue for animals.

She stuffed a wool gown and another set of underclothes into a bag. "Turn around," she said.

"What? Why?"

"I'm not changing in front of you."

Mr. Squibbles' sigh was loud and clear as he shuffled around. She slipped out of her nightgown and into a simple dress. Once she was ready, she picked up the bag and moved to the door.

She peeked out of her room cautiously. She'd said that there were no guards, but she didn't want to take any chances. When she saw that no one was in the hallway, she crept out.

"Come on, let's go," Mr. Squibbles said as he darted ahead down the passage.

Naomi closed the door to her room and stepped quickly to catch up with the mouse. The fact that she was following a mouse no longer seemed surreal.

Her heart was pounding when she arrived at Tavik's door. They hadn't heard or seen anyone in their sneaking, but she still feared being discovered. She tried the handle, praying that Mr. Squibbles was right about Tavik not locking it when he wasn't there. It opened smoothly. She slipped into the dark chamber and closed the door quietly behind her. She raised her candle with a shaking hand. Her eyes went immediately to the bed. For a second, her eyes saw a form there, and she had a small heart attack, but the candle flickered and revealed her imagination had made shadows into warlords.

"Where's the passage?"

"This way," Mr. Squibbles said and darted off into the darkness.

Naomi squinted and crept further into the room. She finally picked out the mouse beside the fireplace on his hind legs. She moved closer, her eyes darting over the mantle. "What do I press to open it?"

"Do you see that discolored stone?"

She placed her hand upon it and pressed. It didn't budge.

"Now count four stones down and three to the right."

Naomi was glad it was dim so that Mr. Squibbles hadn't seen her attempt or current her light blush. She followed his directions to the stone and pressed. It didn't budge either. "Nothing's happening."

"It's old. Push harder."

She leaned into the stone and pushed with all of her weight. It shifted a little but still didn't budge. "Am I doing something wrong?"

"Obviously, you're not pushing hard enough."

She tried harder to push the stone. It just stayed where it was.

"Maybe it needs to be oiled or greased or something," she huffed as she took a step back.

"Let me see what I can do." Mr. Squibbles disappeared through a chink in the wall.

Naomi waited nervously for the mouse to do something. She'd known this was a bad idea. She was going to get caught and then she was going to be thrown into a dungeon. She hadn't been shown one on her tour, but Tavik was sure to have one stashed somewhere in the castle. It probably had chains dangling everywhere, a rack, whips, large beady-eyed rats who loved fingers and toes, an iron maiden, thumb screws, a rusty guillotine, and every restraint imaginable. Tavik had already shown a peccadillo for tying her up.

"Mr. Squibbles, hurry up," she called. She heard muffled swearing through the wall.

Finally, something began to happen. Stones ground together, and the block, that she'd been pressing, slid inward. As Naomi began to worry that someone would come to investigate the strange sounds, the wall began to swing open. As soon as the gap was wide enough, she slipped through. She found a ghostly Mr. Squibbles waiting for her. He'd gotten dust and cobwebs all over himself while getting the door to work.

"We won't be able to close it. The rope snapped for the main pulley," he told her as he brushed himself off.

Naomi looked back into Tavik's room. "But they'll know how we escaped."

Mr. Squibbles' whiskers twitched. "If you stop worrying and start going, we'll be long gone by the time they discover the secret passage. Now move it!" The small mouse took off down the dark passage, disappearing quickly.

Naomi lingered a moment. She was still indecisive over this whole thing. She spared a thought for Yula and worried that the old woman would come to harm due to her escape. Maybe she should bring the old woman with her?

"Mr. Squibbles, wait!" she called, but the mouse was gone.

She thought frantically about what she should do. If she left Yula, the female servant might be punished, but if she was found with Naomi, she would surely be punished. Tavik had not placed a guard on Naomi nor had he seemed to have instructed Yula to watch her. He couldn't punish the woman for something she hadn't known to do; at least that was how Naomi hoped it would be. It was safer if she left her behind. Though the decision made her feel awful, it was the way it had to be.

As if karma agreed wholeheartedly that Naomi was doing a bad thing, her candle snuffed out with her first step down the tunnel. She thought about attempting to relight it but feared she wouldn't catch up with the mouse as it was. She tossed the candle aside, stepped further into the tunnel, found the far wall, and began to follow it. With each step she took, her pace increased until she was running full tilt. She knew she should stop. Her mad dash was foolhardy, but what about any of this made sense? She was following a talking mouse to go see a witch about finding a unicorn.

The passage was pitch-black and littered with debris. Stones had crumbled from the wall, and spiders, mice, and other small things had left their trash upon the floor. Even with her hand on the wall to guide her, Naomi slipped and scraped her hands and knees. She got back up but slowed her pace to a walk, though her heart continued to pound like she were running.

The darkness was claustrophobic. She had no sense of distance. Cobwebs latched onto her face and made her skin crawl. She had to blow her nose and spit them out. She could see nothing: not the end to the passage, not the walls or floor, not her hand in front of her face. She began to panic. It was like she was in one of those sensory deprivation tanks. She couldn't see or hear anything. She hugged the wall. It was all she had.

She called out to Mr. Squibbles several times but received no response. She began to wonder if the little rodent had abandoned her. Maybe it was all a trick. Maybe he had brought her here as a ploy to get her in trouble. Maybe he was now watching with his beady rodent eyes, snickering as she stumbled around in circles.

Naomi started thinking of ways to kill a mouse. She could step on him and crush him under her shoe. The sound of his bones crunching would be very satisfying. She could kill him with a trap. She would bait it with cheese. She could poison him, maybe slip something into his wine. She could lock him in a room full of hungry cats. She could clench him in her fist and squeeze until his ribs collapsed, and his beady little eyes bulged. She could dice him up and make stew. She could drown him in a bucket of water. There were so many ways to kill a mouse. Naomi was sorry she would only be able to use one of them when she got a hold of the little traitor. Where was he? Where was she?

"Mr. Squibbles!"

"It probably not even his real name. Mister, indeed. And what the heck was a squibble?" she muttered darkly to herself.

She stumbled on, clutching her anger tight to keep her fear at bay. Thoughts of dead mice danced in her head. She kept imaging new scenarios until she realized the darkness up ahead was lightening from pitch black to moonlit. She quickened her pace and dashed out of the tunnel into a forested area.

"It took you long enough."

Naomi turned toward the mouse ready to pounce with a murderous rage, but stopped short and felt her jaw drop. She had been ready to commit rodent-cide, but she had not figured on there being a witness—a large, snorting, long-legged witness.

"Where did you get the horse?"

"From the stables. Now do you want to get up here or gawp at the nice horse for the rest of the night?"

She went up to the horse cautiously. When she reached his head and let him sniff her hand, she realized it was actually Stomper. She rubbed his forehead and wondered how she was going to manage this. One riding lesson did not a horsewoman make.

To her surprise, she realized the horse was bridled and saddled.

"Mr. Squibbles, did you have help?"

He sat between Stomper's ears, clutching strands of the horse's forelock. "What, you don't think a mouse could saddle and bring a horse out here all on his very own?"

"Who helped you?"

"Maybe a poor stable boy, who is more superstitious than wise, thought a ghost of a dead general told him to saddle and ready the horse, and maybe the dead general got the horse to come out here with a little animalspeak, and you should thank the dead general."

"Thank you, General. What are your orders, sir?"

"Get on the horse, Naomi. We're wasting moonlight."

She climbed up onto Stomper with little grace, but luckily, he was a very patient horse. She sat on his back uncomfortably and fiddled with the reins. Master Geoff had not let her hold them during her lesson. She didn't know what to do with them.

Mr. Squibbles sighed. She got the feeling he would be doing that a lot during their little adventure. "Nudge the horse gently with your left heel and pull the right rein to turn him around."

She did as instructed, and Stomper slowly wheeled around. "Now nudge him again with both heels," the mouse instructed. The horse began to trot through the woods.

"Can't you use more animalspeak to tell him what to

do? I really have no feel for this," she suggested.

The small animal hunched his shoulders. "Very well. If I'd known you were this helpless, I would've planned this a whole lot differently."

"What would you have planned?"

"Not to have done this at all."

They rode on in relative silence. The mouse would occasionally chitter something to the horse to guide him, and Naomi would yawn. Dew began to set, and Naomi felt clammy. They traveled through the forest following a dirt trail. The insect noises sounded off-key to her, like wildlife calls put through a synthesizer. Stomper moved sedately, but she knew she would not have covered as much ground on her own. The further they went, the more apprehensive she became. The forest grew denser, and the eerie wildlife noises increased. She began to worry about umbreks.

"How much further?" she asked after they'd traveled for what she judged to be an hour.

The mouse didn't answer.

"Mr. Squibbles?" She peered at the mouse sitting between Stomper's ears.

"Um," the mouse nervously laughed.

"What?"

"Well, you see, the house is around here somewhere…"

"You don't know *where* it is?"

Mr. Squibbles' ears flattened. "I knew where it was, but she must've moved it."

Naomi couldn't believe this. "What did she do, make it grow legs and have it walk away?"

"No, that would be silly. She couldn't have gone far, though. She likes these woods. We'll find her. Don't worry."

"Don't worry, he says. We'll find the magically moving house. It can't have wandered off too far. I hate this world," she muttered. Stomper snorted in consolation.

"There, that light! It's her. It has to be. Nobody else would live out here." Mr. Squibbles said something to Stomper, and the horse sped up to a trot, heading toward the light.

Naomi didn't let herself believe it. She sat stonily and kept her eyes firmly on the house. It could be a woodcutter's cabin or a hunter's lodge. She was already formulating a ruse to tell the owners when the house turned out to be some poor family's home. She would claim to be lost—which was the truth—who had been set upon by umbreks—a several days old truth—trying to find her way back home. Naomi realized she wouldn't have to lie much at all.

When they reached the house, Mr. Squibbles leaped down from the horse before Naomi could stop him.

"Agatha, get your wrinkly ass out here! I've brought her!"

"Mr. Squibbles!" Naomi exclaimed.

If the witch were home, she didn't want to be hexed before she even reached the doorstep. The door to the cottage swung open, and an old hunched woman stood in the light. She raised a lantern up, and Naomi's eyes met the dancing eyes of Agatha. Everything that she'd gone through came rushing up in her throat in one word. "You!"

Agatha's smile widened into a toothy grin. "Welcome to my home."

"Do you know how much trouble you put me in? I was forced to marry Tavik!"

"That was the plan."

"Plan? I didn't agree to any plan!"

"It was better that you didn't know."

She slid off Stomper and marched up to the witch. "You better be ready to tell me stuff. Stuff like how I can get home."

Agatha nodded. "Come inside and we'll discuss it." She

held the door open for her.

Naomi looked inside and felt like the fly being invited in by the spider, but shook off her misgivings and went in. She turned to look at Stomper. She wasn't sure if she should tie him up or not. Before she could decide whether to go back outside, the door swung shut on its own.

"Have a seat, Naomi."

The cottage was warm and cozy except for the random animal bones that hung from the ceiling. They added a certain deranged something to the place.

Agatha settled down into a cushioned chair and motioned for Naomi to take the other.

"So, Mr. Squibbles brought me," Naomi said, unsure of anything else. The mouse in question had darted off into the shadows of the room.

Agatha picked up a long pipe and lit it with twig from the fire. She nodded her head as she puffed it.

"Yes, I said I'd send for you."

"Is Mr. Squibbles really a mage trapped in mouse form?"

Agatha grinned around the pipe's mouthpiece. "No, he's my familiar. He thinks humans will take him more seriously if he tells them that he was once human."

From the darkness, Mr. Squibbles' voice floated out. "It's because humans are ignorant speciesists: can't accept that another animal might be as smart or smarter than you."

"I think you're much smarter than me, Mr. Squibbles," Naomi said in the direction Mr. Squibbles' voice had come. She turned back to Agatha. "So you two are going to help me?"

To her amazement, Agatha blew out a plume of smoke in a long spiral. It swirled out like a corkscrew and slowly dissipated. "Yes, I'm going to help you. If you need a unicorn to get home, I'll help you get one."

"How?" Naomi asked.

"Let me know one thing first. How committed are you to getting home?"

"Very committed. To the point I should be fitted for a straitjacket."

The witch obviously didn't understand the reference, but Naomi's tone was convincing enough. "And you're not a virgin?"

She shook her head.

Agatha sat back in her chair. "It would help matters if we had one."

"I don't suppose you know any?" Naomi asked.

She threw her head back and laughed. "No, not personally. Not many virgins come my way."

"Wooh, wooh, aiv noe."

Both women turned in their seats. Mr. Squibbles came out of the shadows with a piece of bread in his paws and his cheeks puffed full with food.

"Iaa loow fleuar un fis."

"You do, do you?" Agatha said.

"What did he say?" Naomi asked.

"He knows where we can find a virgin."

"Where?"

"Fwavik."

"What?" Naomi asked.

"He said Tavik."

She didn't understand. "There's a virgin with Tavik?"

"Nwo! Wit is Fwavuk."

Naomi still didn't understand. "Tavik is holding a virgin?"

"No, Fwavuk!"

"Huh?"

"My dear, the virgin is Tavik," Agatha said.

CHAPTER NINE

"Unicorns find humans irritating. The whole have to be a virgin thing is just an excuse to not have to talk to most of you."—Mr. Squibbles

Naomi stared at the witch a moment and then began to giggle. "That's ridiculous. Tavik isn't a virgin. How could he be?"

Agatha's eyebrows rose. "Slept with him, have you?"

Naomi hunched her shoulders in embarrassment. "No, we made a deal, but surely—"

"Squibbles' nose is rarely wrong."

"He can smell virgins?"

"Aund wyou cyan't?" the mouse asked incredulously.

Naomi threw her hands up. "Well, what good is that going to do us? We can't kidnap him and use him as unicorn bait!"

Agatha stared at Naomi. She was grinning. It was unnerving.

"You're crazy," Naomi said.

"No, I'm a witch."

Naomi was getting a sinking feeling. She was very much not going to like this, of that she was sure. "Come on, let's be serious."

"You said you were committed."

"Yes, but this is bat-shit crazy. I've only at cuckoo on the loony scale."

"Squibbles, I need you to get us back into the castle. We're going warlord hunting."

"Wohkay," the mouse said. His cheeks still full and unconcerned by the witch's plan.

"No, this is absolutely insane. Do you know what he'll do if he catches us? He'll *kill* us! He may be a virgin, but he's a homicidal virgin!"

"Who said we're going to get caught?" Agatha asked.

"How are you going to sneak around the castle? Tavik knows you, and I'm sure the servants do, too."

Agatha puffed on her pipe. The smoke didn't rise. It settled around her thickly. Naomi got a skin crawling electrical feeling as the witch continued to draw on the pipe. The smoke increased and shrouded the witch. All Naomi could see was a blurry outline, but it began to change. The electrical feeling increased. With a small thunderclap, the smoke dissipated, and in Agatha's seat sat a black cat with yellow eyes.

"Do you think anyone will question your new pet?" Agatha asked from the cat's body.

Naomi was really becoming uncomfortable with how comfortable she was getting with talking animals. "You just better hope Tavik isn't allergic."

"If we're to make it back before anyone notices Naomi's gone, we'd better hurry," Mr. Squibbles said, having finally emptied his mouth.

Agatha jumped down from the chair. She meowed at the door, and it swung open for her. She waited in the doorway for Naomi to follow. She shook her head and rose. She was going back to the castle. If Stomper started talking to her on the way back, she would know she had gone completely mental and was in that straitjacket she'd mentioned earlier, surrounded by nice padded walls.

Naomi climbed back onto Stomper with less grace than before. Mr. Squibbles retook his place between the horse's ears, and Agatha, the cat, hopped into Naomi's arms.

"You know black cats are bad luck," Naomi said.

"I certainly will be for Tavik," the witch replied.

Mr. Squibbles said something to the horse, and the large steed turned and headed back to the castle. Naomi felt odd carrying her would-be savior in her arms, especially as she began to purr. To break the silence and reassure herself that she was with a witch and not just a cat, she cleared her throat and asked, "How exactly did you end up enemies with Tavik?"

The purring stopped, and Agatha's fur bristled. "It's hard to explain. We've always been at odds. He believes the only way to solve anything is with bloodshed and war. I've done all I can to limit that."

"Like helping all the women and children escape from Harold's Pass?" Naomi said, remembering Agatha's comments when they first met.

The cat nodded. "Yes. I just barely managed it this time. I'm getting too old to whisk away that many people in the dead of night."

"Isn't there anyone to stand against him? Another lord or king or someone?"

"There used to be."

"But they were worse," Mr. Squibbles said.

"Worse?" Naomi asked.

There was a low growl from Agatha. Mr. Squibbles looked back at them from his position on Stomper's head. "Don't try and argue it, Agatha. The rulers before Tavik were heartless. Yes, he creates strife and kills, but at least he doesn't torture and enslave like the others did."

116

"He is merely the lesser evil. The key word to remember being *evil*."

Hearing Tavik referred to as evil felt strange to Naomi. Yes, he had scared her a number of times and had hurt her once, and she could be considered enslaved by being forced to become his wife and fill the role of Lady Naomi, but still there was something about him that made her balk at calling him evil. He'd allowed her to learn how to ride, and he didn't lock her in her room. And there was their agreement. No sex. Why did he want to remain a virgin? He'd seemed interested enough that one time.

They arrived back at the entrance to the secret passage. Even knowing it was there, Naomi couldn't tell where it was. The way the foliage grew and rocks formed, it was completely invisible.

Mr. Squibbles stayed on Stomper when Naomi and Agatha dismounted. He would return the horse to the stable.

Naomi crept cautiously back into the passage, following the witch, but it was as dark as before. She moved slowly to avoid slipping again. She had no desire to add to the scabs on her knees and hands. Agatha, noticing her trouble, said a word and a spark of light formed that floated up to guide them. Naomi grinned down at the cat. The idea that magic existed and could be useful was quite comforting. It meant things were possible. Hope was not a far-fetched idea.

Naomi worried about the wedged door of the secret passage, but after they passed through it, another single word from Agatha closed it without a sound. There was no evidence any longer of Naomi's adventure, except for a black cat. She shook her head. She knew that the mission they were on would not go as smoothly.

"Tell me, do you even have a plan?" she asked the cat as she climbed into bed.

"Something will come to me. Don't worry."

Agatha closed her eyes and curled up at the foot of the

bed.

Yula woke Naomi far too early for her liking the next morning, but then, anything before noon would have been too early for her. She moaned and tried to burrow under the bedcovers, but Yula began tugging on her feet to get her out of bed.

"What is so important that I have to be awake?" she asked from under her pillow.

"Breakfast, of course."

She rolled her eyes and tried to cocoon herself in blankets, but Yula caught her arm and pulled her toward the breakfast table. "Did you not sleep well, milady?"

"I feel like I didn't sleep at all," she answered, scrubbing at her eyes. She began to pick at her food.

"Do you wish to miss your lesson with Master Geoff?"

Naomi chewed grimly on her food. "No, I wanted horse-riding lessons. I shouldn't shirk them after all the trouble everyone went to for me."

There was a meow at her feet. Agatha had followed her from the bed and looked clearly hungry. Naomi began scraping eggs from her plate to a saucer to share with her.

"Who is this?" Yula nodded down at the black cat.

"My new cat, I guess. She came to my room last night and made herself quite at home."

"And what name have you given her?" Yula crouched and extended her hand for Agatha to sniff.

Naomi froze. They hadn't discussed names. She couldn't say Agatha, obviously. Tavik would kill them both, and while Agatha may have nine lives, Naomi definitely only had one. "Kitty."

Yula's brow scrunched together. "Kitty?" She obviously didn't think much of the name. Agatha meowed to distract her. Yula scratched under her chin, and Agatha raised her head to give her better access. The sight was slightly disturbing to Naomi. Her mind kept trying to picture the scene if Agatha were in her real form.

She went down to the stables feeling half human. She met Master Geoff and Stomper. The horse greeted her affectionately. She hoped the stable master didn't pick up on their improved familiarity, but she needn't have worried. Master Geoff looked to have been perturbed by something else prior to her arrival. She cocked an eyebrow at him.

"Is something wrong?"

The stable master smiled tightly at her. "Nothing to worry about, milady. Just someone played a grand joke on one of my stable boys. The poor lad is still scared half out of his wits due to it."

She already knew about the joke he was referring to but thought it prudent to inquire. "What happened?"

"Someone hid in the stables and told the boy he was a ghost and made him saddle Stomper here."

"Oh, what a terrible prank."

"Yes, I'm going to have to put a guard on the stables to keep it from happening again."

Naomi nodded. She wondered how they would get Stomper the next time they needed him. Mr. Squibbles could not possibly trick a couple of grown men.

She decided to push this worry from her mind and focused on her second riding lesson. Master Geoff noticed how much more comfortably she sat and complimented her on it. She accepted the praise as innocently as she could.

She returned from her lesson twice as tired as before, and she was beginning to feel sore from all of her riding. She hoped Yula would let her nap for the rest of the day. She was barely keeping her eyes opened as it was. Of course, napping was out of the question when she returned to her room. Tavik was waiting for her. With a quirk of an eyebrow, she saw that Agatha was in his lap, purring loudly as the warlord petted her.

"Tavik, welcome home," she said, stifling a yawn.

"How are your lessons?"

"Geoff has some hope of making a horsewoman of me yet. Are we having lunch together again?"

"No, I came to ask you something."

The statement had the effect of a large espresso upon Naomi. That had not been a casual statement. There had been a shot of suspicion in it. Naomi blinked and waited for Tavik to continue. "I found something very odd when I returned to my quarters," he said.

Naomi made herself not react as her mind raced. Did the entrance of the secret passage not close properly? As blankly as possible, she asked, "What did you find?"

He nudged a pale pink candle that lay on the table. It was the one she'd cast aside when she entered the secret passage. She hadn't paid it any mind at the time because she hadn't thought she would be coming back and hadn't thought about it when she and Agatha had returned.

Going for total ignorance, she asked, "What's wrong with it?"

Tavik chuckled slightly. "I don't have pink candles in my room, and none of the servants would use one of these. They are only used in your room."

"Huh. Maybe a servant dropped it while cleaning your room?"

"You think that's what happened?" he asked, clearly not buying her theory for a second.

She shrugged her shoulders. "I don't know."

"Have a seat, Naomi."

She was getting a bad feeling again. "I'm fine. I would rather stand, you know, because of sitting on the horse."

"Have a seat."

She gulped and scooted over to the chair across from him. "How did your business go? Did everything go all right?"

"What did you hope to find in my bedchamber?"

Her face fell. He knew it'd been her. She was in trouble

now. Agatha jumped down from Tavik's lap and went over to her and began to brush up against her legs. She purred loudly. She figured the witch was trying to reassure her.

"I wasn't looking for anything."

"But you were in my bedchamber."

What could she say? He already knew that she'd been in there. How could she divert him from what she had really been doing and still not get into trouble?

"I was scared. I missed you."

He sat back in his chair and crossed his arms. She couldn't tell if he believed her but continued on regardless. "I don't know what you want from me. I've never been a lady or lived in a castle. It's all so strange to me. I wanted to see you, but you weren't here so I went to your bedchamber as the next best thing. I'm sorry I invaded your privacy." She hung her head in pretend shame.

"And if I had been here, what would you have done?" he asked quietly.

She bit her lip. Oh geez, she did not have any answer to that.

"You forced me into an agreement on our wedding day. You specifically said separate beds. Have you reconsidered that demand?"

Her eyes widened. That day at lunch, she may have had a momentary lust for the warlord, but she needed him to stay untouched. How had he stayed a virgin so long, anyway? She glanced at Agatha for any clue on how to proceed. Yellow eyes stared back at her without an ounce of help in them. She twisted the cloth of her skirt. Closing her eyes, she answered.

"No, the agreement stays. I'm better now. I won't bother you ever again."

"Don't feel you have to keep the agreement on my account," Tavik teased.

She lifted her eyes to glare at him. Things were just not

adding up. He had agreed to separate beds when he had not really needed to. He had not wanted a wife in the first place. He was a virgin. If he hadn't come on to her the other day, she would have thought he was a very suppressed gay man, but he had shown his interest in her clearly. What if the other day were an act? What if he was so deep in the closet that he didn't know what he was? It almost made her feel sorry for him. Oh, the poor virgin gay warlord. Who was worse off than him? His wife.

"It's probably for the best that it stays," she said softly.

Tavik rose from his chair and stepped over to her. She looked up at him in apprehension.

"Close your eyes, Naomi."

She stiffened at the request, and then she saw the blindfold dangling from his hand. She grimaced and did as she was told. He tied the blindfold across her eyes securely.

"Swivel your chair toward me."

Goose bumps were already rising on her arms. She carefully turned her chair toward him. His hands settled on top of hers on her lap. His breath brushed her forehead.

"Lift your face."

She tilted her head back. His lips grazed her cheeks, her nose, and her chin with soft touches. She breathed shallowly through her mouth under the gentle kisses. His mouth slanted over hers and gained access easily. She gave in to the kiss. He certainly kissed her like he liked girls. She was ashamed at the feeling of relief that caused her. His sexuality should not matter to her. The fact was it would be better if he were gay. There would be no chance of her tempting him then. He pulled on her arms to get her to stand. She rose without breaking the kiss. He began backing her to her bed. He switched her wrists to one hand and wrapped his other around her to hold her close. Any lingering thoughts of Tavik being gay were swiftly blasted away by the bulge she felt against her hip.

"Gods, you make me do dangerous things," he

murmured against her mouth.

"Why is this dangerous?" she whispered back. His answer was another kiss and another step back toward the bed.

As she took another blind step back as Tavik kissed her, she felt something furry tangle with her feet. She faltered to try and get clear of it, but Tavik had already taken a step for them. She lost her balance and began to fall. In the back of her mind, a voice cried, "*Timber!*" She landed on her back without her arms to offer any buffer, and then a second impact as Tavik landed on top of her, squashing her.

She groaned in pain and tried to shift him off her. "God damn it, Kitty!" Her hand went to remove the blindfold so she could glare at Agatha, but Tavik's hand intercepted hers and jerked it away from her face.

"This is why it's dangerous," he said.

"What is the big deal? Why can't anyone see your face? Are you terribly scarred, disfigured, what? It doesn't matter!"

"It does matter. I'm sorry." Holding her hands immobile, he leaned forward and gave her a another kiss, but it wasn't a kiss to ignite passions. It was a kiss of farewell. He rose to his feet and was gone. She waited a moment and heard the door to her chamber close. She reached up and snatched off the blindfold. Agatha crouched under the bed, glaring at her. She glared back just as hard.

"What is the big idea? Are you trying to kill me?"

"And I want to know what you were trying to do! We need him to stay pure."

"Are you sure Mr. Squibbles was right? Because he certainly doesn't act like a virgin."

"I'm sure."

"Well, maybe there's another virgin in the castle. Have you considered that? Maybe we should expand our options."

"Why, so you can remove Tavik as a possibility?"

Naomi blew out a breath in aggravation. She rose up and went to her window to look down onto the courtyard. Maids beat on carpets. A blacksmith toiled with a hammer on a piece of hot metal. Children chased chickens. Everyone was going about doing normal, mundane things while she argued with a talking cat and plotted how to kidnap her virgin husband. She wanted to beat rugs.

Agatha leapt up to the windowsill. "I doubt we have much time before Tavik returns to his troops and escapes our grasp," the witch said.

Absently, Naomi stroked the feline's head. "What do you suppose we should do?"

"Our best option is to drug him. We can carry him down through the secret passage and be long gone before anyone knows anything."

"They've placed a guard on the horses due to Mr. Squibbles' little theatrics the other night."

"That will make things a little more difficult, but we will be able to get around it."

"And how do you suggest we drug Tavik?"

"Surely he would accept a drink with his wife?"

"I wouldn't count on it."

"Enough of this gloominess. We must stay confident. We will succeed."

Naomi turned away from the window in frustration. "I don't know if you've noticed, but we're a team of a mouse, a cat, and a captive woman. What will we succeed except total and utter failure?"

"That's the spirit," grumbled a squeaky voice. Naomi looked at their new arrival.

"Do you have any bright ideas? How about we throw a net over him and conk him on the head?"

"Do you still want to get a unicorn or not?" Mr. Squibbles asked.

124

Naomi dropped her head but nodded.

"We need Tavik, then."

"Really is there no other virgin we could get? Maybe instead of kidnapping someone, we could just ask them to help us?"

The mouse shook his head. "The only other virgins in this castle are children. Do you want to take a child?"

"You know that he's the worst person to take. He's not only the most dangerous, but a lot of men will come looking for him. How can we be sure we'll make it to a unicorn before they catch up with us?"

The cat stood up on her back legs and placed her forepaws on Naomi's knees to look up into her face with large unwavering eyes. "You have such little faith. I am a powerful witch, capable of many things that would surprise you. I bet you are capable of a few things that would surprise you as well. We will succeed. How, may not be apparent at the moment, but we will accomplish this because we are capable, determined, and just a bit crazy."

Naomi gave the cat a small smile at the statement. Just a bit crazy. Yes, she was certainly that. She felt a little better. Agatha was an amazing woman. She was sure she could do lots of things that would astound her, and Agatha was more than willing to help her. If Naomi couldn't have much confidence in herself, she should at least have some in her new friends.

"I'm sorry. I do believe you, and I'm grateful for all the help you've given me. I wouldn't have a chance without both of you."

Agatha and Mr. Squibbles nodded, accepting her apology. "So what do you have in mind?" Naomi asked.

Agatha opened her mouth to reply, but her head whipped to the door. Yula cracked the door open and peered in. Naomi groaned.

"Milady, who is in here with you?" she asked tentatively.

Hoping Yula hadn't heard anyone but her, Naomi chuckled thinly and indicated Agatha. "Just the cat. I know it's silly, but I just started talking to her and couldn't stop."

Yula pushed the door open and slipped in. She looked around the room. "I thought I heard other voices."

Naomi laughed again. "I may have been answering myself with a pretend voice. I'm not insane. I swear."

Yula didn't look convinced that Naomi had not been talking to someone else, but the only other being in the room was the cat and she was keeping mum. Mr. Squibbles had run back under the bed as soon as the door began to open.

"Was Lord Tavik here?" Yula asked.

Naomi rolled her eyes as she nodded. "Yes, his grand lordship graced me with his presence."

Yula smirked at her but didn't comment. She took the seat vacated by Tavik. She continued to grin at Naomi until she began to wonder what she found so amusing. Her comment hadn't been that droll. She waited for the servant to let her in on the joke, but Yula's grin only widened into a Cheshire cat smile.

"All right, I give up. What's so funny?"

"You seem to be missing a ribbon."

Naomi looked down, and saw that the ribbon that laced up the front of her dress was gone. The front of her dress gaped open. She hadn't noticed Tavik tugging it open during their liplock. She looked around the room and found Agatha playing with the ribbon near the bed. When she bent down to pick it up, she whispered, "You could've told me."

Agatha merely reached up and batted at the dangling ends. Naomi snorted at her behavior. She returned to her seat and began threading the ribbon back into her dress. Yula's eyes still danced in amusement.

"I have no idea how this happened," she muttered.

Yula chuckled at her expense.

There was a tap at the door. Yula went to see who it was. A maid stood there. She spoke softly to Yula for a few moments. "Milady, Lord Tavik requests your company for dinner tonight."

"Who'll be dining with us?" she asked.

"It's to be a private dinner in his chamber."

Agatha immediately went to the door and meowed to be let out. Naomi assumed she was going to consult with Mr. Squibbles and create a plan to kidnap Tavik. She hoped the two would remember that she would most likely be tied up for the meal and unable to slip something into his food, and Tavik would probably notice a cat or a mouse trying to get at his cup or plate as well.

CHAPTER TEN

Taking a unicorn's horn won't kill him, but he'll die before letting you have it.

Yula pulled the brush through Naomi's hair and quietly said two hundred. Naomi thought fifty strokes had been more than enough, but Yula had paid no attention to her opinion. She was more excited about the private dinner than Naomi. Naomi had tried to dampen her zeal, but Yula was having none of it. She kept muttering things like how nice holding a baby again would be. Needless to say, Yula's excitement was freaking her out. When Naomi saw her reach for the perfume bottle again, she hopped up from the chair.

"I don't need any more perfume! The cooks can probably smell me from the kitchen while chopping onions!"

Yula wielded the perfume bottle expertly out of her reach and still managed to dab the pestle in Naomi's cleavage before she could stop her. "We want you to smell nice everywhere," she countered, but she put the perfume down. She picked up the hairbrush again. Naomi began backing away with her.

"Stay away, Yula. You've gone a bit bonkers."

"Just a few more strokes, milady. We want you to look your best for Lord Tavik." Yula tried to dart behind her with the brush, but Naomi skipped back and stepped on the bed to get away from her.

"No, we do not! I looked perfectly fine for Tavik an hour ago!" She felt quite ridiculous delivering this protest standing on the bed, but she was not going near that woman until she put down the hairbrush.

"At least put on a little more jewelry. I think Lord Tavik especially liked that ruby pendent. He stared at it quite a bit at the banquet."

"Are you sure it was the pendent he was staring at?" Naomi knew the pendent had rested in her cleavage.

"Well, we should at least give him an excuse to look there," Yula said coyly.

Naomi stomped her foot in frustration and toppled forward when the bed bounced. Her hair fell across her face, and she felt the combs that were holding it shift out of place.

"See, this is what you get for being obstinate," Yula scolded.

Naomi muttered curses to herself as she rolled off the bed and let Yula put her hair back to rights. Tavik better come get her soon because the evening would probably be ruined if she killed Yula.

She sat still as Yula rearranged her hair. The older woman had a serene look on her face. "You really care about him, don't you?" Naomi said.

Yula stopped brushing her hair and looked at her through the mirror. "No, I don't. The fact is I often hate him."

"You do? But you look after him. Take care of him."

"It's what I have to do to stay close to him."

"Why?"

She began brushing her hair again. "Because I'm more likely to find my sons if I'm with him."

Naomi felt a jolt. She hadn't ever suspected that Yula had a family. She couldn't believe she hadn't asked. Maybe she was more a "lady" than she thought, since she hadn't wondered about something so important to another person.

"What happened?"

"Lord Tavik's men go to the towns and enlist the young men. It's either enlistment or pay for exemption. We were too poor to pay the exemption fee. They were swept up into the army three years ago. I couldn't follow them. The soldiers wouldn't let me. I finally latched onto a camp and became one of the cooks. I asked everyone about my sons, but no one knew them. When I was offered the job of cooking for Tavik, I took it. He visits all of the camps. I'm sure to find my sons someday. I pray that they are alive and well."

Naomi looked down at her hands. She remembered her request to keep Yula with her. She hadn't known how selfish her request had been. "So you want to go back with Tavik when he leaves?"

"I don't know, milady. I enjoy being with you, but I want to find my sons, and I can't do that if I stay here. Don't worry about this now. It's time to go."

She escorted her to Tavik's room. When she raised her hand to knock, Naomi caught it and turned her around to face her. "I'm going to help you find your sons. You will see them again."

Yula smiled at her, but it was a touch sad. "That's kind of you to say, but don't trouble yourself with my problems. Have a lovely dinner with your husband."

"How can you say that? He took your family. Don't you want him punished?"

"The gods will punish him for any crimes he has committed. Remember, he is your husband. You can't trouble yourself with these things."

"So I shouldn't care that I'm married to a warmonger?"

"You're his wife. You can't look at him that way."

"He is what he is, Yula."

"Yes, he's your husband. He is the man that controls your fate. Don't go against him. Be his wife. He seems to care for you. Don't give him a reason to stop."

Yula reached past her and knocked on the door. Tavik called out to enter. Yula opened the door, and with her hand firmly on Naomi's back, propelled her into the room. Naomi had to clench her jaw to keep from protesting her forced entrance.

Dinner was already set. Tavik stood by the fireplace, waiting. He was dressed in a long shirt and soft pants. She looked around the candlelit room. Effort had been made to make the room look softer and romantic. The draped cloth, the flower garlands, the scented candles were appealing, but she also found all the preparations somewhat sardonic; after all, she wouldn't be able to enjoy them from behind a blindfold.

"This looks lovely. What's the special occasion?"

Tavik pushed off the mantle and walked over to the table. He held out a chair for her. "Can't a husband think dining with his wife is special enough?"

She slipped into the seat and put her hands in her lap. With relief, she saw the glint of yellow feline eyes from under the bed. She smiled demurely and reached for her wineglass. *Be polite, be cordial, maybe even flirt a little*, she instructed herself. She didn't know what the plan was, but those actions would surely help it go smoothly. She still clenched her jaw when the blindfold appeared. After Tavik had tied it, his fingers trailed over her hair. They swept forward and brushed her neck and under her jaw. She swallowed nervously.

He leaned down to whisper into her ear, "What were you looking for when you came to my room?" His breath on her neck sent shivers down her spine, but they weren't good shivers.

She leaned away from him to try to maintain her composure. "You," she lied.

"But I wasn't here."

"I know." Her mouth was dry. She reached blindly out for her goblet and knocked it over. She felt the wine spill onto the lap of her dress.

"Let me," he said.

She stilled as a napkin brushed over her lap. Tavik's breath tickled her neck. It was going to be like lunch all over again. There was a low growl, and Agatha knocked Tavik's hand away by jumping into Naomi's lap.

"I didn't know she was in here," Tavik said in surprise.

Naomi patted the cat shakily. Agatha meowed petulantly. Naomi could just imagine the scolding look she was receiving from the feline.

"She likes to follow me everywhere."

"She's a fine-looking cat," Tavik said. Naomi heard Agatha hiss, and felt Tavik suddenly jerked back.

"She doesn't seem to like me at the moment."

She grabbed Agatha to hold her still. "Did she hurt you?"

Agatha let out a low growl.

"It's nothing."

Naomi smirked and shook her head.

"What?" he asked.

"We certainly are a pair. Just can't seem to keep our hands off each other."

Tavik leaned into the back of Naomi's chair and stroked her shoulders. Agatha growled louder. Naomi's hold on the cat tightened. He chuckled. "She acts like your chaperone who is very displeased with me."

"I wouldn't say she's my chaperone," she said, thinking of whose purity they needed to keep intact.

"Maybe she's your familiar, and you cast a spell on me."

If only he knew, she thought. "I'm not a witch."

"How can I be sure?"

She rolled her eyes from behind the blindfold.

He seemed to warm to the idea. "Yes, maybe you cast a spell that makes me want to do things that would be very bad for me." His hands flexed on her shoulders.

"Yes, this is all part of my diabolical plan. While I was tied up that first night, I cast a spell, which I strengthened while being chased by umbreks. Yula is my second-in-command. Mrs. Boon and Geoff are my allies as well."

He chuckled. "And what is the goal of your diabolical plan?"

"To corner the market on lederhosen, of course."

Tavik guffawed. She smiled thinly. He moved his hand to the back of her neck and turned her head toward him. She could feel his breath on her lips. Agatha dug her claws into Naomi's lap. She squeezed the cat to stop her.

"What's for dinner?" she asked. She winced at how breathy her voice was.

She felt him shift to extend his arm round her to lift off the tops of the platters. The smell of warm food hit her salivary glands, and her mouth watered.

"Lamb, potatoes, green beans, and stuffed mushrooms appear to be our menu. What would you like?"

She tilted her head down. She really didn't want to be fed like a baby, especially without ocular input to help with the judging of distance, mouth opening, and general expectation of what she was eating before she tasted it.

"What's wrong?" he murmured, and if he were going to reach over her shoulder to feed her, she was going to get food all over her dress to go with the wine. She was sure of it.

"I would rather feed myself," she said.

"You will have trouble."

"Not if I'm not blindfolded."

He sighed. "You don't want to do this."

"The first time was fun and kind of kinky, but this is no way to eat day-to-day. It's demeaning. I can feed myself just fine without blindfolds and ropes."

She felt him leave her back. She listened to him move and sit on the other side of the table. "You can remove the blindfold." With Tavik out of her immediate vicinity, Agatha jumped down.

Naomi reached up behind her head and untied the blindfold. When she lowered it from her face, she saw him sitting across from her with the helm firmly in place. If she were to eat, he would not. A piece of lamb and some vegetables were already on her plate. She picked up her utensils self-consciously. He was going to watch her eat. Having someone watch her, and not eat always made her feel self-conscious, like her table manners were being scrutinized, and she felt guilty that she was eating and the other person wasn't. But this was what she'd asked for. If she didn't eat, he would likely replace her blindfold so he could partake, and her stomach would grumble, and she would be grumpy. She preferred self-conscious and guilty to grumpy.

She cut into the lamb and ate a bite. Tavik sat silently across from her, inscrutable in his helm. He had one hand resting on its side on the table in a loose fist while the other rested on his hip, bent in a relaxed position. She hoped he didn't start toying with his goblet or utensils because the guilt would really kick in then. She slanted her eyes to the bed to seek out Agatha or Mr. Squibbles as she chewed. She wondered what their plan was and if she were to play a part.

Tavik noticed the direction of her eyes. "Dear Calax, I should have chosen a different room."

Naomi stopped chewing in surprise.

"No, this is fine," she protested around her food. She dabbed her lips to make sure she didn't have any sauce on her mouth. "I thought I saw something moving under your bed earlier. I was just checking to see if it were still there."

Now he turned to look underneath his bed. She wished she'd come up with a better story, but talking about his bed made her extremely nervous. "Was it the cat?" He got up and crept over to the bed. He crouched down and looked underneath.

"No, I'm sure it was my imagination," she lied.

"We've had a problem with mice lately. Mrs. Boon was telling me that they had been causing havoc in the kitchen. She has never seen rodents with such ingenuity. It's like they've grown smarter."

She inwardly groaned. Mr. Squibbles had been getting industrious while foraging and maybe had even unionized his brethren. The idea of mice going on strike with little placards gave her a moment of amusement, which was shattered when Tavik lunged beneath the bed and grabbed something.

Agatha let out a yowl and lunged at his crouched form. The witch in cat-form planted all four claws in his back. He shouted and shot up. In his closed hand, a pair of whiskers peeked out. His hand reflexively clenched. Naomi heard the crunch of many small bones. Tavik dropped the mouse from his hand. It landed with a lifeless thump. Naomi felt sick.

"Oh my God, you killed him," she said.

Tavik wasn't paying attention to her. He was trying to reach around to pull Agatha off his back, but couldn't reach her. He was going around in circles with the cat just out of his grasp.

"Get your damn cat off of me!" he demanded.

Naomi went to him, but she didn't grab Agatha. She began slapping him on his arms and shoulders. "You killed him!"

"Naomi, what are you doing? Stop it!" He grabbed her by the arms and shook her. "What is the matter with you? Get the cat!"

She could just make out Agatha's eyes from over his shoulder. They were filled with rage. He hissed as feline claws ripped into his back.

"Don't you get it? You killed him!" Naomi yelled into his face.

"So? It was just a mouse!"

So? Just a mouse? Was? She didn't know which part angered her more, but each part certainly angered her. She struggled to free her arms and kicked at his legs. Tavik didn't seem so much hurt by the attack as extremely aggravated by it. Agatha was hurting him. Drops of blood had appeared on the floor.

"Naomi, get this damn cat off of me, or I will kill it."

Naomi didn't reach for Agatha. She threw Tavik's hands off her and backed away. "You would kill her, too, just like him. Why not kill Yula, also? She's my friend. She cares about me. And if that isn't enough, kill Stomper as well! I like him, and he seems okay with me."

Tavik barely spared her a confused look as he continued to struggle to reach Agatha. "What are you babbling about?"

"I'm talking about my friends! Did you notice your name didn't come up?"

Tavik shook his head. "Sit down and calm yourself. I'll have someone fetch Yula to help you back to your room."

"Room? You mean cell! And I won't sit down."

She rushed back at him. She was going to claw his eyes out. He just didn't get it. He'd killed Mr. Squibbles. It didn't matter to him. Of course it didn't matter. He was a murderer. He slaughtered people every day. She managed to slap and punch him a few times before he grabbed her wrists again. She struggled to free her hands. Determined to hurt him. He held her off easily.

"Naomi, calm down."

"No!"

Her struggles were easy for him to control, but at least if he was preoccupied with her, Agatha could shred his back without impediment. Naomi was determined to do some damage of her own. She kicked out at him, but she doubted her feet were even badly bruising him. He was inhuman. If umbreks couldn't hurt him, what could Agatha and she hope to accomplish? And Naomi realized, he was pushing her toward the bed.

"No, I'm not getting near your bed. Let me go!"

"You need to sit down."

"No!"

But he forced her back. She had to take a step or else lose her balance. She stepped back, and her foot came down on a lump and with a sickening horror, she realized she had stepped on the small corpse of Mr. Squibbles. With a sense of déjà vu, she slipped and went down, taking Tavik with her. This situation, though, was nothing like the last time. She landed on her back. He caught one arm on the bed and kept himself from landing flat on her. Seeing him above her like that, she reached up and grabbed the helm and wrenched it off. She threw it across the room. It hit the far wall with a very loud clang. For a moment, everyone froze.

She stared up at Tavik's face. He was shaved bald. She'd known that already. His eyebrows were black, wide, and sharply arched. His mouth wasn't too much of a surprise either, having kissed her before. It was large with firm lips. If he smiled, he would be handsome. His head was pale due to constantly being covered by his helm. It made the tattoo centered on his forehead starkly visible. It was dark blue and was a demon's face with evil slanted eyes and long fangs. And now she was as dead as Mr. Squibbles.

Tavik's mouth thinned to a narrow line. "I wish you hadn't done that."

He let her go to reach behind his back and grab Agatha by the scruff of her neck. He tossed her across the room. She landed near the mask and scrambled away to hide. Her eyes weren't narrowed in rage anymore. They were wide with fear, but they couldn't be wider than Naomi's. She stared up at Tavik. She couldn't move. It felt like rigor mortis was already setting in.

He pushed himself to his feet and held out a hand to her. She took the offered hand limply. He pulled her up without a word and set her on the bed. All the protest had left her. She couldn't stop staring up at his face; after all, it was the reason she was going to die. He grimaced and went across the room to the table. He sank into a chair and stared at her.

"Well, what now?" he asked.

She didn't answer. She was trying to compose her last words.

"Naomi, what's going on? What did you hope to achieve by this? And what is this with the mouse?"

The body lay crushed in the middle of the floor. It was the saddest thing she had ever seen. The small crumpled corpse didn't compute at all with the strong-willed, often foul-mouthed rodent she had come to like and trust.

She dropped her head. "He was my friend,"

"The mouse? Naomi," he sighed. He sounded very sad for her, not in the way that he was sorry for her loss, but that the loss meant anything to her, like she was pathetic.

"He was helping me! He was one of the few beings in this castle who really cared about me and what I wanted. He didn't think it was all right to tie me up like some Christmas goose. He was going to help me get back to my

138

family. You might not believe this, but I had a life before I was forced to marry you. A life that meant something to me! I have two loving parents, a brother, a job, a home, and a future that I would really like to get back to!"

"You were conspiring with a mouse." Tavik shook his head. He reached over and picked up his goblet. He drank it like he really needed it. She crossed her arms and slouched. She didn't need to explain herself further to him. He was going to kill her in the near future for the simple offense of seeing his face. If he thought she was crazy, what the hell was he?

"I don't even know what your stupid tattoo means. That's why you wear the mask, right? Because you don't want people to see it? Well, now I've seen it, but I don't have a freaking clue what it is. So just remember that when you're killing me. I'm dead because I saw your stupid tattoo, and I have no idea why it's a big deal, and I don't care. I don't care about you or your stupid, ugly tattoo."

Tavik rubbed his head while shaking it. "I'm not going to kill you. My tattoo is important. I wish you hadn't seen it, but I can't erase the memory from your mind."

"I'm sure you would if you could. It's not like I'm really your wife or anything. What's wrong with erasing one memory anyway? Why not just give me a lobotomy? Then I'll sit here nice and quiet like a good little enslaved wife, though I may drool a little, but that's okay; you can just put a bib on me."

Tavik rubbed his head more like he had a headache. "Naomi, we agreed at the very beginning that you wouldn't see my face in return for not sharing my bed. Obviously that deal has been broken. We need to make a new deal."

She arched her eyebrows. "I don't know how I'm supposed to uphold any deals, seeing as how I'll be dead."

Tavik jumped up and sent the chair toppling over. "I am not going to kill you!"

Naomi shrank back on the bed. His outburst seemed to have unsettled Tavik, too. He blinked a moment and shook his head. He grabbed the wine cup and took another hearty drink. When he lowered it, he frowned, rubbed his eyes, and looked at the cup still in his hand. He sniffed the rim.

"How did you—" And then he keeled over onto the floor.

CHAPTER ELEVEN

A unicorn weighs more dead than alive.

Naomi stared in shock at Tavik's prone body. He lay sprawled on the floor unconscious. She wheeled around, looking for Agatha. The black cat crept out from under the bed.

"What did you do?" Naomi asked.

"I didn't anything," Agatha answered.

"I did it," a small, squeaky voice said.

"Mr. Squibbles!" Naomi exclaimed.

"That's me." The familiar poked out from a rumpled napkin on the table.

Naomi's eyes darted to the small furry corpse on the floor. "Then who—"

"A stupid field mouse who insisted on following me. I told him to stay away, but he was so stupid he wouldn't listen to me. Serves him right, idiot."

Agatha leapt up onto the table and patted the mouse's head with a paw. "Oh, Mr. Squibbles, you make me so proud. A witch couldn't ask for a better, smarter, cleverer familiar."

"And I will remind you of that repeatedly," he said.

"You poisoned him?" Naomi asked

"Don't worry. I didn't kill him. I just gave him enough to stay asleep for a very long time."

"Now what do we do?" She stared at the prone body. He seemed bigger unconscious.

Agatha chanted some sort of spell. The fog appeared, and she changed back to human, thankfully with the clothes she'd been wearing. The old woman nudged the body with her shoe. "We'll have to carry him."

"But he's heavy," Naomi complained. She couldn't help fussing over such a trivial thing. If she didn't fuss, she felt she might start going into hysterics or something.

"We could use some help," Agatha said.

A lightbulb went off over Naomi's head. She knew who she could ask for help, and no matter the answer, she would feel better for asking.

She scurried down the corridor and tapped softly on the door. Yula cracked the door to see who it was. Her hair was braided, and she had on a nightgown.

"Lady Naomi, what is the matter?" She opened the door wider.

Naomi slipped inside and closed the door softly behind her. "How would you like to do something really crazy and stupid?"

Yula arched an eyebrow. "What?"

"I'm kidnapping Tavik and sneaking out of the castle. I need help carrying him through a secret passage. Agatha's helping, but another pair of hands would come in really handy, so to speak."

Yula's eyebrow arched higher. "Agatha, the witch that Lord Tavik hates? The one he suspected you of conspiring with? You are conspiring with her? Naomi." She sounded disappointed in her.

Naomi hunched her shoulders as guilt crept over her. "I didn't plan to conspire with her."

"You swore to him that you weren't in collusion with her."

Naomi straightened. She couldn't back down now. It was impossible. "And I wasn't when I swore. But I will do whatever I have to do to get home. We're getting out of here tonight. Agatha's going to help me get a unicorn."

"But how did this come about? How did you conspire with her? I never saw anything."

"She was the cat."

"Kitty?"

"Yeah, I know it seems impossible, but she's a witch. They can do that sort of stuff. And she has a talking mouse that helped me."

Yula began patting Naomi's head. "Do you feel ill? Did you fall out of bed? Did you eat something rotten?"

Naomi swatted Yula's hand away. "This is real. Will you help? I know it's asking a lot, and I'll understand if you say no, but I need to know your answer quick."

Yula turned away and hugged herself. "You will surely get into trouble."

"I surely will, but I don't care. I have to do this. Yula, this is the only chance I have to be reunited with my family. If you had the chance to see your boys again, wouldn't you take it?"

The servant whirled around to face her. "I would die for the chance to see my boys."

"I know, and I know that I really have no right to ask you to come with me, but I didn't want to leave you behind without at least giving you the choice."

Yula turned away again. With calm practicality, she took out clothes and dressed. When she was done, she walked over to a chest and swung it open. She picked out one thing. It was a rabbit rag doll. It was old and discolored, with long floppy ears and a smile stitched on its face. She tucked the toy under her arm. "No woman should be separated from her family. If I can help you reunite with yours, maybe there will be hope for me."

Naomi led the way back. Agatha had gotten the door to the secret passage open and had one of her floating, glowing balls ready. Tavik had been turned over to his back and lay with his arms crossed over his stomach on the floor.

"Dear Calax, his face!" Yula shielded her eyes with her hands.

Naomi noted her reaction with concern. "Are you sure you're up for this?"

Yula steeled herself and lowered her hands. She took a deep breath and let it out slowly. She nodded, but she kept her eyes averted from Tavik.

Agatha motioned them over to the body. She put her hands underneath his arms. "Grab his legs," she ordered.

"Wait." Yula went and retrieved the helm. Its crash with the wall hadn't even dented it. Naomi was kind of upset with that. She'd really wanted to mess it up. Yula put the helm over Tavik's lolling head. Naomi and Agatha both directed scrunched eyebrows at her. She shrugged her shoulders. "He will feel better with it on, and I think once he wakes up, he will not feel very well at all."

Naomi shook her head. Yula still tended to Tavik's well-being. She supposed it was all right, but she didn't think they would be able to coddle the warlord much longer. He probably wouldn't let them. She dreaded what he'd do when he woke up.

Yula and Naomi each grabbed a leg and heaved. Tavik was no featherweight. All three women instantly began to huff as they scuttled out of the room with their burden.

They were a quarter of the way down the secret passage when Agatha called for a break. She bent over at the waist and let her arms dangle down to the floor. She had been carrying the brunt of the burden. Naomi took pity on her and switched places. She picked Tavik up under his arms and began walking backwards while the two older women carried a leg each.

"May I ask why we're taking Lord Tavik with us? Is he to be ransomed?" Yula asked between pants.

"No, he is to be bait," Agatha replied. She seemed very pleased with the way things were turning out.

"Bait for what?" Yula asked.

"The unicorn," Naomi supplied.

Yula stumbled, and Tavik's foot slipped from her hands. Naomi's arms screamed as she staggered under the sudden extra burden.

"What good is he for a unicorn?" Yula asked.

"Seeing as how he's a virgin, he'll come in very handy in attracting one for Naomi," Agatha said.

"A virgin?" Yula asked incredulously. She put her hands up and shook her head. "That is ridiculous. He isn't a virgin."

"Yula, pick his leg back up," Naomi wheezed. She could feel her knees starting to buckle.

Instead Agatha dropped her leg and turned to the other woman. Now Naomi was the only one holding him. Her body screamed at the strain. As she struggled to hold him up, Agatha put her fists on her hips. "Slept with him, have you?"

"Guys!"

Yula seemed offended by Agatha's question. She crossed her arms and stared down her nose at the witch. "No, I have not, but he is a strong, able-bodied young man. Of course, he's not a virgin. Why, Naomi is his bride. She can tell you that."

"Actually, all I can tell you is that he's a good kisser, and I am about to drop him if you two don't come back and help," she wheezed.

"But you two slept together," Yula said.

"Yeah, we slept together as in we slept in the same bed and kept our hands to ourselves. Do you two want me to drop him?"

"But this is unheard of," Yula said, still clearly amazed by Tavik's chastity.

"It actually makes perfect sense," Agatha said.

"How so?"

"Fine." Fed up, Naomi dropped him. His helm-covered head clanged loudly when it hit the floor. She lifted her arms and stretched.

"You saw the tattoo. You know what it means."

Naomi's ears perked up. She still didn't know what the tattoo meant, and she had the feeling she should probably find out.

"It means nothing. No one would dare scrape their knee to *him.*"

"You know that tattoo. It's his mark. Tavik has sworn himself to him."

"But that's outrageous! No one in their right mind would worship Errilol anymore. One would be doomed."

"He has sworn allegiance to the Lord Destroyer," Agatha insisted.

"Then we should get as far away from him as we can, not bring him with us!"

"Bring him. Leave him. Don't we have to move to do either of those?" Naomi was still ignored.

"He's the only full-grown virgin available to us. We have to use him to entice the unicorn."

Yula shook her head in disbelief. "Oh, this is perfect. We are going to use a worshiper of Errilol to get ourselves a unicorn."

"You know, we could debate this as we haul heavy butt here," Naomi suggested.

Neither woman so much as glanced at her. Their eyes were locked on each other. Jaws set, eyes narrowed, a spot of color high on each cheek. She was invisible to the two arguing women.

"Well, it's the god's own fault for demanding virginity of his acolytes. He had to know they would be useful in unicorn hunting."

"Where is Mr. Squibbles, anyway?" Naomi wondered aloud. She looked around. Was the mouse getting horses? She hoped he didn't ditch them if they didn't appear by dawn.

"No, I doubt he thought anyone would be crazy enough to kidnap a warrior imbued with Errilol's infernal rage. In fact, if the idea had occurred to the god, it probably made him guffaw."

"Well, I wonder if he's laughing now."

Yula finally turned to her. "Naomi, you can't be serious about this?"

Naomi looked up. She'd been picking her nails while the two women argued. "I would get serious if I could get some help hauling lead-ass out of here."

Agatha nodded and went to grab a leg again. Yula hung back, shaking her head. "What have I gotten myself into?"

"Think of it as a grand adventure," Agatha suggested.

Yula's mouth thinned, but she retook her place with the other leg. Naomi looked up at them but didn't grab his arms. "Are we really going now?"

Both women nodded. She bent to grab him. "You're both ready?"

They nodded.

"Now I don't want either of you to stop to argue again," she said.

The two women looked at each other narrowly.

"I mean it. No one says another word until we're out of this tunnel."

"Naomi, let's go," Agatha said.

She bent down and heaved up her portion.

The three women huffed and puffed down the rest of the secret passage without a word passed between them. When they arrived at the end of the passage, Naomi looked around but didn't see Mr. Squibbles with any horses. Her brow scrunched as she searched harder in the dark.

"Up here."

She looked up and dropped Tavik again. It was going to be pure luck if he didn't have a concussion after all of this, but that was the least of her worries. Seeing Agatha's cottage floating above them sort of took precedence over everything else. She stared at the underside of the house and experienced that little world tilt she'd felt when first seeing the two moons. She rubbed her eyes and still saw the same thing. The cottage was above them, floating. Clumps of dirt rained down intermittently and roots dangled. She couldn't see anything suspending the cottage over them. There weren't any balloons or wings.

"What in the world is that?" Yula exclaimed.

"That is my home. You're very welcome to come inside," Agatha said. Thick ropes descended to them. Naomi grabbed one numbly and looked up.

"We're going to the northern plateaus in that?" she asked.

"Do you have a problem with my home?" Agatha asked.

"I have a problem with it flying."

"Pshaw, it's perfectly safe. Cottages are very buoyant, don't you know."

"You don't say," Yula said in a dazed fashion. Naomi was glad she wasn't the only one amazed by the hovering real estate.

"Are you all coming up or not?" Mr. Squibbles demanded.

"Who is that talking to us?" Yula asked, searching the open door and windows for a figure.

"That's Mr. Squibbles. He's a mouse and Agatha's familiar. I hope foul language doesn't offend you."

"What?"

They tied a rope around Tavik and watched as he was pulled up to the flying house without any visible help. The rope Naomi still clasped gave a little tug on her hand.

"Just get a good grip and the rope will do the rest," Agatha said.

148

Naomi clasped the rope tightly but nearly let go when it began to pull her up. She white-knuckled the rope and squeezed her eyes shut. She expected the house to crash to the ground any moment, and her with it.

Once she was up, she scrabbled through the doorway into the cottage. Tavik lay in the center of the room. Mr. Squibbles peered up at her. "What took you guys so long?"

"Yula and Agatha stopped to argue in the passage."

"I have a feeling those two are going to be fun together," he said in an ominous tone.

When they were all inside, Agatha began battening down the house for flight. It involved closing and locking cabinets and putting anything loose into a crate or bin.

"Squibbles, have I forgotten anything?"

"Other than provisions and a proper plan, I would say no."

Agatha grinned. "Good, let's get moving." She reached up and unlatched a ship's wheel which swung down in front of her. Naomi hadn't noticed it before, but then, who looked for a ship's wheel in a cottage? The witch peered out the open front door and spun the wheel around one turn. The house swiveled in the air. Naomi suddenly feared she would be sick. Demerol was something else she missed from home, and while she was adding to the list, she put vodka on it. She would have given her left arm for a bottle of vodka. She knew this whole situation would've made a lot more sense drunk.

"Take a seat, ladies. We'll be flying through the night," Agatha said.

Naomi looked at their unconscious hostage. "Shouldn't we tie him up?"

Agatha cast a dismissive glance at Tavik. "If it makes you feel better, go ahead, but he would be a fool to attack me in my own house. A witch's cottage is her sanctum. I have a lot of spells laid out in this place that would make even the most blood-crazed berserker think twice before taking me on."

Naomi was glad Agatha felt so secure in her home, but since she didn't have any such assurances, she used the rope that had brought them up to restrain Tavik. By the time she was done, he looked like he'd been mummified with hemp.

Yula stood with her nose pressed against one of the windows. "Oh, my lady, come look!" She pointed out at the land racing below them. "Isn't it wondrous?"

"It is pretty amazing that the cottage can fly."

"And us, we're flying too!"

Naomi shrugged. "I've been on airplanes. They fly even higher in the air and take people to distant places on my home world. Flying is pretty mundane there."

"I don't see how this could ever be mundane," Yula murmured as she watched the racing scenery below them.

"As soon as anything becomes commercial, it's mundane."

Feeling very tired, Naomi lay down on a love seat and closed her eyes. Fighting with Tavik and carrying him down the passage had exhausted her. She'd always had an easy time falling asleep on airplanes, and the same could now be said about flying cottages, too.

She dreamed about flying. She was sailing through the air like Peter Pan. She loved it. She'd never felt so free. She looked down upon the dark forest flowing past below her and felt like she was queen of the world. She looked up at the night sky and marveled at how close the stars appeared. Her eyes went to the moon, only it was not one of the ugly moons, but Earth's moon. It was full and hung heavy in the sky. She thought it was the most beautiful thing she'd ever seen. A unicorn appeared on the face of it. She shot up to reach him, but the moon never seemed to get any closer no matter how far she flew and flew. The unicorn tossed his mane and whinnied. She called to him to come down, but the unicorn didn't listen. She was impure. The unicorn didn't listen to impure things. She screamed louder, but he continued to ignore her. She flew higher and higher. It didn't grow colder in the higher elevation. It remained toasty and nice, but the climate didn't matter. All she cared about was reaching the unicorn. She stretched out as far as she could in her desperation. The unicorn laughed at her antics. She grumpily wondered how she could have ever liked unicorns when she was young. They were infuriating beasts, entirely too judgmental of a person's lifestyle, but judgmental or not, she needed him if she were ever to see that moon in her night sky again. She reached further. She felt her fingers graze the unicorn's tail. She lunged again and fell hard onto the floor. Unicorn, moon, and stars vanished. A wood floor, breakfast smells, and the sound of a crackling fire replaced them.

Naomi sat up from the floor and looked over to the hearth, where Yula tended a skillet with eggs frying on it. Agatha sat at the table studying a map with Mr. Squibbles, and Tavik had been moved to a chair across from the witch. He seemed awake, but it was hard to tell with the helm on and all of his limbs tightly tied.

"Good morning, milady. Breakfast will be ready shortly," Yula said.

Naomi nodded and got up off the floor. She went behind Agatha to look at the map. She noticed Tavik's head swivel to follow her. He was definitely awake, then. She tried to ignore him, but goose bumps went up her arms at his silent stare. Maybe it was a good thing he had the helm on. His current expression was probably scarier than it.

The map was hand drawn. In the upper portion, there were the northern plateaus. "How's it going?" she asked Agatha.

"We made good time during the night. If we keep this up, we'll reach our destination by early tomorrow."

"So the cottage can fly several days without landing or anything?"

"It could, but I thought I would set her down midday

to give ourselves a break."

"Sounds good." She scooped up Mr. Squibbles from the table and walked across the room with him.

"Has Tavik said anything?" she whispered.

She had to hold the mouse to her ear to hear his hushed reply. "He said he was very disappointed with Yula. She didn't take that well."

Naomi clenched her jaw. "How dare he. He has no right to reproach her."

"He watched you the rest of the time. I think if he ever gets loose, you're the first one he'll go after."

Naomi nodded. She didn't want to think about what Tavik would do if freed. She slanted her eyes to him. His helm was pointed at her still. She walked across the room and ripped it off.

"Lady Naomi!" Yula cried.

"He doesn't need that with us. We've all seen his face. No point in hiding it, and it just annoys the hell out of me."

He looked up at her with cool blue eyes. He didn't say a word. Agatha's eyes bobbed back and forth between them. A little smile curled her lips when she turned back to her map.

When the table was set, there were five places. One was just a small saucer for Mr. Squibbles, but Tavik got the same place setting as the women. Naomi realized that he would not be able to feed himself. She wasn't sure if they should feed him. Maybe it would be better to keep him weak with hunger, but Yula seemed steadfast on the dining arrangements. When Naomi took the seat beside him and picked up his fork, she got a little thrill of revenge.

"You know, to make this completely fair, I should blindfold you."

He turned his arctic eyes to her, and they bored into her. "Would I get the same dessert as you did?"

Her back stiffened at the mention of past events. "No, I'm afraid that's not on the menu."

He shrugged. "Then blindfolding me wouldn't be fair."

She bristled at his reply. "And what the hell do you know about fair? Do you think it was fair to truss me up like a Christmas goose whenever it suited you? Do you think it was fair to force me to marry you? Do you think it was fair to draft Yula's sons into your army?"

"The only people who ever believe anything can be fair are small children who have lived sheltered lives," he replied.

She clenched his fork in her hand. She could stab him in the eye and say, well, fair didn't exist. Sucked for him.

Agatha circumvented Naomi's murderous plans by standing up from her seat and rapping him on the head with the wooden spoon for the eggs. Bits of cooked egg sprayed across his face. "I think it would be *fair* to say you shouldn't make any of us angry. We are the three women who hold your fate in our hands, and we do not think much of you. Who knows what might happen if you were to upset one of us. You could end up riding outside, dangling from a rope. It can get very cold out there, and permafrost can only be cured by amputation."

Tavik slouched back in his chair and cast a dark look at the witch. Naomi speared a piece of sausage and held it to his lips. He angled his eyes back to her, and she smiled sweetly. "Open wide."

CHAPTER TWELVE

"A truly wise man never plays leapfrog with a unicorn."—
Tibetan proverb

After breakfast, things quieted down in the flying cottage. The table had been cleared and everything put away. Naomi stood at one of the windows, looking out at the passing scenery. She wasn't sure why, but a sense of unease had settled upon her. Everything was going according to plan, what there was of a plan. No one could possibly be following them. Tavik was still tied up. Why she felt something wasn't right eluded her.

Agatha stood at the wheel, holding it steady. Mr. Squibbles slept on the witch's shoulder. Yula was dusting. Tavik still sat at the table. No one had replaced the helm, and he had not demanded it back, which was good because if he had, Naomi would have pitched it out the open door. She was considering blindfolding him, though. His unblinking stare followed her wherever she moved.

She got up and paced the room. She wanted to talk

about the plan, but Agatha had dropped cues not to reveal anything to him. Naomi had no idea how this whole thing was going to play out once they reached the northern plateaus. The only thing she could figure was they would tie Tavik to a tree and hide until a unicorn showed up. It seemed ridiculous and highly likely to fail. She wasn't sure why keeping him in the dark was important but played along.

"If you're bored, there are some games in that cabinet," Agatha said.

Naomi stopped pacing to check out what sort of games the witch would have. An assortment of odd-shaped objects lay nestled in the cabinet. She began drawing each out to take a look. She pulled out a stone board that had checker squares scratched into it. There was a small tied bag with the pieces for it. It looked like the game might be similar to checkers. She pulled out a stack of cards in another tied bag. She shuffled through them. Odd pictures were drawn on each of them. It looked like none of the cards repeated. She pulled out a bowl with small round stones piled inside. There were toys in the cabinet as well: a stuffed bear with a lopsided smile, a blocky wagon with fat wheels, hand carved animals. A child had obviously played with these. She wondered where the child was now. She put the toys back and only kept out the items she supposed were games.

"Any suggestions? I don't know how to play any of these."

Agatha bounced the shoulder the mouse slept on. "Squibbles, hop down and show Naomi how to play Cirrant."

"I don't want to play Cirrant," he mumbled as he turned over and tucked his nose under his tail.

Naomi looked over at Yula, but she was on her hands and knees with a wash bucket and rag and hadn't even looked up when they spoke. By the time they reached the northern plateaus, the cottage would sparkle and gleam if

Yula had anything to do about it. Unwillingly, her eyes landed on Tavik. He was still staring at her. Agatha's eyes shifted to him as well. She arched an eyebrow to her as if to say, if she wanted to ask him, ask him.

She did not like that idea. Feeding him had been fine, and while playing games with him when he was tied up wasn't necessarily cruel, it was pathetic. She decided she would amuse herself with a tried and true Earth pastime. She took the stack of cards over to the table. Tavik arched an eyebrow at her. She didn't pay him any attention. She set the deck on the table and picked up the first two cards. She balanced them on their edges to form her first triangle. She would build a house of cards. No need for instruction or other players, and it could take up hours.

She couldn't believe she was this bored. She should relish the break in action, but in actuality, it made her antsy. She focused on the house of cards and blocked out everything else.

The house of cards was now a card castle with four stories and a bridge. Tavik had sat there silently watching her at her idle pastime without ever saying a word. She appreciated this as it allowed her to utterly ignore him. Mr. Squibbles had finally finished his nap and had taken on the daring enterprise of sneaking through the castle's foundations. She couldn't see where he was currently among the cards.

She carefully began the fifth story of her masterpiece. She had never built one this tall. She was kind of impressed with herself. She grinned as she laid down another layer of cards. She sat back to enjoy her success. Suddenly the table lurched, and the card castle tumbled.

"Ack! I'm buried alive," Mr. Squibbles cried.

Her jaw dropped at the total destruction of her idle pastime. Not a single card was still standing. She looked at Tavik. There was an evil smirk on his face. He had caused the "table-quake." She narrowed her eyes as she glared at him. She would get him back for that.

156

"Naomi, clear that mess away so I can start setting out lunch," Yula said.

Naomi began picking up the cards and dug out Mr. Squibbles, who quickly scurried away to avoid any further calamity.

Yula laid out a large spread for lunch. Naomi retook her seat from breakfast for Tavik-feeding.

"Don't give Lord Tavik any of the soup. I put carrots in it, and he can't eat those," Yula warned.

"Why, would they kill him?" she asked.

Yula shook her head. "Oh no, they just give him an upset stomach."

Naomi chuckled darkly. "Darn, I was hoping we could kill him with a carrot. I bet that would be fun to watch." Yula gave Naomi a nervous look and moved the pot of soup out of her reach.

"Tell me, Tavik, how long have you been in service to the god Errilol?" Agatha asked.

He stared at the witch silently. Naomi poked him in the ribs. "Answer her, politely."

He didn't even turn his head to glare at her. He seemed to be locked in a staring contest with the witch.

"Your family must be so proud," Agatha commented, her voice dripping with contempt.

"I have no family," he replied flatly.

"Then Naomi's motivations must seem completely foreign to you. You see, this is all spurred by her fervent wish to return to her family. She misses them. I bet her parents are very proud of her."

Tavik swung his head to look at her.

Naomi hunched her shoulders, feeling like a pawn in the argument and not liking it. "I don't know if they're like really proud of me. I mean, I guess they are because I have my own place, an okay job, and no criminal record, but I'm probably more proud of them than they are of me. I mean, they raised me, gave me a good home, helped me get through college, and they never made me feel like I owed them for it, even though I know it was hard for them sometimes financially." She shrugged her shoulders, not feeling like she was saying it right. "I miss them. They make me happy, and I love them."

"You are a good girl," Yula said softly.

"Damn, now I want to visit my mom," Mr. Squibbles grumbled.

"Interesting, because I still do not," Tavik said. His face was unreadable. His eyes were again locked on Agatha, and she stared back with a grim look on her face.

"I miss my boys. They were good boys. Whenever I would go out to chop wood, one of them would pop up to do it for me, and the oldest didn't even live at home anymore. He was apprenticed to the blacksmith, but he still would come by to help around the house."

"Do you know where Yula's sons are?" Naomi asked.

He looked down at her for a moment. They stared at each other. She tried to keep her face blank, but she really wanted to give Yula something for helping her, and nothing would be better than knowledge of her sons. He stared back at her, and she thought for a moment she saw his eyes soften, but then he turned away, and she couldn't be sure. Yula stared at him with an open face. Her hope was clearly stamped on it.

He grimaced and shook his head. "I could ask one of my captains to check into it for you. I can't offer a guarantee that they'll discover where they are, though."

Yula deflated at this less than hopeful news. "I've asked at the different camps, but could never get information. No one knew them."

"Do you still have something of theirs?" Agatha asked.

She mutely nodded.

"Give it to me; I may be able to help you."

Yula's face broke into a true smile. She rushed to her small bag and retrieved the stuffed rabbit.

"They both played with it. Is this good enough?"

Agatha took the toy and smoothed its ears back. She smiled and nodded. "Yes, but I need to collect a few things before I can try the spell. We'll do it tonight."

"Oh, thank you," Yula said, clutching the witch's hands.

Naomi smiled. She had high hopes that Agatha would be able to help Yula. The witch had shown how formidable she was; after all, they were flying through the air in her cottage.

"There's no need to thank me. Family's important. It's all most people have."

Naomi noticed that Tavik clenched up at the witch's statement. It took him a couple of seconds to loosen his jaw to take the beef off the fork she offered him.

"I never met any of your family or heard anyone talk about them. Are they still alive?" Naomi whispered.

Tavik's eyes turned to her with a coldness that made her instantly regret her inquiry. "I have no family," he said again.

She nodded and didn't ask any further questions.

The flying house settled in a small field after lunch. Everyone except Tavik exited swiftly to walk around and stretch their legs. Yula looked back at the cottage with pity.

"We should let him come out and relieve himself. I would think he needs it."

Naomi looked back at the house too. She frowned. "It would be too easy for him to escape. He could overpower us in a snap."

"He will not escape," Agatha said.

"You can't be sure. It's too much of a risk," she argued.

"So he should just piddle on the floor? That'll be nice," Mr. Squibbles said from Agatha's apron pocket.

"What will we do to keep him from escaping?" Naomi asked.

"We could put a leash on him," Mr. Squibbles suggested.

Yula looked sickened by the idea.

Naomi, though, was okay with it. "It could work. Who's going to leash him?"

Everyone looked at her. She began backing away and shaking her head. "Oh no, I am not holding the leash on Tavik. He already wants to kill me first."

"Come on, Naomi. He's your husband, so you're the one who gets to walk him," Mr. Squibbles said.

"Oh, sure. Use the old matrimony argument: To love, honor, and imprison."

Yula crossed her arms. "It's either let him outside to relieve himself or mop up after him, and I just spent all morning on my hands and knees cleaning that floor."

"You know no one asked you to do that. I keep a very tidy home," Agatha said.

Yula pressed her lips together and turned her back to the witch. Agatha's eyes narrowed.

"Naomi, go, before these two start scratching each other's eyes out," Mr. Squibbles said.

"I'm going. I'm going." She did an about face and headed back to the cottage.

Tavik lifted his head when she entered. She suddenly realized she had no idea what to do. Leashing him just ensured he couldn't run away, but he could still run at her. She planted her fists on her hips and glared at him. Her frustration seemed to amuse him, if the twitching at the corners of his mouth were any indication.

"I'm supposed to take you outside so you can relieve yourself."

"Very kind of you."

"You only have to pee, right?"

He couldn't hold back his grin. "Yes, I only have to pee."

"Thank God."

She found another long length of rope. She went over to him and put a hangman's noose around his neck. "Stand up."

He rose and stood straight with his shoulders back. He was still very large and intimidating. She was so dead. She tugged on the noose.

"Follow me, hop-along."

He shuffled a couple of inches and stopped. "This is ridiculous."

"Better ridiculous than dead." She tugged on the rope. "Now come on."

"Plan on holding it for me?"

"No, you can sit."

"Untie my feet at least."

She shook her head. "Uh, no. You could tackle me or something, and I would rather not find out what the something could be."

"I give you my word of honor that I will not tackle you or something," he said dully.

She shook her head again. "I don't think I can trust you."

"Have I ever broken my word to you?"

She tilted her head and contemplated his question. "You have kept it, but I don't think you have any compunction to keep it now. We kidnapped you."

"Naomi, I would never harm you. I gave you that oath and do not ever plan to break it."

She gave him a speculative look. He seemed sincere, but she couldn't believe him. If she were him, she'd be looking for any chance to escape. Wait. That had been her! And look, she'd escaped. He was bigger, stronger, and was from this world. His chances of escaping were much higher than hers. He wouldn't need a talking cat and mouse to help him. She looked at his bound feet. But it would take them hours to get out of the cottage like this.

Knowing it was a bad idea, she went with it anyway.

"Sit down."

He sat without another word. She knelt and untied his feet. Knowing she was making a mistake, she heaved a deep breath and placed her hands on his knees to push herself up. As she rose, he opened his legs, and she found herself pitched forward into his lap. Her face was level with his, and she froze.

"You promised," she said.

He grinned. "What did I promise?"

She opened her mouth to answer, and suddenly she had Tavik's tongue in it. She flailed back, but he followed her. He was merciless. His hands were tied behind his back, but she felt like the powerless one, and it didn't feel too bad. Damn, the man was a good kisser, but she knew she shouldn't indulge. He needed to stay chaste. She pushed him away and skipped back finally. She raised her hand and wiped her mouth.

"That definitely falls into the 'or something' category."

He looked very pleased with himself. "Pity, I thought you might let that pass."

She bent and picked up the leash. She gave it a good tug. "Come on."

Mr. Squibbles sat on a rock near the door. "What took you two so long?" he asked. He noticed Naomi's flushed face and bruised lips. "Naomi," the mouse scolded.

"It's his fault," she said, pointing at Tavik.

"Humph, I think I'll go with you two. Obviously, you need a chaperone."

"We're married," Tavik argued.

"Doesn't matter," Mr. Squibbles said. He crawled up Tavik's body and took up residence on his shoulder. "Well, let's go pee," the mouse said.

Naomi led the way to a small copse of trees that would give Tavik some cover while he did his business. She wasn't worried about him running off anymore. Her lips still tingled. Maybe she shouldn't be the one holding his leash. He'd brought up their marriage like it mattered. She never really thought of them as husband and wife. More like prisoner and jailor. But were they something more to each other? Everything was so topsy-turvy here. She did trust him in an odd sort of way. He had always kept his word to her, the recent incident in the cottage aside. But she still didn't understand this business with the tattoo and the god. And all the pillaging and fighting. She couldn't disregard that either.

Tavik came to stand in front of her. "I need my belt undone."

She meant to only glance down at his waist to check his belt, but her eyes kept going down to stop a few inches below that article of clothing. Get a grip, she told herself. He was going to go to the bathroom, which, eww, not sexy. She grabbed hold of the belt and tugged it loose. Instantly, the pants began to sag. Her eyes shot back up to Tavik's face.

He smiled crookedly at her. "Are you sure you wouldn't like to help?"

She thought about hitting him, but she didn't need to. Mr. Squibbles stood up on his hind legs and bit him on the earlobe.

"Ow!"

"Go do your business," the mouse ordered.

She grinned wryly and turned around. She realized that she would hear every sound he made. She hummed to distract herself. After a few bars, she realized her subconscious liked a good joke. She was humming the wedding march.

"He's done," Mr. Squibbles announced.

Naomi turned back around as Tavik ducked out from among the trees. He'd pulled his pants back up. All she had to do was refasten his belt. As she reached to do that, he stepped back and weaved to the side, playing keep away. She couldn't help giggling.

"Keep still," she laughed.

He had a grin on his face, as well, as he continued to dance away from her reaching hands. His pants sat precariously on his hips.

"Enough, children, we need to get back to the cottage," Mr. Squibbles said.

Naomi giggled again and lunged for the belt. Tavik hopped back, and his pants slipped. She quickly turned around to face the other direction. She wasn't sure if she'd seen anything, but there had definitely been skin, too much for there to have been any sort of underwear. Tavik went commando.

"See, this is what happens when you don't listen," Mr. Squibbles scolded.

"I didn't see," Naomi sputtered.

Tavik sighed. She could hear him struggling to pull his pants back up. He growled softly in frustration. Naomi's shoulders slumped. She knew what that meant. She turned reluctantly back around. She kept her eyes firmly up on Tavik's face. He was leering at her again. She frowned. She walked up to him, closed her eyes, and bent down. She jerked the pants up, none too gently.

"Careful, you might want to use that later," he warned.

She glared at him. Mr. Squibbles bit him on the ear again.

"Will you stop that!" he thundered at the mouse.

"Yes, when you behave."

Fun over, she refastened the buckle and tugged on the rope to take Tavik back to the cottage. Yula and Agatha were already back, preparing to leave. They must have resolved their brewing argument and had collected different plants.

"Are we ready to go?" Agatha asked. Naomi nodded. She sat on the loveseat, and Tavik sat down beside her. She didn't bother retying his feet, nor did she move from her place beside him. The loveseat was not big enough for there to be any space between them, but the lack of room didn't faze Naomi. She relaxed in the chair with a sigh, Tavik's warm body a comforting presence. Agatha pulled down the steering wheel, and the cottage lifted off. "Next stop, the northern plateaus," the witch announced.

Tavik's back stiffened slightly. They'd kept their destination a strict secret. Agatha must have thought it didn't matter anymore. He turned to Naomi. "You don't look northern," he said softly.

"I'm not," she replied and left it at that.

As the cottage flew through the afternoon, Naomi began to yawn. She dozed off and didn't wake up until the cottage touched down again. She raised her head from Tavik's shoulder. She glanced at him apologetically and wiped at the drool spot she'd left.

"Sorry."

He slanted his eyes to her and gave her a small smile. Feeling a little too close to him, she rose from the loveseat and stretched. "What's the plan?" she asked the other women.

"We should scout out as much of the area as possible before nightfall, and then I'll perform the finding spell for Yula."

Naomi nodded. "Sounds good. What are we looking for?"

Agatha motioned them over so she could speak without Tavik hearing. "Hoof marks that are cloven, gashes made by a single horn on rocks, fragrant feces."

"Nice-smelling poop?" Naomi repeated.

The witch nodded. "Highborn ladies pay a great deal for the excrement of a unicorn."

Naomi shook her head. "Now I've heard everything." She suddenly shot a look at Yula, remembering the perfume she'd forced on her. "Did you dab me with poo?"

Yula shrugged her shoulders. "It smelled nice if it

were."

Naomi shuddered. She was not wearing another drop of perfume while in this crazy world. Nothing could be trusted.

"What should we do with Lord Tavik?" Yula asked.

"He will stay here with me and Mr. Squibbles. You two be careful out there. Stay alert for predators."

They nodded, both remembering their brush with umbreks.

They put on heavy cloaks, mittens, and caps to keep warm on their scouting expedition and slipped from the house. Tavik came to the door to watch them go. Naomi heard Agatha tell him to go back to his seat. She felt a stab of worry. The witch seemed to truly dislike him. She hoped he was still in one piece and human shaped when she got back.

The Northern Plateaus were sparse country. There were no trees, and the ground was permafrost. A cold wind whipped across the plateau and stung their cheeks and noses, telling them that the fall season would be very brief.

"Let's make this quick," Naomi said.

Since the space was so open, they could see for miles. Naomi began walking and looking at the ground for possible unicorn signs. Yula trailed after her.

The plateau was immense. There was too much ground to cover in one day. She hoped they found something soon because combing the entire place was a daunting prospect. The bleakness of the area brought her spirits down as well. Her feet quickly went numb from the cold, and the rest of her was not long off. The wind made her wince every time it blew. Why the unicorns would roam here was beyond her, unless the inhospitality was a defense against being hunted.

They crept across the plateau for a couple of hours. They found no signs of unicorns or of any other wildlife. Naomi began to fear that this whole expedition had been one very bad wild-goose chase. As the sun began to dip, they turned back to the cottage, which was a distant speck. They had covered a good amount of area, but it had been no use. They had found no cloven hoof prints, horn scratches, or aromatic feces.

"I wonder if Agatha knows of anywhere else to search," Naomi said with her head bent as she continued to search the area doggedly on the way back. She didn't expect to find anything but couldn't give up.

"Milady," Yula called.

She kept going, too focused on the ground. "Obviously there are other plateaus, since it's called the Northern Plateaus and not the Northern Plateau, but I wouldn't mind giving up here and going somewhere a little warmer and less likely to have unicorns. I hate the cold."

"Milady, look over there!"

She finally turned to Yula. "Did you find something?"

She was pointing at something. Naomi followed her wavering finger. Standing, not five yards away, was a unicorn.

"Actually, I think he found us," Yula said.

CHAPTER THIRTEEN

A baby unicorn is called a foal, just like a baby horse, and their mothers love them just the same.

From roughly fifteen feet away, the unicorn stared at them. He held his head high, his coat shimmered in the deepening dusk, and from the center of his forehead, his horn extended with a warm, golden glow. There was no mistaking him for anything else.

"I looked over, and there he was," Yula said.

The unicorn seemed curious about the two women. Naomi wondered if maybe all the virgin business was nonsense. He'd appeared at out of nowhere for them. She cautiously approached the beast with her hand out. He bowed his head and pawed at the ground. The horn was pointed right at her. She halted her approach.

"It's okay, big guy. I won't hurt you. Just want to make some travel arrangements," she said.

The unicorn backed away with his horn still lowered

toward her.

"Be careful, milady. Unicorns have gouged men in full armor. He will skewer you for sure if you're not careful."

She thought Yula might have a point—or rather the unicorn had a point, a sharp point which was pointed at her chest. She put her hands up and backed off. The unicorn raised his head and watched them start back across the plateau to the cottage. She glanced back frequently as they walked.

"Is he following us?" Yula asked.

"I think so. Maybe he's hungry. Not a whole lot to eat up here."

The unicorn stayed well back but kept pace with the two women. Naomi couldn't wait to get Tavik out there to deal with him. They jogged back to the cottage in high spirits, but when they were close enough to see through the windows of the home, they looked back, and the unicorn was gone.

Naomi stomped her cold feet in frustration. "I knew that was too easy."

"At least, we're sure that unicorns do roam this plateau," Yula offered.

Naomi nodded with a sigh. "Yeah, you're right. Let's go get warmed up." They hustled into the warm cozy cottage.

Agatha stood over a pot bubbling in the fire. Naomi couldn't help stopping to recite the famous lines. "Double, double, toil and trouble; fire burn, and cauldron bubble."

"What?" Agatha asked, looking up from the pot.

Naomi shook her head with a grin. "Nothing."

"Did you find anything?"

Both women nodded their heads, and their eyes danced. "It practically followed us home," Yula gushed.

Agatha made hushing motions as her eyes darted to Tavik. He stood by a window, looking out. It was in the opposite direction of the way they'd come back. He cast them a bored look and turned back to the window. Naomi studied him for a second. He didn't seem any worse for wear after his isolation with Agatha. She'd half expected to come back to find him singed and drowned.

"What's that you're cooking?" Yula asked, walking over to the pot.

"Stew seemed like the perfect thing for a night like this." Yula picked up the large wooden spoon sitting across the top and stirred the contents up. "Don't worry. I didn't put any carrots in it. Tavik watched me the whole time. Didn't you?"

He didn't respond. He was being super quiet. It was making Naomi nervous.

She sidled over to him. "Hey."

He looked over at her. "Your cheeks are rosy."

Reflectively, she put her fingers to her face to feel them. "Yeah, it's getting really cold out there."

"You should be careful. There are dangerous beasts in this area."

"They seem to be everywhere," she said, a touch wryly.

He nodded and looked back out the window. She watched him for a few seconds more, and then wandered away. Maybe he just wanted to be left alone.

The women set the table for dinner and chatted amicably. The cottage had a palpable cozy feel to it. As they puttered around the room, Naomi smiled.

"It's nice having company again," Mr. Squibbles murmured to her from a shelf.

"Agatha doesn't get much company?"

He shook his head. "There were years where we didn't have a single soul grace our doorstep. It was a lonely time. We used to have visitors regularly, villagers who would need a charm or some scrying done. Then they stopped coming."

"Why?"

"He forbade it."

Her eyes darted to Tavik and then back to Mr. Squibbles. "Why?" she whispered.

He dropped his head. "I shouldn't say. It's a bad business."

She absorbed this information with concern. What could the bad blood be between the witch and the warlord? Was it only the Errilol business?

The group settled around the table for dinner. Agatha ladled out the stew and passed the bowls around. Naomi once again sat beside Tavik to feed him. She stirred the stew and found herself making sure there were no carrots in the bowl. She loaded a spoon and brought it to his mouth while her other hand hovered underneath to catch any drips. He gave her a wry look and took the spoonful. She knew he was thinking about their switch in roles and how much she had protested it when she had been the one tied and fed, but then again, he wasn't blindfolded.

Agatha was telling Yula about the finding spell. Once they were done with dinner, they would scrub out the pot, boil some water, and use the plants they had gathered that afternoon. Naomi hoped the spell worked.

"You shouldn't trust her. She only has her own interests at heart," Tavik said softly.

She had to swallow her mouthful of stew before she could answer. She loaded a spoon for him and kept her voice low to answer. "She's the only one who seems to know how to get me home, and though ditching me at the castle for you to find didn't seem like the best move on my behalf, it has worked out all right, and she sent Mr. Squibbles to me and now I'm here. I think she can get me home."

"How did you end up in Harold's Pass?"

She knew she still couldn't tell. She shook her head. "It was very bad luck."

"Was it bad luck?"

She paused. She knew he meant to insinuate that

Agatha had a hand in her arrival, which really was impossible, but was it *bad* luck that had brought her there? The fact that she'd ended up on *another planet* was pretty damn amazing. She'd witnessed *real magic*. She'd just met a *unicorn*. A lot of people would be absolutely amazed by one of these things happening to them, never mind all of it. They wouldn't be calling it bad luck. They'd be counting their lucky stars. Then she looked around the table. She liked and cared about Yula, Mr. Squibbles, and Agatha. She didn't regret meeting them. She turned back to Tavik. Weirdly, she didn't regret meeting him, either. Maybe it would be fairer to call it all a fluke?

"What are you two whispering about?" Agatha asked.

Naomi didn't know why, but she blushed. "Nothing important," she answered.

The witch gave them a speculative look. Yula hid a knowing smile by taking a bite of stew. And Mr. Squibbles didn't pay them any mind. The mouse was paws deep in broth and happily nibbling on a potato the size of himself.

Naomi cleared the table while Agatha set up for the spell with Yula's help. Once the dishes were clean and put away, she retook her seat by Tavik to let the other women work and because she wanted to ask him some more questions.

"Why did you forbid the villagers from going to see Agatha?"

He had tilted his head down to hear her and kept it bent as he thought about his answer. She thought that he deliberated too long for his response to be completely truthful. "I didn't want her causing trouble."

Naomi glanced at Agatha and smiled a little. "She's certainly capable of mischief, but she can help people too. Why prevent her from doing that?"

"Because she's not interested in helping anyone but herself."

She really didn't understand why he kept harping back

to that. "How is helping me self-serving?"

He turned and looked at the witch bent over the once more bubbling pot. "It will become apparent soon enough."

Her eyebrows scrunched together at his vague assurance. She decided to switch topics. "Tell me about this god of yours. Yula was really upset by your tattoo."

He rolled his shoulders and stretched his back as he thought about his answer. Naomi realized that his hands had been tied behind his back for over two days now. His arms were probably killing him, if he could feel them at all. She rose from her seat and moved behind him. She began rubbing his shoulders like she had that first night. He released a grateful sigh and relaxed under her hands.

"Errilol is not openly worshiped any longer. He is a god of war but not a god of victory. He loves the strife and chaos of battle and the pain and despair of bloodshed. All of his temples have been destroyed or abandoned. People stopped worshiping him when they realized that he did not care about them. He only cares for conflict. He does not protect his devoted. He couldn't care less if they live or die."

"Why would you swear yourself to him then? He sounds more like a demon than a god."

"Because unlike other gods, he makes himself known. He imbues me with his power so that I may kill my adversaries. Even if he doesn't care about me, he does answer me when I call. It is with his might that I have survived. Other gods promise salvation and refuge but do not always deliver. Errilol promises neither but is a reliable source of strength."

She shook her head. "I don't think the fact that he's dependable is enough to sell him to me. The fact that he's so eager to answer your prayers is scarier than not answering them."

He shrugged under her hands. "I can't justify my

173

reasons any better than what I have said."

"The fact that you would scrape your knee to that fiend is horrifying. Errilol is a god to stand against, not with," Agatha said, revealing that she'd been eavesdropping on their conversation.

Tavik stood up to face the witch. A muscle in his jaw twitched as he locked eyes with her. "Errilol made me the man I am."

"I wouldn't be so proud of the man I was if I were you. Having your people fear you and wonder if you are a fiend is not something to be proud of."

He clenched his jaw. "I became the man I needed to be."

Agatha scoffed. "And what need, pray tell, required you to become a barbarian who has slain hundreds of men and destroyed countless lives?"

Tavik's eyes narrowed. "I don't know. Why don't you ask my mother?"

Agatha's eyes grew wide as her face thinned. She sucked in a breath through her teeth. "How dare you. I taught you to respect your fellow man and care about the people around you. How dare you insinuate that I prompted your descent into this madness!"

Naomi and Yula's eyes caught each other's in a wide stare. "She's your mother?" Naomi asked.

Agatha's eyes didn't leave Tavik's angry face. "I have no son."

He jerked as if hit. Naomi winced in sympathy. She crept from behind him over to Yula. "Did you know this?" she hissed to the other woman. Yula dumbly shook her head.

When Naomi looked again, she saw that Tavik and Agatha had stepped toward each other to better shout at one another. Both were beyond angry. Tavik's body was a mass of tense muscles while Agatha's face was red, bordering on fuchsia.

"You can deny me all you want, but it was the only way to save the town!"

"No, it wasn't! There are always other options. I was working on something!"

Tavik kicked the table. It slid across the room and banged the wall so hard a number of items fell off their hooks. Naomi and Yula backed further away from the two. "There wasn't any time! The army was approaching!"

The witch crossed her arms and gave him a narrow look. "Well, where's the army now?"

In a cold voice, he said, "Every solution has a price. You taught me that."

Her back stiffened. "I also taught you that if the price is too high then you turn away!"

"THERE WASN'T ANYWHERE TO TURN! They would've razed the town, burned the forest, and drawn and quartered you! I was supposed to turn away from that?"

In response, she silently turned her back on him.

Tavik let out a snarl of frustration and paced the floor like a caged animal. Naomi wanted to do something to help but didn't know what. She was still reeling from the realization that the two were mother and son. Tavik's eyes fell on her and flashed with anger.

"At least be honest with Naomi and tell her your real plan."

Agatha still kept her back to them. Naomi jumped in to try and explain again. "I told you we didn't plan this initially. It was a fluke that I came to Harold's Pass. If it weren't for your mother, some bastard soldier would've raped and killed me. She saved my life."

"But what about leaving you at the castle as Lady Naomi? Was that just a fluke?"

"It was the safest option," she said, but even she wasn't sure of that. It had seemed like a dirty trick at the time.

"She can change herself into a cat, and her house flies. Leaving you for me to find was the best she could do?"

Naomi didn't have an answer for that. Her eyes turned to Agatha's back.

"She left you for me. Why do you think she did that?"

She had no idea. "Agatha?"

The witch shook her head and wouldn't turn around.

"She knew what would happen. She planned the whole thing."

Naomi had asked her about unicorns! She had to have known Tavik was a virgin. But she would've had to have planned the whole thing in like an instant, and who planned to kidnap her own son to catch a unicorn? But Tavik still didn't know about the unicorn part of the plan and that part made the whole thing especially convoluted. She had to choose her words carefully as she asked, "You're saying she planned to get us married, so we could kidnap you? Doesn't that seem kind of silly?"

He shook his head. "That wasn't the plan."

"It sounds like the plan to me," Mr. Squibbles said.

"You forgot one key thing. I'm her son. And what does every mother want for her son?"

She looked over to Mr. Squibbles for the answer, but it was Yula who spoke up. "Happiness. Every mother wants her son to be happy."

"No, that's what a good mother wants. We're not talking about someone like you, Yula."

That was a serious burn. Naomi couldn't believe Tavik had just said that in front of his mother. She looked over at Agatha for her reaction. The witch was shaking her head with her hands on her hips. She slowly began to turn around. "I suppose I am a bad mother if one judges me by my son—a demon worshiper and warmonger. Silly me for hoping I could change that."

"You thought that I'd abandon everything once I had a

176

pretty wife to warm my bed."

He thought Naomi was pretty? That made her feel nice, though it was probably the wrong thing to be focusing on.

"I thought you might finally see the folly of your ways!"

"No, you expected me to fuck her."

"What! Now wait a minute," Naomi said.

Agatha threw up her arms. "I really am an awful mother. Just look at my son."

Tavik growled in frustration and stomped over to the door and put his head against the doorjamb. If he wanted to open it, he'd have to use his teeth.

Naomi cast her eyes to the familiar. He was looking back and forth between mother and son.

"Do you know what they're talking about?"

He shook his head.

Yula came over to join their huddle. "So she wanted you to sleep with him?"

"I don't know! She always stopped him when he was about to do anything before."

"Well, she was in the room. What else was she going to do?" Mr. Squibbles said.

"So I was supposed to sleep with him?" she asked the mouse.

"Heck if I know anymore. Definitely won't get a unicorn if you do."

Deciding to table the whole sex with Tavik question, she asked, "How do we smooth this over?"

"Trust me. You don't want to get in the middle of that."

"They won't do anything to each other," Yula said, but she didn't sound too sure.

"Were you watching the same argument as me?" asked Mr. Squibbles.

Yula's eyes darted between the mother and son. "Of course, they wouldn't hurt each other; they're family."

Mr. Squibbles snorted. "May I remind you that she

kidnapped her own son? She wouldn't think twice about cursing him if he made her mad enough. She probably has a few on the tip of her tongue right now."

"Then maybe we should calm them down," Naomi suggested. "Yula, you talk to Agatha. Mr. Squibbles, help her. I'll talk to Tavik."

"Are you sure you can handle him?" he asked.

"Of course, he's my husband." She knew that didn't mean anything, but someone had to go talk to him, and she was the best candidate.

Tavik still stood at the door. His left eye was twitching, and he was grinding his teeth. He looked murderous. Naomi didn't want him to direct any of that anger her way. She liked all of her limbs just where they were. She crept to his side and waited for him to acknowledge her, but his eyes stayed firmly trained on the door's wood grain. She took her chances and stroked his arm. His eyes snapped down to her, and she cringed. He stepped back from the door, and she slipped in front of him. She was surprised when he stepped back in and bent his head to rest it on top of hers. She wrapped her arms around his waist and rubbed his back in slow circles, hoping a little comfort would help.

"Hard to believe we're family, isn't it?" he murmured into her ear.

She squeezed him before answering. "No. Only people who love each other can get this mad at one another."

"Yes, but how long do you think it takes for the anger to burn all the love away?"

"Has it burned all of your love away?"

He buried his face in the crook of her neck in answer. She ran a hand over his head gently. From across the room, soft sobs traveled to them. Hearing them, Tavik shuddered in her arms. God, they were tearing each other apart, Naomi thought, looking over Tavik's shoulder at Agatha. Yula was hugging her and patting her on the back as the witch's shoulders shook.

Naomi braced herself against the door and slid down to sit. Tavik moved to the floor with her. She looked at his face and saw how ragged he still was. "Lie down," she said softly.

He grimaced and began to move away to do so, but she pulled him back and patted her lap. He laid his head down and snuggled into her stomach. She felt him sigh against her. She caressed his head and hoped he fell asleep.

She watched Yula's progress with Agatha. The witch was wiping her eyes and nodding at what Yula was saying. She glanced their way and saw Tavik stretched out on the floor with his head in her lap. The witch rolled her lips, her eyes watering again, and wandered over to the pot.

Quietly, they went back to work on the spell. Naomi heard Yula softly protest that they could do this another night, but Agatha didn't pay any attention to her. Naomi dozed off as the two worked. She didn't dream.

The next morning, Naomi didn't want to wake up. She could feel pins and needles pricking her body in her unconscious state. She knew if she woke up those pins and needles would become knives stabbing her all over. Unfortunately, someone dropped a large metal pot, which jolted her awake and straight into pain. She flailed about, unsure what to clutch first. Her back, her head, her legs, even her eyelashes ached. It was a good thing Tavik's head was no longer in her lap or else he would surely have been harmed by her spastic motions.

She rubbed her eyes and looked around for him. He was seated at the table, giving her a sympathetic look. She waved and tried to stand. It took a bit of fumbling before she could gain her feet.

Yula apologized for startling her awake and offered her

a hot pad for her muscles.

"Yes, please, thank you, you're wonderful," Naomi croaked as she lowered herself into a chair. She wondered if her hair had turned gray overnight. She sounded eighty.

Yula gave her a cloth bag full of hot uncooked rice and went back to bustling over breakfast. Naomi sighed and pressed the hot pad into her lower back. She looked over at Tavik.

"You could probably use one of these, too."

He shrugged his shoulders. "I'm used to sleeping on hard—" but before he could finish, Yula pushed him forward and dropped a hot pad behind him. When he leaned back, she saw his face relax in comfort. "—surfaces," he said as he sighed.

Yula was a domestic dervish: she beat eggs, fried bacon, and baked bread. After watching her for ten minutes, Naomi felt tired enough to go back to sleep. Agatha and Mr. Squibbles weren't around. When Yula swept by, Naomi tugged her skirt to get her attention. "Where's Agatha?" she mouthed. Yula indicated the door with her head and went back to work.

Naomi looked over at Tavik and studied him. He didn't look as ragged as last night, but he still looked worn out. She bit her lip. After what she'd learned, it didn't seem right to keep him tied up. Agatha was his mother, for God's sake. He wouldn't attack his mother—at least, that was what she thought. She lurched up from her seat, her body screaming to return to the hot pad, and went behind his chair. She reached down to untie his hands. He grew completely still when he realized what she was doing. After the rope was undone, she raised her hands and massaged his shoulders and biceps. When she moved to go back to her seat, he jerked her into his lap. He wrapped his arms around her and hugged her tight. She hugged him back dazedly.

"Thank you," he breathed into her ear.

Her cheeks became very warm, and she ducked her head. "I probably should've done it sooner."

When Yula saw that Tavik was no longer bound, she gave her a nod of approval and began setting out breakfast. Naomi unwound Tavik's arms from her waist once the food was out. He let go of her reluctantly but pulled her chair closer to his and kept his arm across the back of it.

Finally, Agatha returned from whatever she had been doing and stopped short at the sight of Tavik feeding himself. Naomi carefully watched the witch's reaction. She hoped her decision wouldn't upset her but couldn't believe that a mother would rather see her son tied up than not.

Agatha merely nodded curtly at them and took a seat across the table. Mr. Squibbles jumped off the witch's arm to go to his own plate. Tavik and Agatha ate, staring at their food. Yula and Naomi exchanged concerned glances as the tension persisted between the family members. She didn't know what to do. Agatha obviously hated the fact that Tavik had devoted himself to Errilol, and he seemed to think he had to do it to protect her and others from some danger in the past, but he was still devoted to the war god. She didn't understand why he was still faithful to him. He'd admitted that Errilol was not a kind or just god. Why he hadn't severed all ties with him was beyond her knowledge. She wanted to get a chance alone to ask him.

"Have you figured out why we've brought you here?" Agatha abruptly asked.

Naomi jumped and dropped her fork. She looked to the witch in surprise. There was no glimmer of benevolence or even mischief in her eyes. They were red, though like she'd been crying again. Naomi felt a sympathetic stab of pain for her, but hoped she wasn't about to do something cruel.

Tavik lifted his head from his plate to consider the

question. He looked out the window at their location. "You seek to capture a unicorn."

"And do you know why we want a unicorn?"

Naomi got a sinking feeling in her stomach. "Agatha," she said softly, hoping to dissuade her from saying more.

Yula had also stilled and looked nervous. Tavik looked at his mother for a moment. "You want an alicorn," he said.

She snorted. "No, we have no intention of killing a unicorn. But we need a unicorn's help. Can you guess for what?"

Naomi stared at the witch, wondering why the old woman wanted to make everything worse. Tavik looked over at Naomi and noticed her pallor. He removed his arm from her chair and turned to look squarely at her. He wanted the answer to come from her. Naomi wished then Agatha had just blurted it out. Having to tell him herself was terrible. Like a betrayal.

Naomi bowed her head as she composed herself to answer. She had to steel herself to look back up into his eyes. "I need a unicorn's help to send me home."

"I'll take you on ship or wagon wherever you wish to go."

She shook her head and bowed it again. "The only way I can go home is by unicorn. Please, Tavik, help me."

He lifted her chin and brushed his thumb across her lip. "What if I don't want to let you go?" he said.

Tears welled up in her eyes. She wasn't sure what exactly was upsetting her. She knew she was supposed to go home. That was the plan from day one, but to have to ask him to help her made her feel awful.

"Please," she said.

Tavik didn't reply.

Agatha slammed her utensils down. "You will help her whether you want to or not."

He turned dead eyes towards his mother. Naomi

182

grabbed his jaw and turned his face back to her. She didn't want them to fight, especially if it were over her.

"Tavik, it's your decision," she said.

Agatha gasped, and Yula's jaw dropped. Naomi, though, felt strangely calm.

CHAPTER FOURTEEN

Unicorns don't like the color orange.

Everyone was silent at the table for a moment. The only sound was the crackling fire and the howl of the wind outside.

"Are you mad? He will never help you!" Agatha declared.

Naomi stared into Tavik's eyes a few moments longer and then calmly turned away. She didn't know what had possessed her to say he could decide whether to help her go home, but she would stand by her decision. She would not force him to do this for her.

Yula cleared the breakfast dishes. Mr. Squibbles jumped into the serving woman's apron pocket to stay out of everybody's way. Naomi rose from the table and began putting on her winter gear.

"Where are you going?" Tavik asked, standing up also.

She shrugged. "Out for a walk."

"I'll go with you." He swung Yula's cloak onto his shoulders.

Agatha turned her back on them. It hurt Naomi to see her do that. She admired the witch. She hoped they'd be able to mend their differences.

"Wait for me," Mr. Squibbles said as he struggled out of Yula's apron pocket, but Yula knocked him back in and sealed it with her hand.

"Be back by lunch," Yula said by way of farewell.

They picked their way across the plateau silently. It was an even bleaker place in the morning sunshine. Small twisted shrubs and prickly scrub grass were all that grew there. Again, Naomi wondered why unicorns might want to roam. If it were only for the isolation, her heart went out to them. To be reduced to roaming such a harsh place when they could go anywhere was awful. The pair made their way to the edge of the plateau and looked over the rocky drop. The wind whipped and tugged at them. Tavik put an arm around her waist to ground her. They stood like that for a while, huddled beside each other.

Tavik finally broke the silence. "You won't be able to come back if you leave, will you?"

Naomi shook her head and burrowed deeper into her cloak. He pulled her into his arms and held her close, letting her put her face against him to escape the wind.

"I don't want to let you go," he told her.

She nodded silently and pressed herself closer. She hadn't had a conscious thought since leaving the cottage. She was just going on autopilot now as she waited for what happened next to occur.

"Naomi, look at me."

She lifted her head and looked at him. He smoothed away the few loose strands of hair that whipped across her face. "What do you want?" he asked.

She scrunched her eyes closed and leaned her forehead

against him to avoid answering. He lifted her chin back up to look at him. She tried to duck her head again, but he laid his hand the length of her jaw and held her steady.

"I don't want to say," she murmured.

"You have to."

She squeezed her eyes shut. "I'm sorry, Tavik, but I have to go home," she choked out.

His hold tightened around her. "I know," he whispered. He turned his head and kissed her softly on the cheek. Tears slid sluggishly down her face, leaving frost tracks behind them. His warm lips kissed them away.

She sniffled and looked miserably down the plateau's side. She wanted to know when the idea of leaving began to hurt. The pain had begun gradually, but when? Her mind flickered back through past events, but she couldn't find the defining moment. She liked these people. She wasn't ready to let them go—but she wasn't the one letting go. She was the one leaving. It was her choice. She'd been so gung-ho to go home once upon a time. Now she stood on the brink of departure and was looking back with regret. She wiped angrily at her face. She was almost at her goal. She hadn't asked to come here. She hadn't wanted to. She had every right to go home. Home was sane, safe, and had all sorts of comforts that didn't exist here. She shouldn't feel bad about leaving, but she did. She felt awful.

"Let's go back," Tavik said. He turned them toward the cottage, but she balked. She didn't want to go back to the cottage. It wasn't time. She wasn't ready.

Tavik wasn't going to wait for her. He scooped her up into his arms in a bridal carry and began striding back. Naomi reflexively tried to wiggle out of his grasp. His hold tightened. It dimly reminded her of the last time he'd carried her. Their wedding day. She looked up at him and saw a muscle in his jaw twitching. She ran her free hand along the muscle to soothe it. He had frost tracks on his face, too.

Naomi emitted a small teary hiccup and wrapped her arms around his neck and drifted into a no-man's-land in her head. She was going home. This was supposed to be a happy day. She couldn't stop crying.

She came back to herself when Tavik stopped outside the cottage. She was in no state to appreciate the fact that he'd carried her almost a mile without slackening his hold or slowing his pace. He set her on her feet and gently pushed her forward.

Agatha sat at the table, poring over her map again. She looked up at their entrance and gave them a sullen glare. "Well?"

"Naomi's going home," he announced.

Agatha blinked a moment in surprise at the news. She looked back and forth between the pair, then back down at her map.

"The best chance of attracting a unicorn is at night. You should rest up now. It may be a long vigil," she said to the map.

Tavik wordlessly moved to the bed in the far corner. Naomi hung back.

Yula sidled up beside her. "You should spend what time you have left with him."

Naomi blinked and looked at her. "Did you find out anything about your sons?"

A spark of pleasure appeared in Yula's eye. "I know where both of them are. Ryan, my oldest, has become a blacksmith for one of the armies, and Warrick is an infantryman in the same army—and one of them is married. Agatha couldn't tell which one, but I now have a daughter." Naomi smiled, happy that Yula had learned good news. She patted Naomi's back. "Now go rest," she said.

Naomi looked at the bed where Tavik lay. Yula and Agatha had used it the previous nights. He'd lain down fully clothed. His eyes were closed. She moved over and got into the bed as gently as possible to not disturb him if he'd already fallen asleep. He opened his eyes, though, and opened his arms. She slipped into them, and the two fell asleep holding each other.

Her phantom unicorn came back to taunt her. He stood perfectly still for her now as she approached. She reached out her hand, and he didn't move. As her hand grazed his cheek, he lowered his head and rammed his horn through her heart.

She shot up in bed with a gasp. Her hands instantly checked her chest for a stab wound. Tavik sat up too and blinked sleepily at her.

"Are you all right?"

She nodded but pulled her knees up and wrapped her arms around them, not wanting to lie back down. He ran a comforting hand down her back. "It was just a bad dream," she told him.

He leaned back against the wall and pulled her back to lie against him. She allowed herself to be uncurled and laid her head on his chest. "How long before dark?" she asked.

He looked toward the windows. "A few more hours."

"Oh."

He kissed the top her head, and they watched the day slip slowly away from the comfort of the bed. Yula and Agatha were in and out. They conferred in hushed tones, not wanting to disturb the two younger people.

Naomi watched Yula tidying the cottage. "You won't hold any of this against Yula once this is over, will you?" She felt Tavik shake his head above her.

"No, I won't. I will have to re-assume the helm when I go back. Errilol is too distrusted to allow the people to see his mark, but I know I can trust her not to breathe a word of this to anyone, even to her sons."

"So you'll let her go see them?"

"She may go and stay with them if she wishes. I can't

defend why I didn't ever help her find her sons or show any interest in doing so."

Naomi didn't reproach him for his willing oversight. They had all been through so much the past couple of days. It would be cruel to start slinging guilt around; especially since she felt she could be slapped with a hefty dollop herself.

"Why haven't you stopped worshipping Errilol?" she asked.

"I can't."

"Why?"

"Once you're sworn to Errilol, there is no breaking the oath. Even if I die, I will be his."

"What about sex?" Naomi asked. During their argument, Tavik seemed to indicate sleeping with Naomi would do something, and if the god required virginity, would that break the oath?

Tavik squeezed her. "No, it wouldn't break the oath. It would anger the god and I would be punished, but he would still rule me."

"Oh."

Tavik stroked her side and they didn't speak further.

The sun set as the four humans and one mouse took their last meal together. The mood was somber. Once everyone took their final bite, Agatha produced the clothes Naomi had been wearing when she'd arrived at Harold's Pass and said that she should probably put them back on. It felt strange slipping back into her sweatshirt and jeans. Once she was dressed, Tavik fingered the ribbed hem of her sweatshirt for a long time. He wouldn't tell her what he was thinking.

Agatha had been looking over the map and finally rolled it back up. "It's time. We should move a good ways from the cottage. Naomi, show me where you last saw the unicorn. Everyone dress warmly. I don't know how long we'll have to stay out there. Hopefully a unicorn will appear promptly and let us get this over with."

Naomi grimaced as she put on a cloak. She wanted to drag her feet but wouldn't let herself. If she couldn't say stop, then she shouldn't delay.

Everyone trudged out of the cottage and headed away to look for a unicorn.

To attract the unicorn, Tavik had to distance himself from the women. In theory, the unicorn would allow him to approach and communicate with the beast, but the only records they had of unicorn encounters were of kills. None of them knew how the unicorn would react when asked to perform a favor.

The night was very cold, and they couldn't start a fire because it would keep all the unicorns away and attract less pleasant creatures. The three women huddled together to stay warm, but they had quickly given up the hope of maintaining any feeling in their toes, noses, or fingertips. Naomi couldn't imagine how cold Tavik was off by himself. He didn't huddle and shiver like them. He stood tall and stared ahead. She peered hard around the plateau for a glimpse of shimmering white, but the plateau was empty and silent. She prayed they would not have to wait out there long. She didn't want anyone to catch frostbite for her.

After several hours, Tavik began walking back toward them. She noticed his break in position with relief.

"Tavik, stop!" Agatha shouted.

Naomi jerked to face the witch. She couldn't be serious. They were slowly freezing to death. Enough was enough.

"Look." Agatha pointed into the darkness.

Naomi looked where she directed and felt her heart both fall and flutter. Standing maybe ten yards away was a unicorn. Tavik noticed the beast too and faced it. The unicorn pranced around. Steam rose in thin wisps from his gleaming white coat and huge clouds drifted from his mouth.

"Approach the unicorn slowly," Agatha instructed.

He looked over his shoulder at his mother. Naomi couldn't be sure in the wan light of the moon, but she thought he rolled his eyes. She hid a smile. Her eyes darted back to the unicorn. It was cautiously edging toward him.

Tavik stood his ground and let the unicorn come to him. The unicorn reached out its neck. Naomi's heart skipped as her nightmare came back to her. Her eyes were glued to the horn tip. Her breath caught every time it dipped down toward Tavik's chest.

"Why, the little squirt brought carrots," Agatha breathed.

Naomi turned to the witch incredulously, not believing that she had just called Tavik a little squirt. Yula chuckled. She turned back and watched the unicorn nudge Tavik's shoulder, obviously wanting more carrots. He pushed the unicorn's head away good-naturedly. The moonlight gleamed off Tavik's teeth as he smiled.

"Don't take all night, Tavik!" Agatha called.

The unicorn's head shot up to look at the three women. Naomi feared Agatha would scare the beast away with her shout, but Tavik quickly recaptured his attention with another piece of carrot. She thought she heard him say something to the beast but couldn't make out any of the words. The unicorn stepped back as if to consider a request. She held her breath. This was it. Either the beast agreed or—they would just try again with a different unicorn. She didn't know if she could do this over and over every night if they had to go through a number of unicorns to find one to take her back to her home.

Her eyes stayed with Tavik and the unicorn, and although she didn't blink, it took her a second to process the fact that he'd turned and was motioning her to come to him. Yula gave her a helpful push, and she suddenly found herself in motion towards them. As she got closer, she discerned the unhappy smile on Tavik's face. She stopped a yard away and stared dumbly at them. He motioned for her to come closer. She crept closer slowly. He lunged forward and grabbed her arm and jerked her to them. She stumbled into him and scrambled to turn around to face the unicorn. The unicorn tossed his mane about in displeasure. She pressed back against Tavik, afraid that the horn would come at her.

He rubbed her arms to soothe her. "Calm down. He won't hurt you."

She tried to calm down, but she wasn't as sure as Tavik; after all, the unicorn's horn was pointed at her.

"He says he'll send you home. All you must do is picture it, and when he pricks you, you will be sent there."

"He said all that?" She felt him smile against her ear.

"More or less."

"More or less!" she squawked.

"Essentially."

She directed a glare over her shoulder at Tavik and heard him chuckle. "I am going to miss you, Naomi," he said and softly kissed her ear. She sucked in a breath and felt it freeze her lungs. Her heart was pounding.

"Close your eyes and picture your home," he repeated. She did as instructed and imagined her kitchen. "Now hold out your hand." She lifted her arm blindly. She steeled herself but began to panic. She hadn't said good-bye properly to anyone. They hadn't wanted to do it in case it didn't happen that night.

She reached with her free hand for one of Tavik's larger ones and threaded her fingers with his.

"I'll miss you, too," she said.

He squeezed her hand and let it go. He must have stepped away. She couldn't feel him near her anymore.

She felt the point land on her middle finger and steady. She bit her lip and willed herself not to open her eyes. She desperately kept the image of her kitchen in her mind. This was it. She was about to leave. The horn point lifted from her finger. *I'm going home*, she thought. She wished the thought made her happy.

The strange howl that sliced through the frigid air felt like a physical blow. Naomi's eyes flew open. The unicorn's head jerked toward the sound. Tavik was suddenly at her side again and took her by the arm. The unicorn wheeled around toward the source of the awful sound.

"Tavik, what is it?"

He turned her toward Agatha and Yula. "Run! Go back to the cottage!"

The unicorn neighed harshly and stamped the ground. Naomi started to sprint toward the two women, who were madly motioning for her to hurry. The howl sounded again, this time in multiples, and closer. When she was a few feet away, the two other women picked up their skirts and started running in the same direction.

"Is it umbreks?" Naomi shouted.

"No, that sounds like golgoffs," Agatha panted.

"Golgoffs?"

"Worse than umbreks."

Naomi looked over her shoulder for Tavik but didn't find him running behind them. He'd stayed with the unicorn. She skidded to a halt and scrambled to go back to him.

"Tavik!" she screamed.

"Naomi, go!" he shouted. He stood with empty hands as large murky objects raced toward him. The unicorn stood by his side with head lowered, ready to fight.

Yula grabbed her arm and began pulling her back. "We must get back to the cottage!"

"I'm not leaving Tavik!"

"You have no hope of fighting them without weapons, and even with weapons, the odds are against us," Mr. Squibbles said from Yula's apron pocket.

"He'll be killed!"

"Errilol will protect him," Yula argued.

She struggled to get free of her. "Errilol protects no one. He enjoys death, even the deaths of his followers."

"Agatha has weapons that can kill the beasts, but she'll need our help," Mr. Squibbles said.

Naomi looked toward the cottage and saw the witch madly scrambling around inside and tossing things about. Yula let her go. Together they raced to the cottage. They stopped at the doorway, though, and hovered there. They didn't want to get hit by any of the flying objects the witch was tossing around.

"What can we do?" Yula asked.

Agatha pointed at a sword, said a word of magic, and it whizzed out of the house.

"Tavik, sword!" Naomi screamed. He turned just in time to catch it. He threw the sheath aside and turned back to the golgoffs. The large beasts closed in on the unicorn and him.

Agatha threw more things around the room.

"What are you looking for?" Yula asked.

Agatha lifted up a scarf to reveal a crystal ball. "This!" she exclaimed and held it up. The witch ran back outside with the crystal ball.

"What are we supposed to do?" Yula demanded.

"Pull down the cottage's wheel," Mr. Squibbles commanded. Yula jerked the wheel down. The cottage began to lift off the ground.

"I'm not leaving Tavik!" Naomi shouted and jumped out of the house before it floated any higher.

"Naomi!" Yula screamed.

She scrambled to her feet.

"Here, take this," Mr. Squibbles called. A tower shield fell flat beside her. She picked it up and staggered a moment under its weight. It had to weigh at least fifty pounds. How the mouse had dropped it out the doorway to her was a mystery that would have to be figured out later. She heaved the shield and put her arm through the brace. It came up to her chin. She began jogging as best as she could back toward the others.

When she finally got a clear view of the golgoffs, she had to wonder if evolution worked a little differently on Terratu. Umbreks had been bad enough, but golgoffs looked like Rob Zombie had designed a Muppet. They were seven feet tall with shaggy hair like a buffalo, but stood upright with massive arms. They had thick tusks that curved down from their mouths, sharp slicing claws tipped each paw, but for some reason, their fur was neon orange.

Agatha stood at the edge of the fray with her crystal ball. She held it high overhead and began chanting indecipherable words. Fog spilled out of the sphere to blanket the field. Naomi went to her side to guard her. She seemed very vulnerable with only the crystal ball. The witch looked at her but didn't stop her chanting. Naomi thought maybe she couldn't stop chanting, not if she wanted to continue producing the fog.

There was a roar that made Naomi jump, and it hadn't come from a golgoff. She watched Tavik charge one of the orange monsters. He leapt on it and sent it to the ground. He rose up with his sword and plunged it into the beast's chest. He threw his head back and roared again. The sound wasn't human. She gasped when she saw his eyes. They were consumed with a burning green light.

"Is that Errilol? Has he summoned him?"

Agatha nodded and continued her chanting.

The unicorn was holding its own. He blinked in and out of the field, striking the golgoffs with his horn wherever he appeared, winking out again before they could turn to strike him. Hard to believe some guys with dogs were ever able to kill one.

Tavik was climbing off the golgoff he'd killed when another blindsided him with a massive claw and threw him into the air. He flew several yards away. With the shield, Naomi ran to help him. He landed face down.

"Tavik, are you all right?"

He didn't stir.

The golgoff that had thrown him was snorting and scratching the ground. He was getting ready to charge. She held the shield tighter, but the golgoff had to be at least three times her weight. It'd make roadkill of her.

"Tavik!"

A low chuckling came from him. It made the hair on the back of her neck stand up. "Tavik, get up!"

The golgoff charged. She crouched behind the shield and braced herself. It was all she could think to do. The golgoff's paws slammed the earth as he ran at her. She could feel the impact of his steps through the ground. "Oh God, this is going to be bad," she said to herself as she screwed her eyes shut and waited for the slam.

The ground shook and suddenly stopped. She felt a little bump on the shield and then there was a distant thump. She peeked over the shield to see the golgoff yards away, sprawled on his back.

She turned back to Tavik and found him standing behind her. "Are you all right?"

He didn't reply.

"Tavik?"

Before she could protest or even offer it as she would have done, he grabbed the shield and wrenched it off her arm. She screamed as her shoulder was nearly dislocated. He put his arm through the brace and hefted the shield. He looked down at her, and the burning green eyes stared through her. That wasn't Tavik in there anymore.

"I'll be back for you," he said, and went after the remaining golgoffs. She didn't romanticize his statement for a second. He wasn't coming back to help her. He was going to finish her off once he was done. What were they going to do?

Her ears perked up as she heard a change in Agatha's chanting. The fog took on a strange odor that made her face feel numb. "Stop that, witch!" Errilol shouted from within the fog.

Naomi stumbled toward Agatha, not sure what she would do, but knowing the witch was still too vulnerable. Several golgoffs still stalked around. The unicorn was attacking them, but its horn only wounded them. None of them were close to dead. Naomi's steps were sluggish as she moved to Agatha. The fog was no longer a simple fog. It had sleeping gas in it. She covered her mouth to try and lessen the effect.

Naomi heard pounding footsteps and turned to see Tavik running toward Agatha. He was going to attack her. She ran to intercept him. Her legs burned as she sprinted.

He didn't see her coming at him. He was only a couple paces away from Agatha when she tackled him from the side. They went down. Naomi climbed on top of Tavik.

"Tavik, wake up! You gotta get rid of Errilol!"

His eyes, though, still burned green. "I'll leave when everything's dead."

He raised the sword to stab her. She grappled with him for it, but she could never hope to win an arm wrestling match against him.

"Tavik!" she screamed, madly holding onto his arm to keep him from striking her with it.

He coughed, and a speck of impossible hope formed in Naomi's heart. He was growing weaker. The fog was having a quicker effect on him. When he dropped the sword, she thought it was over that he was giving up, but he'd only dropped it to grab her throat.

Naomi tried to get away, but his hold on her throat kept her from getting up. She clawed at his hand, digging her nails into his skin, but his hold only tightened. Dark blotchy spots began to take up her vision. Everything was beginning to fade. She wasn't going to make it. Her hands slipped away from him. Her face calmed, and she mouthed the only thing she could think of. She let her eyes slip shut and went completely lax.

There was a harsh neighing off to their right, and cloven hooves galloped toward them. Naomi was roughly pushed aside by a large equine head and a blinding horn slashed Tavik's chest. Tavik screamed and let go of her throat. She fell off of him and struggled to breath. She took a deep breath, which set off a coughing fit that threatened to make her head explode or wish it would.

"Naomi?" Tavik gasped.

She turned to him with her fist to her mouth as her lungs continued to turn inside out. His eyes were beautifully blue again. She gave him a pained smile.

They stared at each other until a harsh snarl drew their attentions. Two remaining golgoffs were approaching them from the edge of the fog. Tavik rose, but his body moved jerkily. The fog was still zapping him of energy. He was in no shape to fight, and the unicorn had received wounds in the battle, too. It was slashed across one flank, and it moved jerkily with exhaustion. Standing a few yards away, Agatha still chanted her incantation, but she had grown hoarse. Fog barely spilled from the globe now.

Tavik pulled Naomi up and pushed her behind him. He held up the shield to protect them, but his arm shook under the weight. He didn't have any strength left.

The golgoffs lowered their heads in preparation to charge. They scratched the ground and roared. As they broke into a run, the cottage dropped out of the sky onto them. Naomi stared with gaping mouth at the sudden return of the cottage.

Yula peered out of the open door of the cottage from the ship's wheel. "Did we squash them?" she called.

Naomi began to giggle in relief and then began to cough again. "Deus ex suburbia," she wheezed.

CHAPTER FIFTEEN

Unicorns never say good-bye, but then again,
they never say hello.

Agatha pressed yet another cup of tea into Naomi's hands. She pushed it back. "No, no more. My eyeballs are swimming in this stuff," she croaked. Her throat was still sore, but she didn't actually like tea. She'd dutifully drunk three cups, and she did feel better, but she couldn't handle anymore. Her gag reflex wanted to kick in, and her throat definitely couldn't handle that.

"Don't argue. You're going to drink this cup, too. It's only your fourth," the witch whispered. She'd completely lost her voice due to the chanting. She'd been sipping the tea as well, but Naomi had been keeping tabs, and she was only on her second cup.

Tavik was dabbing at the unicorn slash on his chest with a wet cloth. It was a nasty looking scratch, but it wasn't deep. It wasn't even bleeding. Yula moved around the cottage, straightening the home. Many things had crashed to the floor when she had dropped the building onto the golgoffs. Amazingly, the floor hadn't buckled or anything. Naomi wondered if the golgoffs were as flat as pancakes. She figured the witch would have to move the house soon or else it would begin to smell.

"Why do you think the unicorn attacked Tavik?" Mr. Squibbles asked. He'd been swift to tell everyone that he'd helped Yula. He'd directed her on how to get the cottage airborne and how to set it down soundly on the beasts. Agatha had given him a huge chunk of cheese for his reward, which he had gobbled up, and now his stomach bulged out so much he couldn't see his feet.

Agatha looked inquiringly at Tavik for the answer. Naomi turned too with the mug up to her mouth. She was only pretending to drink it.

"The unicorns recognize more than just chastity as a type of purity. Pure hearts are also highly regarded."

Agatha cocked an eyebrow. "Pure hearts?"

He didn't respond. Naomi lowered the cup, and put her hand over his. He uncurled his hand and let her fingers slip in.

"Tell me it's safer where you're going," he said softly. She lowered her eyes and nodded her head. "And you'll be happy there," he added.

She looked around the cottage. Happy? But she was happy here.

"No, don't think about what you'll miss here. Think only of what you have there. Can you be happy?" She thought about her family and nodded again. Tavik squeezed her fingers. "All I want is for you to be happy," he murmured. He raised her hand to his lips and kissed her palm.

"Will you be happy?" she croaked.

He let go of her hand and stroked the column of her throat. Dark purple bruises had already begun to blossom. They would be in the shape of his hand.

Agatha came up behind him and put her arm around

him. "I'll make sure he's happy, even if I have to beat him with a stick to do it."

"And I'll stop her, so don't worry," Yula declared from across the room. Agatha turned to the other mother, and her eyes narrowed in challenge. She raised her hand and swatted Tavik upside the head. Tavik ducked at the smack and glared at his mother over his shoulder.

Yula shook her finger at the witch. "Don't challenge me. I will win."

Agatha bristled back.

Naomi laughed, though it sounded more like a wheeze. "Careful, Agatha, she might drop a house on you, and even on my world, we know that's a sure way to get rid of a witch."

"Really?" Tavik asked, intrigued.

She turned to him, and her face broke into a huge grin. She threw an arm around his neck, but when her head hit his shoulder, her laughter turned to tears. Her sobs tore at her throat. Tavik held her tight as Agatha and Yula gathered round and patted her on the back.

"It's time," Agatha whispered.

Tavik nodded and picked Naomi up like before when they'd taken their walk out on the plateau. She tried to stop crying, but she couldn't. She was going home, but it didn't feel like that. Her sobs didn't stop, but her voice eventually gave out. She buried her face against Tavik's shoulder.

Tavik carried her out to where the unicorn waited. As they approached, his horn brightened. Tavik set her down gently. The unicorn stepped closer and gently dipped his head toward her. Naomi stood completely still while he touched her neck with the tip of his horn. A warm glow spread over her throat, and the dull ache disappeared. She touched her neck in wonderment. "Are the bruises gone?" she asked. Her voice was back to normal.

Tavik nodded.

"Can you hear him?" he asked.

She turned back to the unicorn. He stood motionless,

staring at them. She tilted her head, and her jaw dropped. It wasn't like a voice in her head, but more a stray thought or an urge. They didn't think in words, but she was able to understand. "He wants to know if I have any other injuries!"

Tavik smiled. "Do you?"

She looked down at herself and really didn't think she had any other aches or pains that would warrant the unicorn's help. She turned to Tavik and raised her hand to his chest, lightly touching the slash the horn had made. The unicorn shook his head. He couldn't heal wounds inflicted by the horn.

"Don't worry about it. It's not bad," Tavik said.

She threw her arms around him and squeezed him tight. He hugged her back just as strongly.

"It's time," he reminded her softly.

She turned her head and said the words that she hadn't been able to say aloud when Errilol was strangling her. "I love you."

He shuddered, but he turned her around to face the unicorn again. "Hold out your hand, Naomi, close your eyes, and think of home."

She closed her eyes. Her hand shook as she held it out. Tavik steadied it with his. The unicorn dipped his horn again, balanced for a second on her fingertip. Tavik stepped back. Naomi's body began to shake again, but she kept her outstretched hand steady. The horn flicked across her middle finger, drawing a single drop of blood. There was a flash of light and sudden wave of vertigo.

Naomi jerked her hand back, but the deed was done. She stood in her kitchen. A broken unicorn horn lay at her feet. A sudden wave of nausea washed over her as she stared at it. Her hands shot out and grabbed the edge of the sink. It was full of soapy water. She dipped her fingers in it and found the water was still warm. Had any time passed?

She knelt down and picked up the broken horn. It was

just a piece of bone now. There was no more magic in it. There was no going back.

She was going to be sick. She rushed to the bathroom and put her face over the toilet, but though her stomach rolled, it did not heave. She picked herself up and brushed back the shower curtain. Unable to think of anything else, she decided a shower might help her. It would at least give her something mindless to do while her mind stayed in free fall. She began to undress, and as she moved around in front of the medicine cabinet, something in the mirror caught her eye. She had to grab another mirror to see it clearly. She turned her back to the medicine cabinet and raised the small hand mirror. There, on her right shoulder blade, was a branding mark. It was shaped like a *T*. It was all she had to remember Tavik. She tried to reach back to touch it, but her fingers could barely graze it. A hollow ache developed in her chest.

She called her parents once she regained her composure. They were happy to hear from her, but they had seen her just that morning. Her mother told her how well the yard sale had gone and who she'd seen. Naomi held the phone numbly as she listened to her relaxed and happy voice. When a couple of tears fell onto her lap, she quickly said good-bye and hung up. She was home, and nothing had changed. No time had passed, and no one had worried about her. She didn't know if she would go insane or if she already had.

That night she dreamed that the unicorn stood before her, but instead of reaching out to capture it, she shook her head and backed away. She didn't want it. She held up her hands to ward it off. She shouted at it to leave. The unicorn didn't hear her, though. She was not pure. It leveled its horn at her. She turned to run away, but he ran her through. She looked down at the horn sticking out of her breast and touched the point with her index finger. The horn pricked it, and a single drop of blood was absorbed. The world began to swirl, and she screamed.

She jerked up in bed and looked wildly around. She was in her bedroom, but that didn't seem right. She knew why. She'd become accustomed to stone walls, tall beds, and Yula's cheerful good morning. Home did not feel like home.

She dragged herself out of bed. She was grateful that it was Sunday, and she wouldn't have to worry about work. She didn't think she could handle the bank. She wondered if she should call in sick on Monday. She needed a mental health day—or maybe a week.

Deciding not to worry too much about Monday, she lounged around the house. She did a little cleaning, but neither the television nor a book could hold her attention. She finally settled beside the front window and stared out. It was a sunny day, and people were going about enjoying the lazy afternoon. She watched people walking dogs, children playing, cars rolling by at sedate paces. The sound of lawn equipment droned quietly in through the closed window.

She was startled when it began to grow dark. She'd been sitting there in a daze the entire afternoon. She hadn't eaten a thing for lunch, and her stomach grumbled.

When the phone rang, it made her jump. She picked it up, and her mother's cheerful voice came through inviting her to their house for dinner. She thought about declining, but she'd missed her family so much. She wouldn't let her depression keep her from them. It would be good for her to see them.

When she arrived, she perked up some as she slipped into the home and called out to her family. Her father answered her from the living room, and her mother came out of the kitchen to give her a hug and a kiss on the cheek. She still looked sad enough for her mother to ask if she were all right and to check her forehead. Naomi quickly told her she was fine and slipped away with the excuse of wanting to see Bobby. Her younger brother was still home for the weekend. He lived in the dorm during the week. He was staying for dinner and to finish his laundry. She crept up to his room, where he was doing homework.

She knocked and stuck her head around the door. "Hey."

Bobby looked up from his textbook and smiled. "Hey. Come on in."

"How's life?" she asked and flopped down onto his bed.

"Going okay. Would be better if I could miraculously memorize all these chemistry formulas for the quiz on Tuesday."

She nodded and rolled onto her back to look at the ceiling.

"You okay?" he asked.

"I had a weird dream. I dreamt I was married to this really scary guy who turned out not to be so scary, but I couldn't stay with him because I had to get back home. I didn't want to go home, but it was like that was the only thing I could do. If I didn't go home, I wouldn't ever see you guys again."

"What'd you do, have a burrito before going to sleep?"

She sighed and hugged herself. "I didn't want to wake up from the dream."

"Why wouldn't you be able to see us ever again?"

"Because the guy was on another planet. If I stayed with him, I'd be too far away to even call and talk to you all. I was scared it would upset everyone if I left and never came back."

Bobby's eyebrows scrunched together as he thought about what she'd said. "There's like a lot of issues in there. Deep Jungian stuff. I mean, I usually just dream about meeting Natalie Portman."

She rolled to her side to look at him. "You going to analyze me?"

He grinned and shook his head. "It seems pretty obvious to me. You're afraid to grow up."

She propped herself up to better glare at him. "Afraid to grow up!"

"Well, yeah! You meet this great guy who you could marry—"

"We were already married," she interjected.

His eyebrows rose. "Even clearer. You have this husband you love, but you leave him to go back to your mommy and daddy when you could stay with him and start your own family."

"But I would never see you guys again!"

"Oh, come on, Naomi, that's nearly impossible in this day and age."

She bristled. "We were on another planet."

"Fine. Say you met like the King of Mars, who was perfect for you and wanted to marry you—are you saying you wouldn't move back with him to Mars to be with him?"

She looked at her brother incredulously. "No!"

"Why?" he asked smugly.

"Kids, dinner's ready!" their mother called.

She rolled off the bed. "Because Mars sucks."

Dinner wasn't formal at the Taylor household. Elbows rested on the table. People happily ate with their hands. Food picked off and passed to others' plates. Naomi dug into her plate with gusto. Yula's cooking had been good, but she had no pasta to work with so had never fixed spaghetti. They chatted and Naomi felt at ease. Naomi realized this might be the first stress-free meal she'd had in days. No one was tied up. There was no impending doom. She smiled to herself, though she still felt a pang of regret.

During a lull in conversation, Bobby announced, "Guess what: If Naomi met the King of Mars and fell in love with him, she wouldn't move there to be with him because she wouldn't want to abandon us."

Both parents stopped to absorb this piece of weird news. Their father nudged Naomi with his elbow. "That's because she's Daddy's little girl." She smiled thinly at him.

"If you were able to come back and visit, I don't see why you wouldn't want to marry the King of Mars," Barbara said.

Naomi rolled her eyes. "I wouldn't be able to come back."

"But if this king were able to come here, and you were able to go there, I would think you would be able to repeat it."

Naomi wished this hadn't become the topic of discussion.

"There would be no guarantee that we could. I could wind up stranded on Mars, and you guys would never hear from me again."

"Yeah, but you said you loved this guy, so why not be his queen?" Bobby asked, wanting to prove his theory.

She glared at him. He wasn't taking the idea seriously. He thought this was just some hypothetical argument when she'd already faced this decision and chosen.

Sensing Naomi's irritation, Barbara said, "Why don't we drop this? No need to have bloodshed at the table."

Naomi looked at her plate and didn't say anything beyond one- or two-word answers for the rest of the meal.

She was in the kitchen helping her mother with the dishes when the matter was brought up again. Barbara was at the sink, washing while Naomi stood by with a towel. "You know, the only thing I've ever wanted was to know that you're safe and happy, but I might give up the knowing part if the rest could happen."

Naomi stopped drying the plate in her hands to look at her mother. "But if you didn't know, what good is the rest of it?"

Her mother turned to look at her. There was a frown on her face. "Naomi, I don't know all the time if you're all right. I had to start dealing with that the first day you went off to school. I had to convince myself that you were okay, and nothing bad would happen to you, and that hope was rewarded every time you hopped off the school bus and began jabbering about how your day at school had been. Then you went off to college and found your own place. I only see you now on visits. It was hard to deal with the fact that you weren't living here anymore. I had to let you go, but I know you're okay even if I don't have hourly updates. I just have hope."

"But what if the possibility of even visits were taken away?"

Her mother handed her a glass. "I would learn to deal with that too, and I would if you were safe and happy."

Naomi looked down at the glass in her hands and began slowly wiping it dry. She wouldn't have been safe— that was the reason why Tavik had wanted to send her back—but she thought she could've been happy.

When she got home, she put Mom's leftovers in the fridge. She was struggling with the nasty realization that her family would've wanted her to stay with Tavik. Sure, they might not have been overjoyed with her moving to another planet, but they would've seen her off and wished her well. It was a difficult realization. Her family would let her go if it made her happy, and she was starting to realize that she could let them go. But all this was moot now. She'd made her choice, and she had to deal with it.

She went to her living room to submerge herself in television, but stopped short when she saw a mouse sitting on the coffee table.

"Hello, Naomi."

She rubbed her eyes and looked again. The mouse was still there.

He stood on his hind legs and peered up at her. "Now you're supposed to say hello back. It's just general good manners. You do remember me, don't you? You better not come after me with a broom. That'd be just rude."

Next Naomi pinched herself.

"Are you about to faint? Maybe you want to sit down."

It was him. It was really him. She sat down on the couch. She did feel a little dizzy. "Mr. Squibbles, what are

208

you doing here?"

"Thank the dark gods for small favors. You had me worried there for a moment when you seemed shocked to see me."

"I am shocked."

"I would think you'd have gotten over that by now." He lifted his nose and sniffed the air. "Got any wine and cheese?"

"Wine and cheese?"

"Do you really remember me? Yes, wine and cheese."

She dumbly went to the kitchen. She poured a saucer of Merlot and chopped some cheddar. She went back to the living room and set them down before him. She sank back down onto the sofa and stared as he took a moment to savor his refreshments.

"How is everyone? How did you get here?" she finally asked. She was still having trouble believing the familiar was there.

Mr. Squibbles wiped his mouth with his paws before answering. "Everyone is not well. I'm here to ask you to come back, and I got here the same way you did. I hitched a ride from a unicorn horn."

"How can we go back?" That word had become Naomi's favorite. How, how, how?

He merely shrugged his shoulders and told her, "With the horn you have."

Her eyes went to the broken horn that sat in the glass case on her mantle. "We can't use it. It's broken."

"You're right. We can't use a broken horn, but we may be able to use a mended one."

Her eyes grew round as she turned to stare at the mouse. "There's a way to fix it?"

The mouse nodded. "I got the spell straight from the horse's mouth, or rather, the unicorn's."

She could go back? She hadn't considered the possibility, and that was strictly true, but she had daydreamed about going back. She'd tried to stop herself and would deny it if asked. It had seemed just too impossible, but here was a talking mouse telling her it was.

"What do I have to do?"

He tilted his head up at her, and his front teeth showed. She assumed it was his equivalent of a smile. "It would be good to write this down. The list of ingredients is long."

None of the items Mr. Squibbles rattled off would be impossible to obtain, but it wasn't like she could just hop over to the grocery store and pick them up.

The other things Mr. Squibbles had said began to nag at her. "What did you mean everyone is not well? What's happened?"

He heaved a heavy sigh. "Tavik is in peril. He has stopped pillaging and conquering."

"But that's good, right?" Naomi asked.

"Yes, but we've lived at war for so long that no one knows quite how to handle peace. Bands of ex-soldiers roam the land, plundering towns, and Tavik won't take up his sword to stop them."

The news made Naomi's stomach twist with worry. She couldn't believe Tavik would just give up like that. She knew her departure had upset him, but he had seemed resolved to it. He was so strong and determined. Surely, she wouldn't have weakened him so much.

Mr. Squibbles quickly offered what little good news he had. "Agatha has come out of her woods to help Tavik's remaining men keep order. She even visits the castle now."

Naomi gave Mr. Squibbles a thin smile at this added news. "I'm sure Mrs. Boon loves that."

"You look tired, Naomi. Why don't you go to sleep, and we'll start work tomorrow."

"Shouldn't we do something now? Time is of the essence and all that, right?" she said, but talk of sleep made her want to yawn.

"How much time had gone by when the unicorn delivered you back?"

She shrugged. "No time really. I don't think but a few minutes may have passed."

"That's right, and that's how it will be when we go back. It won't be hardly any time at all has passed."

"How much time had gone by before you came here?"

"Four months. How long have you been back?"

"Less than two days."

The mouse nodded. "The unicorns are very clever. It's amazing that they've been nearly hunted to extinction."

She nodded sluggishly. She was growing very sleepy. She heaved herself up and stumbled into her bedroom. She had barely any energy to think before her head hit the pillow but to wonder why the unicorns would help them. It hadn't sounded like Tavik even knew that Naomi had been sent for, so who had spoken to the unicorns and got their help or…and Naomi's mind slipped away into sleep.

She dreamed that night of unicorns. They spoke to her, and she understood what they said, but when she awoke the next morning, she couldn't remember what they'd told her or what she had said in return. She scratched her head and tried to make herself remember, but the dream was like water. It slipped away faster the harder she tried to pin it down.

She heard the television from the living room. Still struggling to remember her dream, she shuffled into the room to find Mr. Squibbles had found the remote and was channel surfing.

"Good morning," she yawned.

"Naomi, your world is very strange. This box is amazing. What's it called?"

"Television, and it will rot your brain."

With a little squeak of alarm, Mr. Squibbles shut it off. She shuffled into the kitchen to scrounge up some breakfast. Something was nagging her in the back of her mind. She was forgetting something. She looked at the kitchen clock and jumped. It was nine fifteen. She was supposed to have been at work at eight. She looked around the kitchen in panic. She grabbed the phone and called the bank. She spoke to one of her coworkers and apologized, saying she wasn't feeling well and couldn't come in. Luckily, she didn't abuse her sick day privileges so her coworker didn't harass her too much for not calling in sooner. Naomi thanked her for wishing her well and hung up.

She stared at the phone after replacing it in its cradle. She needn't worry about her job, she realized. If she wanted to do the right thing, she should just call and say she quit. She doubted she was going back to work ever again. The thought actually perked her up. She hadn't loved the bank. It'd been an all right job but nothing special.

As she poked around in her cabinets, she began to make a list of what she would miss. Not the material things, like she had done while on her first stay in Terratu, but important stuff like the people who she would never see again. The thought of saying good-bye to her family and friends made her wonder if she were doing the right thing. Tavik might need her, but this was her home.

The other half of her brain reminded her that she had friends on the other planet and a possible new family with Tavik. She decided to not think about it for now. She looked at the list of ingredients that she would have to get for the spell.

A metal nail
A bucket of fresh milk
A strip of non-dyed cloth
Five acorns
Nine drops of her blood
A fist-sized rock from a stream bed
Seven fresh roses with thorns
A handful of rich earth

She knew she had nails in her toolbox and a roll of

medical gauze in her first-aid box, so she didn't need to worry about those. She picked up her purse and keys, told Mr. Squibbles to be good, and went out in search for the other items. She went to the local park first and got the acorns and the stream bed rock. The organic supermarket had unpasteurized milk. The price took her breath away, but she got it anyway. The florist couldn't supply her with roses with thorns. They only had specially grown thornless roses. She knew where she could get regular ones, but she'd hoped to avoid involving those she'd have to say good-bye to.

She parked outside her parents' home. Her mother came out to greet her. "Naomi! What a nice surprise! Are you off from work today?"

She nodded and looked toward the rose bush against the front of the house. "The roses are doing really well this year."

Her mother turned to look at them too. "I'm using a new type of fertilizer."

She couldn't bring herself to ask for the roses. She looked at the house, and her eyes settled on the window to her old room. They hadn't changed it. They used it as a guest room, but it still had Naomi's childhood furniture in it. It was where she'd grown up—or not, as Bobby would like her to believe.

"Mom, can we go inside and talk?"

Her mother looked at her, and her eyes crinkled a little when she nodded and led the way inside. They settled in the kitchen. Her mother poured them each a cup of coffee. Naomi held the mug in her hands and blew across the rim to cool it as she tried to think of how to say what she wanted, but her mother beat her to it.

"You've met someone."

She froze and stared at her. "You can tell?"

Barbara smiled and nodded her head. "I know that distracted look. Only a man could make a woman think so hard. When can we meet him?"

Naomi grimaced and sipped her coffee. *Here goes nothing*, she told herself. "You can't. He lives really far away, and I want to go be with him, but with it so far away, I don't know if I'll be able to visit you guys ever again. I wouldn't be able to call or send letters either."

"Where are you going, Timbuktu? Call us collect. We won't mind."

Naomi shook her head. "I wouldn't be able to call. At least, I don't think so." *Unless Agatha has some spell*, she finished silently to herself.

"You wouldn't be in trouble, would you? This man isn't into anything illegal, is he?"

She was sure she'd land in trouble once she returned to Terratu, but she didn't want to tell her mother that—but then again, she didn't want to lie. "Things can get difficult where he lives, but I'm pretty sure I can handle it. He isn't into anything illegal. He's sort of in the government." *More like he is the law*, she mentally corrected. She really needed to watch her words. She didn't want to lie to her mother, but telling her these half-truths didn't sit well with her either.

"Well, how did you two meet? What's his name?"

Naomi's eyebrows rose at the way her mother just breezed right along with the subject. "His name's Tavik. We met sort of on a blind date. His mother set us up." She was going to burn in Hell for all these half-truths, but if she told her the truth, her mother would be feeling her head and calling the doctor.

"Tavik? Well, that's an unusual name. When did you two meet?"

She shrugged. The unicorn horn made judging time very difficult. "A couple of weeks or so ago."

"A couple of weeks? And you want to move away and be with him? Are you sure?"

She nodded.

Her mother reached across and patted her hand. "You know you'll always have a home here."

Naomi smiled but couldn't be too reassured by the idea. She highly doubted she would be able to run home when the going got tough.

"Mom, can I pick some of your roses and take them home?"

Her mother looked a little surprised by the request but nodded her head. "Of course, take as many as you want."

She got a pair of clippers from a kitchen drawer and went outside to cut seven roses. As she was carefully wrapping a paper towel around the stems, her mother came out.

"Why don't you come by for dinner again tonight? I know your father and brother will have questions. Your father will probably have a very tough time accepting this."

Naomi nodded and took the flowers back to the apartment. She told Mr. Squibbles that she had everything and would be ready to do the spell after she had dinner with them. She took a shower and took care of a few small things at the apartment. Soon enough, it was time to go back to her family's house. She realized that she was quite nervous to see them again like when she'd brought her first high school boyfriend to dinner. Except this time, she was facing her family alone. She sort of wished she could bring someone with her. Even Mr. Squibbles would have been appreciated, but she thought a talking mouse would steal the spotlight from her impending departure. Actually, that might not be such a bad idea. No, she knew she had to face her family and explain to them what she was about to do. She couldn't hide behind the talking mouse. He wasn't big enough to hide behind anyway.

CHAPTER SIXTEEN

Unicorns are not indigenous to anywhere.

"What do you mean you're moving away and can't say where? How will we reach you?"

Naomi winced and hunched her shoulders. "It's not like you could call me anyway, Dad. There aren't any phones."

"What!?"

She winced again. "It's a real rustic place. The phone companies haven't gotten there yet." The idea of the Verizon guy walking by Agatha's cabin, asking, "Can you hear me now?" while umbreks stalked him in the shadows gave her a moment of amusement before her father brought her crashing back to reality.

"I can't believe you're just going to move to some grass hut to be with a guy you've known for less than a month. What are you thinking?"

She glanced at the two other family members sitting at

the table. Her mother was being gently supportive while Bobby looked like he wanted popcorn.

"Dear, I think Naomi is willing to sacrifice so much because she loves this man."

"Are you engaged?"

She shook her head. Technically, it wasn't a lie.

"Knocked up?"

"Phil!"

"Dad!"

"Well?" her father persisted.

"No," she said, and pushed some peas around on her plate.

"Then what's the rush?"

"He needs me. He's in a difficult situation, and he misses me."

Her mother's face softened at the last reason, but her father still looked upset by the whole situation. "Am I the only one who thinks this whole thing is all one big mistake? You're going to ruin your life."

Her back stiffened. "Tavik needs me, Dad, and I want to help him. I know going there is a major risk, but I want to do it. I want to be with him."

Her father turned his face to his plate and moved his food around. "I don't want to lose my little girl."

"Phil, you're not losing her. You're letting her go."

Her father grimaced and swirled his food.

"Have you decided what to do with your apartment?" Bobby asked.

Naomi sat back in surprise with the new mundane consideration. She hadn't really thought about it. She should box everything up and see if anyone wanted it. She looked over at her brother's face and saw the solution sitting across from her. "Can you afford it?"

He wiped his mouth with the back of his hand as he nodded. "A couple of guys and I could totally handle it. It's two bedrooms, right?"

She nodded.

"Will you be taking many clothes?" her mother asked.

She shook her head.

"I could give them to the women's shelter. They'll be put to good use."

She nodded. Leaving shouldn't be this simple, should it?

"What about your job?" her father asked.

"I'll give immediate notice tomorrow."

"Not even two weeks?"

"No."

Her father shook his head. "Bad business. You won't get an excellent reference that way."

"I won't need it. Tavik has a job for me." Though she didn't want to tell her parents that her job title was Lady.

"What about a place to stay? Do you have a grass hut to sleep in?" her father asked, still clearly against the idea.

She smiled wryly and pictured the castle. "Yeah, it's a pretty nice place."

"When will you be leaving?" her mother asked.

She thought about it for a few moments. She had everything she needed and stuff was pretty well taken care of. She shouldn't prolong the inevitable. She steeled herself and answered, "In two days."

Everyone blinked at her.

"So soon?" her mother asked. Her voice wavered.

She nodded again. She twisted her hands in her lap. Her father shoveled more food into his mouth to stop himself from commenting.

"Are you sure, sis?" Bobby asked.

Naomi's eyebrow arched. "It's time for me to grow up," she said.

Bobby stared at her, slack-jawed, with his words thrown back at him. He looked back down at his plate uncomfortably.

Naomi let herself back into her apartment with a relieved sigh. She hadn't been sure if she were ever going to get out of the house. The interrogation had continued, and her father drilled her on everything: Questions about Tavik, his past, his family, his education. When she hadn't known some of the answers, her father's frown would deepen. By the time she left, his looked permanently bowed down and she didn't think there was anything she could do to change that, except not go and that wasn't an option.

Naomi found Mr. Squibbles curled up asleep on the sofa. She stroked his back to wake him.

He jerked up. "What? I didn't eat the scroll!" He looked around quickly and finally up at her. He blinked a moment. "Oh, it's you. How'd it go?"

"About as well as could be expected. I'm ready to try the repair spell. Are you up for it?"

He nodded and climbed into her hand. "Are you sure you have everything?"

She pointed at the ingredients set up in the kitchen. He hopped onto the kitchen counter and crawled through them to make sure they were correct. When he was satisfied, he told her the words to recite for the spell. She wrote them down, and they were ready to begin. First, they needed a small cauldron, as Mr. Squibbles put it. She took out her largest pot and placed it on the counter. She tied the gauze around the horn to hold it together and put the river stone into the pot and placed the horn on top of it.

She reached for the stove dial. "How hot should I make it?"

"The milk needs to simmer."

She turned the dial to low. It was time to begin.

She glanced at her sheet. First was the milk. She poured it in over the stone while saying, "With this simple spell, what was once broken will be mended. With running water and pure milk, the damage will be tended." The stone and the horn disappeared from view in the milk.

She picked up the acorns next. She dropped them in one at a time. "As large trees come from eye-sized seeds, this horn will get the strength it needs." The acorns plopped into the milk.

Now it was time for the nail.

"Iron cold and hard will become hot and molten to meld and fuse what is broken." The nail disappeared into the milk. Small, slow bubbles began to rise to the surface.

She took a moment to smell the roses. She lowered them petals first into the pot. "And these roses will help beauty and dread recombine to make something both dangerous and kind." The stems stuck out of the milk.

She picked up the handful of dirt. "The earth accepts and nourishes all. May it return this alicorn to its original state before its fall." When she added the earth, the milk turned brown.

There was only one ingredient left, and while she had plenty of it, she was a little scared of adding it, considering how unicorn horns reacted to blood.

She picked up a sharp knife and held it against her arm. "With life there is death, but without death there is no life. With my blood, I give this cauldron life to balance the death."

She slid the knife against her arm. The knife was very sharp, and the gash opened easily with a sharp sting. Her blood welled up, and she turned the cut toward the pot. The drops fell, and she watched them slip under the surface, leaving red halos behind.

When she counted nine drops, she pressed a paper towel to her bleeding arm and peered into the pot as she said the last line. "Now the spell is cast and the potion done, may it be enough to render this tragedy undone."

The concoction bubbled and looked very unappetizing. It certainly didn't look magical. "Are you sure this is going to work?" she asked. Out of the corner of her eye, she saw Mr. Squibbles' whiskers twitch. He sat silently on her shoulder. "Well?" she goaded.

"The unicorn said it would work. He would be the one to know."

"You have no idea, do you?"

"Let's just let it sit for the night. We can check it in the morning."

She left the pot on the stove and turned the heat down to the lowest setting. She left Mr. Squibbles with the magical box and wand controller with the firm order not to stay up all night. If people started trying to sell him useless gadgets, it was past his bedtime.

As she got ready for bed, she tried to feel hope about the spell, but she had serious doubts that it'd work. She hadn't seen or felt anything particularly mystical. There hadn't been any whoosh of air, sparkly special effects, or trumpet sounds to announce the spell's successful completion. All it'd done was burble. Well, if it didn't work, there were always the mystical properties of super glue.

When she checked the pot the next morning, her lip curled at the sight. The milk had mostly burned off. The rest had formed a brown nasty sludge at the bottom of the pot. She turned the stove off and contemplated her next move.

"Well, is it fixed?" Mr. Squibbles asked. She picked the mouse up and held him over the pot so he could see the ugly mess. His nose twitched, and his tail whipped about in her hands. "Erg, I suggest we pitch the pot, but first, retrieve the horn."

She pressed her lips together. The mess made her want to heave.

She retrieved a pair of tongs to fish around in the pot for the submerged horn and snagged it. When she pulled it out, the pot emitted a wet plop. The horn was completely covered with the slime, and it dripped slowly off of it in gooey globs. It looked like a very straight turd. The though made her gag. She laid the horn in the sink and turned on the water.

"Well?" Mr. Squibbles asked, running to the edge of the sink.

"Do you think it would damage it if I dipped it in bleach first?"

"What's bleach?" he asked as he stared at the running faucet in fascination.

"Never mind."

Naomi put on a pair of rubber gloves and gingerly picked up the horn to better rinse off the sludge. The pearly white of the horn began to emerge while the gauze remained firmly brown. She picked at the knot and got it to loosen and fall away. The horn stayed in one piece. She ran her gloved hands over where the break had been. A small seam like a scar remained to indicate where it had snapped. She tapped the horn gently to test the bond. She feared at any moment the horn would fall apart, but she had to know if it were truly fixed. The horn didn't break apart. She turned to the mouse for his opinion.

"I guess it worked," he said.

"I am very uncomfortable with guessing."

"There's only one way to be sure."

"I don't want to find out that it's faulty when I teleport only half my body. Could we try any of the other unicorn horn tricks?"

His ears perked up. "I know! Put the tip against your arm and see if it heals the cut!"

She took off the bandage that she'd placed over the cut on her arm and turned the tip to it, but stopped short of touching it. She looked at Mr. Squibbles. "Is there anything I should say or do to make it heal the wound?"

He shrugged. "You have more experience with the healing property of horns than I do."

"What if it doesn't heal me? Oh God, what if instead of healing me, it makes me sick? Like, what if it gives me bubonic plague or a staph infection? What if it's an anti-horn?"

"An anti-horn?" Mr. Squibbles didn't sound like he was taking her concern seriously, but looking at it, Naomi firmly believed this horn was more likely to give her a staph infection than heal a cut. "If you want to wait, I'll understand. This is a life-changing choice and shouldn't be made lightly," he said.

She looked down at the mouse. She had made her choice. She was ready to make a life-changing move. She was just being silly. If she got a staph infection, she'd go to the hospital. They could cure that. Shit, they could cure bubonic plague now, too.

"I'm doing this."

"That's my false lady."

She couldn't help tensing as she touched herself with the horn. Her bottom lip curled into her mouth. She touched the tip to the cut. As soon as it touched her, she jerked it back.

"Well?" Mr. Squibbles demanded.

She turned her arm so she could peer at the scratch, but there was no scratch to peer at. The skin was smooth. She brushed her thumb over the spot, but it was completely healed and showed no signs of having been cut the night before.

"It worked," she breathed.

"What else do you have to do before you can leave?" he asked.

She blinked at her arm, her mind having trouble switching from the miraculous to the mundane. She needed to call work and give notice. She had to call friends and tell them she was leaving. She had to talk to the landlord about switching the lease to her brother. Her stomach churned. The idea of just leaving was more appealing than preparing to leave. She didn't know why. Maybe it was because if she prepared that meant she was really going to do it and there would be no turning back. If she thought about just leaving, she could change her mind.

Naomi knew that her apprehension was silly and

illogical. She was going to go back. She'd already decided, but the idea of saying good-bye to her old home and life was gut-wrenching. She was leaving all she knew for something completely unknown. She didn't know if she could help Tavik and what would happen once she did.

She got ready for the day, deciding that making an appearance in person at the bank was more civil than calling to inform them of her departure. She could pick up the few things she had there while she was at it. She called a couple of her girlfriends and made plans to meet them for lunch. She would tell them the news then.

As she set out to do her tasks, she wondered if she could take Mr. Squibbles up on his offer of just staying for a while first, maybe a year. She could let the people adjust to the idea of her leaving. It was pretty shoddy of her to drop this in their laps and then blithely walk away.

She beat her head against the steering wheel of her car. She was parked outside the bank. If she put it off, would it be easier to leave later? She hated the question because that wasn't what concerned her. What twisted through her mind was the reason she had to go back. Tavik was in trouble. He needed her help. Yula and Agatha needed her, too. Could she stay comfortably in her world while they struggled in theirs? Mr. Squibbles had said that time was not really a concern with the alicorn. Once she left, she would arrive soon after Mr. Squibbles left. Time wasn't an issue, then, but she couldn't be as cold and practical as to accept this fact. Time would still go by for her. If she waited a year, or waited at all, could she face the others when she went back without guilt? Could she face Mr. Squibbles? She beat her head on the steering wheel again. This moral dilemma was giving her a headache physically and mentally.

She straightened in her seat and took a deep breath through her nose. She was tired of contemplating this. She wanted it decided. She opened her car door and got out. She walked up to the bank, went to her boss, got her alone in her office, and gave her resignation. She told the woman she was moving away. She was surprised and touched when her boss assured her she would be happy to be a reference for her without prompting. She thanked her and quickly excused herself. She felt tears forming in her eyes. She went to her desk and collected her personal belongings. She told her coworkers about her departure. They expressed surprise and wished her well. She thanked them and went back to her car, shaking. She'd done it. She'd quit her job. There was no going back now. The ball was in motion.

She started the car and headed to the restaurant to meet up with her girlfriends.

She'd always had friends, but they drifted in and out of her life freely. There was shock at her news, but no tears. They eagerly asked about Tavik. She told them a little, enough to confirm their romantic ideas but not enough to shatter them. She suspected they dreamed that she was going to wed a prince and become a princess with a tiara and everything. They made her swear to keep in touch, and she did swear, but her fingers were crossed under the table.

When she let herself back into her apartment, she felt ready to collapse. She'd stopped at the landlord's to inform him of her departure and that her brother would finish out the lease. Her parents had cosigned with her when she'd gotten the place, so the change of sibling didn't worry him, especially since the deposit would not have to be refunded. She also paid the next four months of rent, which he happily accepted. He'd wished her good luck on her move.

She hung her coat up in the closet. She stopped a moment and fingered the sleeve of her grandfather's coat. If he were still alive, she thought she could've told him everything. She couldn't spill the truth to her parents or even Bobby, but she thought Grandpa Harry would've believed her and accepted everything. He had been the one, after all, to give her the alicorn. She wandered into her living room. She'd been about to call out to Mr.

Squibbles, but stopped with her mouth open. Bobby stood in her living room with a tape measure extended over the sofa.

"Hey, sis. How'd your day go?" he asked.

"What—what are you doing?"

"Rory's got a big screen TV, and I'm checking to see where it'd be best to put it."

She felt a flash of hurt. Her brother was moving in before she was even gone.

Her mother came out of her bedroom. "Welcome back, dear."

She turned to her mother to complain about the brotherly invasion, but her mother was in on it, too. She held a stack of towels from her bedroom bathroom, clearly taking them away to give to some shelter or something. Her cozy home was being stripped from her while she stood there.

"I'm really tired," she told them.

"Then go lie down. We can manage on our own," her mother assured her.

That wasn't what she wanted to hear. She wanted Bobby to put away his tape measure, for her mother to put back the towels, and frankly, for both of them to leave.

She moved to her bedroom and flopped onto the mattress. At least her mother hadn't stripped the sheets yet. She knew that thought was unkind, but couldn't they be a little more paralyzed with grief over her leaving, instead of pushing her out the door? She closed her eyes, deciding that she was grumpy due to exhaustion, and a nap was clearly in order. She yelped when something crawled onto her stomach.

"Hide me," Mr. Squibbles said.

She looked down her body at the mouse perched on her abdomen. She hadn't thought about the possible danger of the mouse with others in her apartment. Her mind suddenly shot to the horn. She'd left it in the kitchen. She scooped up the rodent and raced to retrieve it. Her mother was already there, going through the cabinets. The horn sat on the counter where Naomi had left it. She picked it up and turned to go back to her bedroom, but she stopped and turned back to look at her mother. Her mother had been staring into a cabinet a long time.

"Mom?"

Her mother sniffled quietly and turned a watery smile to her. "Go get some rest, dear."

Naomi moved over to her mother and put her arm around her waist. Her mother leaned her head onto Naomi's shoulder and sniffled again. "I'm going to miss you," she said.

"Oh, Mom," she said, feeling her lip quiver.

Her mother slipped away from her and pushed softly on her shoulder. "Go get some rest. I mean it. I'll order us some pizza in a few hours. Your father will stop by, and we'll have a nice dinner."

Naomi went back to her room and lay back down. She let Mr. Squibbles crawl onto the bed. She stared blankly at the mouse as he came to sit by her head on her pillow.

"We don't need to leave so soon," he reminded her.

"It's done. We leave tomorrow."

He nodded and didn't say anymore. She closed her eyes and drifted off. She awoke when her mother came to the door to get her for pizza.

She entered the living room tentatively. All of her furniture seemed to be still there, though rearranged. Her family was gathered around the coffee table with slices already on plates. She took a seat on the couch between her parents and put a plate on her lap.

"Have you taken care of everything?" her mother asked.

She nodded and took a bite. She chewed it slowly. This was her last slice of pizza. This was her last American meal. "I paid for the next four months of rent. Consider it a housewarming present, Bobby."

His eyebrows shot up. "Thanks, sis."

Maybe she could show Yula how to make pizza. It couldn't be that hard.

She moved and got her purse. She took out her key ring and dropped it into her brother's lap. "You can have the car, too." She knew how to ride a horse now, sort of.

"Sis?" her brother asked. She'd given him practically all of her worldly possessions. She shrugged and retook her seat.

"Can't take it with me," she said. The old saying "Can't take it with you" and what it implied fluttered through her mind. She brushed it aside.

Her father sat on the sofa, stone-faced. His slice of pizza was growing cold in front of him.

"You're making a mistake," he said.

"Phil," her mother said.

Naomi turned and looked at him silently. He could be right, but she couldn't not make this mistake. "I have to do this, Dad."

Her father scrubbed his hand across his face. "Will you ever come back?" His voice was a touch ragged, and though Naomi doubted her mother and brother truly understood the finality of her departure, her father seemed to have an inkling and was struggling with it. She slung her arm around his shoulders and squeezed.

"I hope so," she murmured. Her father slipped his arm behind her and rubbed her back. Her mother put her hand on her back, too.

"We'll miss you," her mother whispered. Naomi nodded mutely. Her throat had closed up.

After that, dinner was a little more somber and quiet, but Naomi wouldn't have given it up for the world. After her family left, she went to bed. She refused to think about the next day.

She felt criminal as she penned a note to her parents. They'd wanted to send her off. They figured that she would be leaving on a plane. She'd had no way to dissuade them without hurting their feelings or raising their suspicions. She wrote that she had left early because she didn't want to say good-bye. She would contact them if she could, but they shouldn't worry about her. She was leaving them, but she would have family where she going who cared about her and would help her just as much as they had.

When she was done, she collected Mr. Squibbles and picked up the alicorn. A stillness had settled over her. Her actions felt like they occurred underwater. She held the mouse in the flat of her hand. She brought him up to eye level.

"What should I do?"

"How did it work the last time?"

"I pricked my finger and the horn absorbed a drop of blood. The next thing I knew, I was in Harold's Pass."

The mouse nodded. "It's that simple, then."

She set her finger on the alicorn's tip. Mr. Squibbles retreated into her shirt pocket. She pressed the tip into her finger until it pricked. A drop of blood welled up, and the horn absorbed it. She felt the strange sensation again of total displacement. Her grip tightened on the horn.

When she opened her eyes, her eyebrows knitted. She stood in the middle of a desert, but the sand was a lavender color. The air was very dry. Mr. Squibbles peeked out from her pocket.

"Oh, crap."

She felt lightheaded, like she wasn't getting enough oxygen. "This isn't right, is it?"

CHAPTER SEVENTEEN

Unicorns make lousy travel agents.

Naomi breathed deeply and felt like she was drowning. She didn't know what to make of the empty scene. Lavender sand stretched to the horizon with nothing breaking it. The sand didn't even create dunes. It was a flat, empty place.

"We need to get out of here before we can't," wheezed Mr. Squibbles.

He was right. She already felt dizzy from the thin air. She jabbed her finger, and blood spilled onto the horn. The purple desert went dark, and when there was light again, her eyes were assaulted by so many shades of green that she looked down to make sure that she wasn't green too, but there was plenty of air. She took deep breaths in relief, but they weren't alone in their new location.

She wasn't sure if the being in front of her was standing or sitting, but it definitely had a tree growing out of its head. It said something in a voice that was incomprehensible; not just the words but the very sounds were impossible to understand. Its voice was like bark grinding and liquid leaves. The being raised an appendage that could have been an arm with fingers, except there were roots and leaves hanging off of it. It pointed one long root at them and said something even louder in its mulching voice.

"What is that thing?" she asked.

"I don't know, but I don't think it's happy to see us."

"Where are we?"

The room was huge. The walls went up and up. She couldn't see the ceiling due to the clouds that were in the way. A dull thumping sound was coming toward them. It sounded sort of like marching stumps.

"Oh shit, I think those are guards. Prick your finger! Prick your finger!" Mr. Squibbles said.

She hastily pressed her pricked finger to the horn. The scene went dark.

She groaned when she looked around at their newest destination. She could tell right off that they had messed up again. This world was gentle rolling hills with large pastel geometric shapes that looked plastic. Each was several stories high. They sat scattered across the hills like a child's discarded toys. She quickly looked around for the possible child that they belonged to. If he appeared, Naomi would be the size of an ant to him and possibly squished like one. She saw no giant child and heard nothing that suggested one was coming. She took a deep breath to calm herself.

"Mr. Squibbles, this isn't working."

"You think?"

"Did the unicorn tell you anything about teleporting back?" she asked.

"No, but then I didn't ask."

"Lovely. What are we supposed to do? We can't keep blindly jumping from one world to the next. The next one might kill us. We could teleport into a volcano or something. I don't want to do that."

"And you think I do? How about you visualize someplace in our world when you do it next?"

"I'm pretty sure I was doing that all along."

"Well, think about it harder. The unicorns can't simply jump blindly like we are."

She pictured Agatha's hut as clearly as possible. She held the image in her mind's eye as she bled onto the alicorn one more time. She closed her eyes as she felt the shift. She cautiously opened one eye and looked straight at the old heavy door of Agatha's cottage. She threw her head back in relief at the familiar sight.

"Thank the dark gods, we made it," Mr. Squibbles said.

That was the second time he'd used that phrase. "Who are the dark gods?"

"No one you don't thank."

Naomi was pretty sure that was bad grammar but decided to not pursue it. She rapped on the door. Agatha jerked it open with a scowl on her face that melted away when she caught sight of her. Naomi scuffed her shoe on the ground and looked up at her through her lashes.

"Heard you could use my help," she said.

Agatha released a whoop of laughter and lunged out to hug her. Naomi staggered back in surprise and relaxed as the witch's laughter infected her. She hugged the older woman back and giggled.

"Amazing," the witch said. "I sent Mr. Squibbles away just this morning, and here you are on my doorstep in the evening." She ushered her into her home and sat her down by the fire.

"Tell me about Tavik," Naomi said.

Agatha leaned back in her chair and rubbed her brow as she stared sideways at the fire. Her actions did not instill confidence. "He's sick. I've tried to cure him, but nothing I do helps. I'm not sure he wants to get better."

"He's sick? Mr. Squibbles didn't say anything about

that!"

Agatha cast a look over at the mouse who was cleaning his whiskers. He didn't bother to look up at his name. She sighed. "I told him not to tell you. I knew you'd say yes if you heard, but for this to work, you had to want to come back for yourself, not out of some feeling of obligation or guilt."

Naomi didn't like that she hadn't been told about Tavik's illness, but she pushed this aside to focus again on what mattered. "Is he at the castle now?" she asked. At Agatha's nod, she stood up. "Then I should go there. He'll want to see me."

Agatha nodded again and heaved herself up out of her chair. Naomi felt a twinge of guilt at making the woman move. She was obviously tired.

"Give me a few moments, and we'll be on our way. You should probably put this on." She handed Naomi a plain gown and a pair of laced boots.

She nodded and began to change. While she shuffled out of her T-shirt and jeans, she sneaked looks around the cottage. It looked the same, though more things were scattered about. Agatha must have been busy making potions and casting spells to help keep things under control. She was tying her boots when a whiff of spicy smoke tickled her nose. She turned and saw the last moments of the witch's transformation.

Naomi raised an eyebrow as the black cat came to stand at her feet. "No need to strain the horse when we don't have to," the witch reasoned.

Naomi shook her head and went outside. The horse was tethered to a small tree by the house. He'd been behind Naomi when she teleported to Agatha's door and had gone completely unnoticed by her. She was pleased to recognize Stomper. She stroked the large horse's neck. He appeared to remember her too and good-naturedly rubbed his head against hers. She climbed onto his back and waited for Agatha to spring up, too.

When everyone was situated, she turned the horse in the general direction of the castle. Mr. Squibbles had taken his usual place between Stomper's ears and quietly directed the horse to where they wanted to go. This left Naomi time to talk more with the witch.

"Does everyone know you're Tavik's mother?"

Agatha shook her head. "Tavik still wears the helm and keeps his secrets."

"What did he tell them about me?"

Agatha hunched her shoulders. "That you ran away. He searched for you but couldn't find you. The consensus is that umbreks got you."

Naomi's back stiffened. It was the most likely story, but the idea that she had left Tavik willingly, while true, just felt wrong. Like she'd abandoned him. With unhappy clarity, she realized that she'd done just that. Umbreks, golgoffs, and an insane god had run her off when he could've used her help. Many would say she'd had every right to leave, that it was too much to ask of her, but she'd regretted it the moment she laid eyes again on her kitchen.

"No one will be very happy to see me, then." And maybe they had every right to be.

"Tavik will be happy."

"But…" she said, sensing more.

Agatha heaved a deep sigh which sounded strange coming from a cat. "Errilol is obviously behind his illness."

"The god doesn't like that he stopped fighting," she said.

"It's a bad business all around. He won't be able to escape the god unscathed. We can only hope the god's displeasure won't kill him."

Naomi felt helpless thinking about how to deal with a god. "What can we do?" She hated how bleak her voice sounded.

"We'll help as much as we can. Don't worry, Naomi. Seeing you will help."

Naomi stroked the cat's head without thinking, but

Agatha's purr told her that her action was not amiss.

She half expected them to go through the secret passage to gain entrance in the castle, but chided herself for being silly. They didn't need subterfuge. She was returning to stay. Mr. Squibbles had directed the horse to the front gates. They stopped before them, and Agatha hopped down. She expected the witch to change back to her human form, but she did not. The guards appeared before she could ask the witch why.

"Who goes there?" one shouted.

She swallowed and wondered how to announce herself. Simple was best, she decided. "Lady Naomi, Tavik's wife," she shouted back.

"Who?" the guard asked, but in the glow of their lanterns, she saw the other guard grab the first guard's arm and whisper into his ear. He squinted down at her.

"What are you doing here?" he demanded.

"I want to see my husband."

"And what makes you think our lord wants to see you?" the guard asked snidely. The man obviously didn't hold her in high regard. Considering what they'd been told, she couldn't blame him, but she couldn't help the frustration that bubbled up in her. They should've taken the secret passage.

"Why don't you ask him?" she snapped back.

Neither guard moved for a moment. The one who'd spoken to her smirked down at her. They could very well keep her at the gate the whole night.

Why didn't Agatha change back? They would let her in. Mr. Squibbles had said that she was their ally now. She glanced down at her and found the cat was no longer at the horse's feet. She'd run off somewhere. Naomi hoped it was to get her help because neither guard was budging from his post.

"Lady Naomi?" called a familiar voice. She felt a relieved smile stretch her mouth as she identified Boris. The steward joined the guards in the lookout and peered down at her. "Are you alone?"

Naomi thought better of informing them of Mr. Squibbles' presence. "Yes. May I come in?"

Boris stared down at her for a few more beats. She began to worry that he would join the guards in keeping her out.

"Lord Tavik will want to see her. Let her in," he told the two guards.

They nodded and called for the huge gates to be opened. Stomper slipped through them, and someone came to take the horse's reins. She dismounted without an offer of help from any of the men standing around her. She felt icy stares directed at her from all sides. Mr. Squibbles had retreated to her bag and stayed out of sight.

Among the assembled servants, the only friendly face she saw was Geoff. He bobbed his head and touched his forelock, but no one else gave her any greeting, and Geoff's motions were rather timid and cursory. There was no smile on his face.

"So you have returned."

She turned and looked up at the stern visage of Mrs. Boon. She stood in the main doorway of the castle. Her hands folded over her white apron, which seemed to glow in the dim light. Naomi gave her a small bob in greeting, but Mrs. Boon didn't acknowledge it.

"Please follow me." Naomi had never heard the word please sound more like a command.

As she moved to follow the woman's retreating back, she felt all of the guards' eyes on her. She was very unwelcome here.

"You look well, milady." The pleasantness of Mrs. Boon's words did not mask her obvious disapproval.

"It feels like I haven't been gone at all," she said before she could think better of it. Mrs. Boon's face hardened, and her eyes narrowed.

"Lord Tavik would disagree."

Naomi cast her eyes to the ground. All of the animosity

was making her feel even guiltier, but once she saw Tavik, everything would be all right, she reassured herself.

Mrs. Boon led her through the castle at a brisk pace. She realized she was leading her to her old chamber as they progressed.

"Aren't you taking me to Tavik?"

"Our lord will come to you." She halted at her door and turned to her. "Yula will tend to you in the morning."

Naomi was surprised to hear her old friend was there. She'd thought she'd go be with her sons. "Thank you, Mrs. Boon," she said.

Mrs. Boon's eyes flicked over her once more. She wanted to say something to the housekeeper to make her friendlier, but thought that no matter what, Mrs. Boon would always look down on her. Mrs. Boon opened her door, and Naomi slipped in past her. She turned to say good night, maybe ask her how she was, but the housekeeper had already closed the door, and Naomi jumped when she heard the lock click. She tried the door, but it was bolted tight. It didn't even rattle under her hand.

She turned from the door to take in the room. The air was a little musty from being closed up for months. She wandered to the window and looked up at the sky. The two moons shone down coldly on her. She wondered how long it would be before Tavik came to see her.

She took off her cloak and draped it over a chair. Mr. Squibbles climbed out of the hood and looked up at her. "An icy reception."

"I can't blame them, considering what they were told," she said, sitting at the table.

She waited for Tavik to arrive. The candles burned low. Her eyes drooped.

"What's keeping him?" she asked. It had been over an hour, she was sure of it.

"I'll go and see." Mr. Squibbles ran under her bed and disappeared.

More time went by. She grew sleepier. She got up and

paced. She found her eyes lingering on the bed longer and longer as she went by it. If Tavik were unwell, he could already be asleep, and no one would want to rouse him. She didn't have to see him that night. They'd have all the same things to say to each other the next day.

She found one of her nightgowns in the chest sitting at the foot of the bed and changed into it. After blowing out the candles, she went to sleep and didn't dream.

Bright morning light woke Naomi. She sat up and looked around. No one had come to get her. She'd expected Yula's cheerful voice to rouse her, but the cook hadn't appeared yet. She got up and stretched. Where was everyone? Agatha and Mr. Squibbles should've come to check in, too.

Her stomach gave a gurgle. Breakfast would be nice. She dived back into her clothes trunk and found a gown to put on. She dressed, and since no one had still appeared to tell her what was going on, she tried the door. It was still locked. Dread started to creep upon her. She knocked on the door, hoping to receive an answer, but no one spoke from the other side. She went to the windows to open one and look outside, but the windows were nailed shut. The nails looked new and hastily installed. She suspected they'd been installed while she stood at the gate. She stared down at the courtyard. There were people down there, moving about their daily activities, but no one looked up at her. She beat upon the window to get their attention, but either they did not hear her, or they ignored her. What was going on?

She sat down at the table to think. Other than something very drastic, she didn't know what to do. Where was Mr. Squibbles? He could surely come to her. She climbed underneath the bed, ignoring how ridiculous her actions were, and put her face to the mouse hole.

"Mr. Squibbles, where are you? What's going on? Mr. Squibbles," she called.

She heard the door unlock, and she scrambled out

from under the bed eager to see Yula.

"Lady Naomi?"

Naomi winced. It wasn't Yula. She straightened and began brushing dust bunnies off of her dress.

"A candle rolled under the bed. I can't get it," she lied.

Mrs. Boon pursed her lips. She set the tray she carried onto the table.

"Where's Yula?" she asked.

"Yula is tending to other matters this morning."

Naomi frowned. She'd wanted to see her friend.

"What about Tavik?"

"Lord Tavik is tending to other matters," Mrs. Boon answered.

Feeling a trend, she asked, "What about Geoff?"

"Tending to other matters."

"It's a shame everyone is so busy. Thank you for bringing me my breakfast. I'm sure you have other matters to tend to."

Mrs. Boon didn't reply. Naomi cautiously sat down in front of the tray. She didn't feel comfortable eating with Mrs. Boon. She wasn't comfortable with Mrs. Boon period.

"When will Lord Tavik be able to see me?" She took a sip of her milk. Mrs. Boon shrugged.

"Our lord is very busy. I don't know when he'll have time to see you."

Her eyes narrowed as she looked at the housekeeper. "He does know I'm back, doesn't he?" she asked.

Mrs. Boon shrugged again, but she thought she detected a malevolent glint in her eyes. "I'm sure someone will tell him."

"He'll want to know I'm here."

Mrs. Boon nodded, but it was insincere. "I'm sorry, my lady, but like you observed before, I am very busy. Please excuse me."

"Wait!" She got up to follow the housekeeper to the door. Mrs. Boon opened the door and moved to close it.

She grabbed the door and pulled it open. Two guards turned toward her.

"You can't keep me prisoner!"

"Of course not, milady. These guards are merely here for your safety," Mrs. Boon assured her.

The housekeeper tugged on the door. Seeing no point in struggling, Naomi let it go, and it slammed shut. She thought she heard Mrs. Boon stumble back and curse. The lock clicked again.

Naomi could not believe how lousy her situation was. She was being kept prisoner in a castle she was supposed to practically rule. She sat down and stared at her breakfast. Tavik didn't know she was back. She was sure of that. How could they keep her a secret from him? The thought that Geoff was in on the subterfuge upset her. She was sure Yula wasn't, but maybe she had gone to live with her sons like Naomi had thought and Mrs. Boon had only mentioned her to make Naomi easier to deal with. She hoped Yula wasn't locked up like her. Where were Mr. Squibbles and Agatha? Did they know this would happen when they brought her back? If not, what were they doing to remedy the situation? If they had known, how could they have led her into it?

She pushed her eggs around on her plate. She felt betrayed, but she didn't know by whom. What if Tavik knew and had ordered this? The thought made her cold.

The rest of the morning passed slowly and unremarkably. No one came to see her, and it looked like no one would bring her lunch. She was going stir crazy. All she could do was pace, and her feet were beginning to hurt due to all the pacing. She flung herself into a chair and put her head in her hands. Where was Tavik? Where were Agatha, Yula, and Mr. Squibbles for that matter? It was like she'd been forgotten.

This was a fine homecoming. She'd given up her nice normal job, nice comfy apartment, and nice loving family for imprisonment, abandonment, and boredom-induced insanity. Nothing about her new situation was nice. It was as far from nice as she could think without physical pain coming into the picture. *See, a silver lining,* she told herself.

"You don't look very happy," Mr. Squibbles said.

Seeing the mouse emerge from under the bed, she dropped from the chair and scrambled on hands and knees to him. Alarmed by her frantic reaction, Mr. Squibbles turned as if to run back under the bed. She stopped herself from lunging at him, but just barely. She took a deep breath to calm herself, but couldn't let it out slowly, instead a rush of questions blasted from her.

"Where have you been? Where is everyone? What's going on?"

The mouse's whiskers twitched, and he sat back on his hind feet. Naomi's anxiety ratcheted up every millisecond he took before he answered. "It seems things have grown worse since Agatha and I were last in the castle. Tavik's illness has worsened. He's confined to his bed. Agatha can't help him."

Her stomach dropped at the news. "How sick is he? What's happened?"

Mr. Squibbles shook his head. "Errilol most likely has upped the ante. The lummoxes have gotten it into their heads that maybe Agatha caused the illness. They found her examining Tavik last night and restrained her. She's being held in the dungeon." So the castle did have a dungeon. Naomi hoped it wasn't as awful as she'd imagined.

"They still don't know she's his mother?"

"And they won't believe it if they're told now."

"What about Yula?"

He shook his head again. "I can't find her. I don't think she's in the castle."

She went to the window to stare blindly out. "What can we do?"

"Don't worry, Naomi. Agatha and I will think of something."

241

A thought struck her. "What about the alicorn? I could teleport out of here. Maybe to Tavik!" She went to get the horn out of her cloak.

"No, it's too dangerous," Mr. Squibbles said.

She held the horn in her hands, not ready to be dissuaded. "We don't have any other options. I'm locked in my room with guards at the door, Agatha's in the dungeon, and Yula's MIA. What else can we do?"

"Just hold off on the alicorn for a little bit. Let me look for Yula again. You were the one who warned that the horn might drop you into a place that would kill you just by appearing there."

"Yeah, but I know where Tavik's room is. I know what it looks like. I should be able to teleport directly there."

"Yes, but Tavik is never alone. Mrs. Boon has healers from the temple of Calax with him all day, and guards are stationed at his door day and night. You wouldn't be able to do anything."

"There has to be something."

"Give Agatha and me more time. We're sure to come up with something."

Naomi tucked the unicorn horn away reluctantly. She hated sitting on her hands, but Mr. Squibbles was right. Accidentally teleporting into a volcano wouldn't help anyone.

"I'm going back to Agatha. I'll come back when we have a plan. Don't worry yourself too much. We'll get through this."

Naomi nodded, and the mouse disappeared back underneath the bed. She turned back to the window and watched the people bustle about below.

The sun was setting when Naomi finally got a human visitor, though she would've preferred umbreks to Mrs. Boon. The housekeeper marched in with a tray of food. She didn't nod her head or give any greeting when she entered, which irritated Naomi. She was not going to be ignored. When Mrs. Boon set down the tray and turned to leave, Naomi was standing at the door, ready to fight her for some answers.

"How long do you think you're going to keep me here?"

Mrs. Boon folded her hands across her stomach and answered in a placid voice, "When Lord Tavik is well again, we'll let him decide what to do with you."

"Who's making the decisions while he's ill?"

"No one is making any decisions right now. Lord Tavik will recover soon."

"You think Agatha put a spell on him."

Mrs. Boon's brow lowered. "And what do you know about the witch? Are you in league with her?"

Naomi knew she should keep her mouth shut, but being locked in her room all day was making her desperate. "Agatha wants to help Tavik. She wouldn't dream of hurting him." *Though drugging and kidnapping him are another matter*, she reminded herself.

"Did you know we thought you were the witch when she appeared at the castle after your disappearance? It just seemed a little too pat. You disappear and a few days later the witch shows up."

"Well, since Agatha is in the dungeon and I'm locked in here, that little theory doesn't hold water anymore, does it?"

"Maybe you're the witch's daughter. I can see a slight resemblance."

Naomi smirked at how wrong and close she had it. "She's not my mother."

"Maybe you're just another witch, and you two are working together to bring down Lord Tavik. I know you're not Lady Naomi. You know nothing about proper nobility."

"You're right. I'm not the real Lady Naomi, but I'm not a witch either. I am Tavik's wife, and he will tell you the same thing."

"Unfortunately, our lord isn't able to vouch for you."

"Why? How bad is he? I want to see him."

"Out of the question. You won't be allowed near Lord Tavik until he is well, and even after that, I doubt he'll want to see you."

"This is all one big mistake. Tavik will be happy to see me, I assure you. Maybe if he sees me now, it'll help him get better."

Mrs. Boon shook his head. "No. You used magic to weaken Tavik and flee him. You only came back now to seize control of his land. It won't work."

"No, that isn't true. I care for Tavik. I'm sorry that I went away for so long, but we both thought it was for the best that I went home. I thought that was where I should be, but I realized that Tavik's my home now. I came back for him."

"But you abandoned him."

She didn't know what to say. Mrs. Boon was right. "He thought it was for the best, too."

Mrs. Boon strode to the door and rapped on it. It was opened from the other side. She turned to Naomi before stepping out. "Whatever our lord decides to do with you, I hope it is fitting for the pain and anguish you caused him. Because, gods help us, he cared for you." With that last statement, she swept out of the room. Naomi stared at the closed door and felt hollow.

She sat down at the meal begrudgingly left by Mrs. Boon. She didn't feel hungry. She felt anxious and useless. The four walls felt like they were closing in on her. She picked at the food and wondered what would happen now.

"Leave any for me?"

She whirled around to look at the mouse. "What's the plan?"

Mr. Squibbles didn't reply.

Her jaw dropped. "There's no plan?"

"Being shackled and kept in a very dark cell is hindering Agatha's witchy genius. Don't worry, she'll think of something."

Naomi felt her stomach twist uncomfortably at the image of Agatha's situation.

"Have you learned anything new?" she asked.

"Nothing encouraging. What about you?"

She shook her head. "They think Agatha and I worked together to make Tavik sick, and that we're trying to seize control, but they're going to wait until Tavik's better to decide what to do with me."

"Or until he dies. I went to his bedchamber. He's very sick, Naomi. He's feverish and delusional. The priests don't know what to do to help him."

The news was bleak. A plan was coalescing in her brain. "Have you or Agatha come up with any ideas to get her free?"

"I'm going to get her a few things for a spell. She should be able to free herself, but we don't know if we'll be able to do much more than that."

"Do it. Don't worry about me. My situation isn't that bad."

"But what if—" he began.

She cut him off. "I can't stand the idea of Agatha sitting in a dungeon. Go get her what she needs. I'll be fine."

He nodded and left.

She waited to make sure Mr. Squibbles was good and gone. She didn't want anyone to talk sense to her. She got the unicorn horn out of its hiding place. She stared at the tip and fixed the image of Tavik's bedroom in her mind. She knew exactly where it was and what it looked like. Once she was sure of her concentration, she stabbed the horn to her finger. She was killing her fingertips with all the teleporting, but she didn't worry about it. She felt the pull that wasn't a pull. She'd closed her eyes again without realizing it. Maybe it was like sneezing; she couldn't do it unless her eyes were shut.

Feeling scared that she may have made one massive mistake, she sent up a silent prayer that she'd teleported to

Tavik's room and not to some strange new world where dogs played poker and fish rode bicycles. Actually, that would be a neat world to check out, but she really needed to take care of Tavik first.

She opened her eyes cautiously.

CHAPTER EIGHTEEN

*Unicorns are peaceful creatures...until crossed.
Then they fight dirty.*

Naomi looked around, and felt relief cascade over her. It'd worked. She'd teleported into Tavik's room, not into some fiery hell, not halfway into a wall, or worse, into Mrs. Boon's chamber, and there weren't any healers or guards there to raise an alarm.

Her head swiveled to the bed. There was someone in it. She didn't recognize him at first. The helm threw her off. In her mind, she'd come to picture Tavik without it. He had told her that he would have to put it back on when he returned to the castle. It made sense, and it didn't, like so much in this world. He worshiped an insane god and hid it from the world by wearing a terrifying mask because his religious beliefs would frighten the townsfolk more. But he didn't worship Errilol anymore. Tavik had broken from the god, and Naomi was here to help him.

She went to the side of the bed. One of his arms lay

above the covers with his hand loosely curled. She picked up his hand. It was heavy and warm in her grasp. She gave it a tender squeeze. He didn't stir. She couldn't tell anything with the helm covering his face. She wondered vaguely how the priests examined him wearing it. They probably hadn't contemplated removing it. She didn't contemplate it either. She just reached out to remove it. She had it halfway off when he stirred. His hand clamped onto her arm. His grip was like a vice.

"Let me take this off, Tavik," she said in a hushed voice. She didn't want to alert anyone that she was there. His head rolled toward her on the bed. The eye holes were just black holes to her. She tried to shake his hand off. His grip tightened. "I want to see your face," she told him.

He didn't release her arm. She felt coldness creeping up her fingers into her hand due to his bruising hold. She put the alicorn down to reach with her other hand. He saw the other hand approaching and jerked the arm he held so that she fell across him.

"Who are you?" His voice was ragged. It held mistrust and rage.

"It's me, Tavik. I came back."

He twisted the flesh under his grasp. She gritted her teeth at the burning flare. "No," he whispered.

She nodded her head. "It's me. Let me see your face. Is Errilol making you sick?"

At the mention of the god, he dropped her arm. "Fever dream," he murmured. He turned his head away from her. She grabbed his now lax hand.

"No, I'm real. I'm really here. I'm touching you. Can a hallucination do that?"

She heard him sigh from within the mask. He turned onto his side, away from her. She wondered savagely what the priests had been doing for him. They couldn't have done freaking much if they'd left the helm on him. They couldn't have examined him, given him medicine, or anything. Had they shut him away in his room, hoping he'd get better on his own?

She pulled on his shoulder to make him roll back onto his back, but even sick, he was still very strong and big, and she couldn't manage it.

She ran around the bed to the other side to make him look at her. "Mr. Squibbles fetched me. We repaired the horn that was broken. We used it to come back. Tavik, it's really me." She tried to keep her voice down, but her desperation was increasing the volume little by little.

If his eyes were open, they stared right through her. He didn't think she was real. He was too sick to tell fantasy from reality. She'd fix that soon enough. She moved back to the other side of the bed and picked up the alicorn. She stared at his curled back. There was a bit of skin showing at the neck of his shirt. She touched the horn to the patch of exposed skin. The horn glowed in her grasp. It felt warm, and the light was gentle, but it was like there was a sensor in her head that showed how healed he was, and the dial hadn't moved any yet. The horn continued to grow brighter. The unicorn had fixed her throat with only a brief touch, but it wasn't doing anything for Tavik.

The alicorn began to feel very hot. Tavik didn't appear to feel a thing. She felt a sob rise in her throat. Why wasn't this working? She had to switch hands because the alicorn was beginning to burn. The light kept growing brighter. The guards were going to notice. She smelled the sickening familiar scent of burning flesh, and again it was her own.

"Why aren't you getting better? You have to get better." Tears rolled down her face. He didn't stir.

The door crashed open. The bright light had finally roused the guards. They had swords drawn. "Stop, witch!"

She stayed rooted in her spot, holding the burning horn. The guards took action and rushed her. They grabbed her and hauled her away. The horn's light flared and went out. She tried to struggle out of their grip to get back to Tavik, but she was weak with pain. She tried to plead with them.

"Let me go. I have to help him."

"And how are you helping him? To an early grave?"

"No, you don't understand. It's not me who's hurting him."

"Who is it, then?"

As if in answer, deep laughter echoed around the room. Everyone froze. The dimly burning fire whooshed to monstrous life. Its color changed from orange to green, and a face appeared within the flames.

"He will always be mine, unicorn mistress."

It was Errilol. That was the only possibility. The god had come to stop her. She was able to free herself from the guards. They weren't paying any attention to her anymore. They were staring at the fireplace in terror. An angry, insane god was in the room with them. They should be afraid. She was afraid too, but she was also furious.

"Tavik doesn't serve you anymore!" she screamed at the green fire.

"That is why he will die."

"No, I won't let you!"

She lurched forward to touch Tavik again with the alicorn, but the green fire belched a ball of flame that flew over Tavik and the bed. It knocked straight into her and threw her and the two dumbfounded guards back into the wall. The force of the god's assault left her breathless, but it hadn't hurt her much. She was still standing, still conscious, and she still had the glowing alicorn. The green fire faded back to orange. Errilol had withdrawn. She sagged against the wall in relief, but she knew that wasn't the last she'd see of him.

More guards had come to the doorway. They were staring at her. They appeared horrified. She pushed herself off the wall to face them. Two strange thumps sounded on either side of her. She thought the two guards had merely passed out. She looked down at them. Black spots erupted in her vision to block out what she saw. The guards were burned beyond recognition. Their flesh was black and charred on top and red and pulpy in the fissures. She stumbled away and fell against the side of the bed.

"Get away from Lord Tavik, witch!" one of the guards in the doorway shouted.

She turned wide eyes at them. They thought she'd murdered their comrades. Their swords were drawn and leveled at her. They were going to kill her if she didn't escape somehow. She fumbled with the alicorn. Her burnt hands were not working. Instead of moving the alicorn to prick herself, she had to stab her wrist on it. It slashed across her arm.

She staggered up the step to Agatha's cottage. All the windows were dark. She moved to pull open the door but cried out when she tried to open her empty hand. Her other hand clutched the alicorn. She couldn't open that hand either. She banged the side of her fist against the door and cried out through clenched teeth at the shock of pain it caused. She turned around and slid down the door. What good was the cottage, anyway? No one was inside. There was no help. Her eyes slipped shut as she passed out again.

Awaken. Naomi lifted her head to find the woods shrouded in mist. It made goose bumps ripple up across her arms. She looked at her hands and saw they were healed. Not a twinge of pain remained in them. They'd healed while she slept. Tears of relief stung her eyes. She wouldn't have been able to do anything with her hands crippled. She didn't understand how they'd healed since the burns were made by the horn, so it couldn't have healed them, but it was a blessing that they were.

She rose to her feet to look around. She didn't know what had woken her, but she didn't feel alone. A glimmer of white caught her attention. A unicorn stepped out from among the trees. Another glimmer of white appeared to her right. She turned her head to find another unicorn. Her mouth fell open as unicorn after unicorn appeared out of the woods.

"What's going on?"

They needed her help. Like before, the knowledge slipped into her brain. The unicorns didn't think in words like conversation. She just knew what they wanted. She was startled by the appeal. She didn't know what to ask first. How could she help them? Why did they need her? What could she do? The unicorns heard her silent questions, and the answers slid into her mind like the mist around her, shrouding her with information. She stood still as she absorbed all they wanted her to do. When they were done, she nodded to indicate she understood and accepted. The unicorns slipped back into the woods, leaving her alone again.

The door to Agatha's cottage was unlocked now. She went inside and began grabbing what she needed. She took a cloak down from a peg and picked up an empty wineskin. She spotted the magic shield that she'd used against the golgoffs. It was as cumbersome as before, but its benefits canceled out all the drawbacks. She pictured the destination the unicorns had given her and pricked herself.

The wind made her stagger. She didn't know the name of the place where she was. The unicorns had only given her a picture. It was a narrow path up the side of mountain. It was dark, so she couldn't see much, but she could picture the path perfectly thanks to the unicorns. She planted the tip of the shield in the ground and huddled behind it. To her amazement, the shield more than sheltered her; it threw the wind back so that the force didn't affect her. Keeping herself behind the shield, she began making her way up the trail. The shield was heavy, and she paused a few times to rest her arm, but as the wind howled around her, she knew she would have been blown off the mountain without it. If Agatha was the one who'd made the shield, she could make a tidy living selling them. Naomi would buy one.

She finally could make out the cave entrance in front of

her. She redoubled her efforts with the goal in sight. Once she was inside and out of the hurtling winds, she put the horn's tip to her lips and blew a warm breath across it. It began to glow and became bright enough to light her way. Another trick the unicorns had shown her, though they of course didn't need to blow across the tip to make their horns glow.

She held the glowing alicorn up like torch and walked further into the cave. There was some light beside the horn. There were markings on the wall that glowed a dull red. She didn't know what the markings meant, but could feel some sort of purpose emanating from them. She brought the alicorn closer to one and both glowed brighter. She didn't dare to actually touch it to the symbol though.

When she went further into the cave and around a bend, she came upon a sparkling spring. It burbled with water that was so clear that only the reflection of the alicorn's light showed it was there. This was her goal. She submerged her wineskin and filled it with the mysterious water. Her hands grew instantly numb due to the incredibly cold water, but she did not shiver. By all rights, the water should be frozen as cold as it was, but it flowed effortlessly. When the wineskin was full, she lifted it out. A fine sheen of frost formed on her hands and the wineskin when they touched the air. She brushed off her hands and the wineskin and put the stopper firmly back. A crisp breeze that felt like a sigh passed over her. She bowed low to the back of the cave, giving silent thanks. A blue light flared in acknowledgment and blessing. She could not see the being at the back of the cave, but knew it was Calax, the god she'd heard so many people refer to in exclamation. The unicorns had sent her here to his home because he was one of the few who would offer help against Errilol.

When she made her way back out of the cave and back down the trail huddled behind the shield, the unicorns were waiting. They watched her silently. Their manes and tails whipped wildly in the artic wind. She brushed her hand over the wineskin and nodded. They nodded back and winked away. She pricked her finger.

She appeared in Tavik's room, ready to fight her way to his bed, but the room was empty again except for him. She couldn't believe that they hadn't posted a guard within the room, but their stupidity helped her. It was one less obstacle she would have to deal with. She took a chair and jammed it against the door to keep the guards out this time. The sound alerted those posted outside, and they began banging on it from the other side, but she turned a deaf ear to them. By the time they broke through, she would be done.

She strode to the bed and took off Tavik's helm. She flung it across the room as she had so long ago. She hoped to never see him wearing it again. He didn't stir at her actions. He was paler than before with a sheen of fever sweat coating him. There was a sickly green glow about him. It wasn't a trick of the eye but Errilol's malice manifesting through him. When she touched him, she wanted to recoil at the sense of malevolence that emanated from him, but she knew she couldn't back down. Tavik couldn't heal himself. She raised his head to put the wineskin's spout against his lips. She filled his mouth with the holy water. He sputtered and flailed weakly, but his eyes didn't flutter. She tightened her hold to keep his head steady. When he finally swallowed, his lips turned blue. She watched the transformation in grim silence.

Errilol leapt to life again in the fireplace. Her eyes slanted to the shield. She'd leaned it against the bed to free her hands, but couldn't stop now to retrieve it and use it to protect herself. Tavik hadn't drunk enough. If she stopped now, Errilol would reclaim him. Tavik's breath came out as cold mist. His body temperature dropped more with every sip he took.

"Stop, bitch!"

She ignored the god and continued to give Tavik the water. Green fire swarmed out of the fireplace. It licked over the ceiling, the floor, and the walls. She didn't budge. The heat scorched the soles of her shoes. Sweat broke out all over her body only to evaporate in the burning room. The bedspread caught fire and flames crept across it, but the flames sizzled out as they touched Tavik. She was semi-protected by the bed and Tavik's form, but the heat of the spreading fire was making her dizzy, or maybe it was lack of oxygen.

Frost spread across Tavik's cheeks. His eyes had fluttered opened. They stared at her, but there was no light in them. Frost began to appear over them. A pang of fear went through her. He looked dead. She bent to kiss his forehead. Her lips were seared by his chill. She poured the last of the water into his mouth. She watched his throat convulse one last time, and then he went completely still. His skin turned white with a blue sheen. She laid him back onto the bed. She crossed his hands and closed his eyes. His eyelashes had ice crystals on them. He appeared ready for a tomb. She wished that thought hadn't occurred to her. She stepped back and realized that the bottoms of her shoes had melted away. Her feet cooked on the burning floor, but the pain was distant, muted. If she'd been fully aware of it, she knew she would be screaming. The guards had stopped trying to break down Tavik's door. That was wise of them. If they broke it down now, the fire might spread to other parts of the castle.

"What have you done?" roared Errilol. She picked up her shield. It was cool to the touch. It hadn't absorbed any of the heat. Agatha really needed to patent this thing. "Answer me!" the god demanded.

"I would prepare if I were you, Errilol. I am coming."

The fire crackled with laughter. "You think you can destroy me?"

"You shouldn't have gone to war with the unicorns. They aren't nice when they're angry."

"I'll wipe them from existence!"

She didn't reply. She pricked her finger and was gone.

She appeared again outside Agatha's cottage. The door was jerked open by the witch. Mr. Squibbles sat on Agatha's shoulder. A relieved smile spread across Naomi's face at the sight of the witch safe and sound.

"Where have you been? What's happening?" Agatha demanded.

"Naomi's out there?" another voice cried, and Yula appeared. Naomi's smile increased at the sight of her other friend. Agatha pulled her into the cottage.

"Tavik's safe," Naomi said.

"You've seen Tavik?" the witch demanded.

She nodded and sank with relief into a chair. She almost missed the time she'd spent imprisoned in her room. Simple pacing hadn't made her ache like this.

"Naomi, your feet!" Yula cried.

She looked down at her burnt feet. She hadn't really let herself contemplate the pain. She knew the unicorns had given her some sort of mental blocks when they'd been in her brain, telling her what to do. They'd prepared her for everything. She was to be their weapon. Vaguely, she thought she should balk at their heavy-handed manipulation of her into their tool, but also knew that they wouldn't be in this predicament if they hadn't helped her. She touched the horn to her feet and felt instant relief as they were healed.

Agatha pressed a cup of wine into her hands. She cradled the cup and sipped from it. The wine felt wonderful going down her throat.

"Naomi, what's happened?" the witch asked again.

"Tavik's safe for now. Errilol can't touch him," she told them.

"How?"

"He's frozen in time. I got some water from the spring of Calax."

"Truly? But how?"

She shrugged. "The unicorns showed me. They need my help."

Agatha nodded. "Yes, I know of their misfortunes, but we must do something about the god's hold on Tavik."

"The only way is to kill him," Naomi said.

"Kill Tavik?" Yula asked, horrified.

"No, Errilol."

Both women looked shocked by the idea. "Kill a god!" Yula exclaimed. Agatha shook her head, denying the possibility.

"The unicorns told me how." Both women stared at her. "I have to go to his place of power and run him through with this horn. It's the only way."

"No, it's impossible. You'll surely be killed," Yula argued. Her voice quavered in fear.

Naomi couldn't deny her assessment.

"Why can't the unicorns do it?" Agatha asked.

"Because they aren't allowed into the homes of the gods. It's a magical law. They can't break it."

"But you can walk right in and slay him?" Mr. Squibbles asked.

"I know it won't be that easy, but I have to do this to save Tavik and the unicorns. Errilol has set out to exterminate them. His priests kill any they come upon."

"And because the priests are virgins, the unicorns don't know what danger they are in until it's too late. That's why they were willing to help us bring you back. They intended for you to do this all along," Agatha said as she pieced it together.

Naomi nodded. "Yes, but we're responsible. The unicorns and Errilol wouldn't be fighting if it weren't for us, and we gave Errilol the idea for how to destroy them."

"Then it's up to us," Agatha said.

Naomi's eyes flew up to glare at her. "No, it's up to me," she said.

Agatha ignored her protest. The witch began rummaging through the shelves that lined one wall. "The shield should be very useful against Errilol, but some sort of concealment will help greatly too."

"Like camouflage?" Naomi asked.

"No, like invisibility."

Naomi and Yula shared a look. Naomi wondered where one signed up to become a witch, because it sure came in handy.

"Ah, here it is," Agatha announced. She picked up a large corked jug. She brushed off the spider webs that clung to it.

"Agatha, I don't know if that stuff is a good idea," Mr. Squibbles said.

"You're not sure it works?" Yula asked. Agatha uncorked the jug, stuck her finger in it, and pulled her hand away. When she held her hand up, she was missing a finger. Yula paled.

"It looks like it works," Agatha said.

"Wait until you have to really use it," Mr. Squibbles grumbled.

"Are there side effects?" Naomi asked.

"It's completely harmless," Agatha assured her. The witch wiped her invisible finger on her apron, and it reappeared.

Naomi glanced at the mouse for his opinion. "Completely harmless," he agreed, "but you don't know how you'll have to use it yet."

CHAPTER NINETEEN

"What use is wizardry if it cannot save a unicorn?"
—The Last Unicorn

"Naked! You want me to face an evil god NAKED!"

"It's the best way to use the vanishing oil, and you'll have the shield. We'll coat that with the oil as well," Agatha said in a far too reasonable tone.

"But I'll be naked!"

"Modesty isn't really an issue when you're invisible."

Naomi shook her head. She'd always thought it was horny, old puritanical men who'd made up all that sky-clad stuff about witches, but Agatha was calmly suggesting she go fight a god in her birthday suit. She didn't know whether to laugh or run away. She contemplated laughing hysterically while running away.

She turned to Yula, who'd been silent after Agatha explained the best way to use the oil. "What do you think about this?"

Yula looked at her in disbelief. "You plan to slay a god.

What does it matter if you face him naked or in armor? He'll destroy you."

"Yeah, but being destroyed in armor is more dignified. Can't I wear armor?" she whined.

Mr. Squibbles tsked from Agatha's shoulder. "You humans sure are funny about your clothes."

"How about we shave off all your fur and see how funny you are?" she snapped. The mouse quickly ducked underneath Agatha's hair.

"Naomi, this is the best way. Fabric absorbs too much of the oil. We would have to use all of it just to coat your blouse."

She slouched in her chair. "Can I at least have some privacy to put this stuff on?"

The witch nodded. "Of course."

She ducked behind a screen and began taking off her clothes. Once she was undressed, she looked down at herself. She'd never been an exhibitionist. In fact, she was rather body shy. She'd never worn a midriff or short shorts. She wouldn't even go out in public without a bra on. Now she was expected to go out stark naked for a showdown with a god. Her mouth quirked. Yula was right. Instead of freaking over the god part, she was spazzing over the nudity. She shook her head at her own illogic. An image of Tavik lying prone in his bed, his skin pale with a blue sheen, flashed in her mind. If she didn't do this, he would stay that way forever. She uncorked the jug and carefully poured out some of the oil.

As soon as it was in her hand, her hand disappeared. Panic locked her jaw. For a moment, she thought she couldn't feel her hand. Agatha had told her it might be best to close her eyes while applying the oil. She understood why now. Looking like an amputee made one very uneasy.

Willing herself to calm down, she closed her eyes and moved her hand to her stomach to start applying the stuff. The oil felt gritty, like there was sand suspended in it. She spread it across her skin, hypersensitive to her own touch. Blindly, she poured more oil into her hand to apply it to the rest of her body. Once she was done, she looked down at herself and instantly felt the panic begin to set in again. She couldn't see her body. She patted her stomach, took a few steps around the room, and wiggled her toes to assure herself that her body was still there. A clump of hair slipped over her invisible shoulder. It was the only part of her still visible. Agatha had said she would give her a cap to put on to conceal her hair rather than pour a copious amount of oil over it.

She ducked out from behind the screen, feeling very exposed and weirded out. She couldn't see herself, but that didn't stop her fear that others could. When Yula looked at her and dropped her jaw, Naomi ducked back behind the screen and peeked out from behind it.

Agatha came up to her and held out her hand. "Here's the cap," she said. It looked like she held nothing.

"Am I really invisible?" she asked as she reach out and felt for the cap. Her fingers skimmed over it. She plucked it out of Agatha's hand and gingerly put it on her head.

"You're mostly invisible," Agatha replied. She reached out and helped her tuck her hair under the cap. Naomi glanced over at Yula and found her watching them with saucer eyes.

"Define mostly," Naomi asked.

"Your eyes are still visible," Yula stammered. She turned to look at her again. Yula cringed a little under her gaze.

"Close your eyes," Agatha ordered. Naomi did as instructed. "Good, they disappear when you do that, but they will be visible when they're open. It can't be helped. The oil would hurt them if we applied it. The soles of your feet will likely be visible, too, since the oil rubs off easily. Remember that. Try not to brush up against anything."

"You'll still be detectable to animals, too. They can smell and hear you just as easily when you're invisible as visible," Mr. Squibbles added.

Agatha turned away and picked up something very heavy. At least, Naomi assumed it was heavy by the way she struggled with it. She couldn't see anything in her hands.

"Here's the shield."

Naomi quickly stepped over and took it from her. She blindly slipped her arm into the brace.

"And the unicorn horn," the witch said, holding out her hand again. Naomi took the now invisible horn with her other hand.

"Thanks, but if animals can sense me and my eyes are visible, how do we know this will trick Errilol?"

"It won't. You'll need to use stealth for it to work. Creep up on him."

"Creep up on a god. Right."

Yula let out a hysterical giggle. Naomi turned to her. Her invisibility seemed to be really freaking her out. "When you speak, I can see the inside of your mouth." Naomi couldn't help flashing an evil smile at her. Yula shook her head. "This isn't right, Naomi. There has to be another way."

She felt a twinge of guilt for causing her distress. "I'm sorry, Yula, but this is our only option."

"Do you even know where to find the god?" she demanded.

She nodded and sighed when she'd realized what she had done. "There's a temple that he resides in."

"I thought all of Errilol's temples were destroyed."

"This one's secret."

"You'll use the horn to get there?" Mr. Squibbles asked.

"Yes."

"So, you'll just teleport directly into his inner sanctum, run him through with the horn, and be done?" he asked.

She sighed. "Unfortunately, no. Like I said, the unicorns can't enter the house of a god; therefore they can't just show his inner sanctum to me so I could teleport there. I'll teleport to the entrance, sneak in, find the god's sanctum, kill him, and then call it a day."

"There will be guards."

Agatha chuckled. It wasn't a nice chuckle. Naomi got a sinking feeling. "I can slip right by the guards. It won't be a problem," she hurriedly said.

"That's right because we'll distract them."

"You aren't coming along," she said. She was determined on this. She wasn't going to put her friends in jeopardy again.

"You need our help," Agatha said.

Naomi closed her eyes. She angled the horn to stab herself in the thigh.

"Oh no, you don't, young lady."

She stumbled back as Yula slammed into her and grabbed hold. She staggered back. Her aim slipped, and the horn glanced off her thigh without drawing blood.

"OW! I'm doing this on my own! You two don't need to be involved!"

Yula held onto the arm holding the horn. Naomi tried to throw her off, but Yula merely grunted and held on tighter.

"Naomi, how badly do you want to save Tavik?" Agatha asked.

She stopped her struggling to blink at the witch. "I'm standing here naked on my way to kill a god. I'd say I want it pretty damn badly."

"Don't you think we want to help Tavik, too?" grumbled Yula.

Naomi looked at the scrunched up face of her friend. Yula's eyes were closed tight as she held onto Naomi's invisible arm. She might find Naomi's invisibility off-putting, but that wasn't going to stop her from stopping Naomi from doing something stupid. Naomi's resolve softened. She knew they cared about Tavik too, even Agatha in her own strange way, but she didn't want them to put themselves in danger.

"I can't ask you to do this," she said.

"That's fine, you don't have to. We're going to help either way," Agatha told her.

Naomi sighed, releasing her ill ease. "What do you have planned?"

Agatha's face twisted into a sinister smile. "You'll see."

Naomi's ill ease slammed back into her.

Naomi crouched behind a bush outside the entrance to Errilol's temple and waited with Mr. Squibbles for Agatha and Yula to begin the distraction. The witch had refused to tell her what she planned, and she didn't have anything to bribe Mr. Squibbles with to get the information out of him. Using the alicorn, she'd teleported them all to a clearing and crept to the temple while they got ready. They were to regroup there if they got separated once it was all over.

While Naomi had brought them there, she didn't know exactly where they were. She figured that she'd brought them south since it was a much warmer and humid climate than where they had been, but she had no way of knowing how many miles they had traveled. The surrounding trees were thick with vines and big, colorful butterflies. Mr. Squibbles warned her that they stung. The news hadn't surprised her.

The temple was a step pyramid like she'd seen on vacation in Mexico, but the entrance was at the foot of the building rather than at the top. Two guards stood at the entrance. They had tattoos like Tavik's on their foreheads. Naomi wondered if Agatha had a tattoo-removing spell. She felt sure Tavik would want to get rid of his once this was over. If he didn't, she'd demand it as an anniversary gift.

The guards were large, muscular men in full chain mail with large, heavy swords hanging from their belts. She wondered how Agatha would distract them. They looked as unflappable as the guards at Buckingham Palace.

"Yoo-hoo, could you help us, please?"

The guards' heads swiveled to the source of the voice. Naomi turned, too, but unlike the stoic guards, her jaw dropped. Standing on the edge of the forest was a woman to make men drool, chest heaving in a straining bodice, flaxen hair floating down to her waist, eyes that caught the sunlight and sparkled, and legs that went all the way up to her neck. She was Pamela Anderson's sister in a Ren Fest dress.

The blonde pin-up poster clasped her hands and batted her eyelashes. In a breathy, husky voice she said, "I am ever so sorry to disturb two important men like yourselves, but you see, my wagon has lost a wheel, and I'm afraid my sister and I can't manage to fix it."

"Your sister?" one of the guards asked.

The medieval Playboy Barbie looked around, and her brow scrunched in irritation. She reached behind her and jerked another woman up beside her. If breast size was any indicator, they were definitely related. The other sister hid behind the first, though by the way she was dressed, one wouldn't think she would want to hide. Flaunt seemed to be what her wardrobe was about.

"Yula, tell these nice men that we need their help."

Naomi's brain popped with the name drop. "P-Please, sirs, help us," Yula stuttered. Her voice was so low that they could barely hear her.

The guards broke from their posts and moved closer to talk to them. "Where is your wagon?" one of the guards asked.

"Just over here," Agatha said, pointing back into the jungle. The guards turned to where she pointed. Naomi saw her chance, and with the guards occupied, she slipped into the temple. She wondered what Agatha and Yula had planned for the guards. She knew there was no broken wagon, but she figured Agatha had some magical ace up her sleeve, or in her cleavage. She could probably carry quite a bit in there.

Naomi paused just inside the temple to let her eyes adjust to the darkness. A passageway stretched out straight before her with hallways bisecting it. At the end of the passage was Errilol, she was sure of it. She hugged the horn and magic shield tight as she crept forward.

Torches burned low and cast more shadows than light. She had no idea what she would find at the end of the passage. She ducked to the side twice when she heard the low rumble of male voices headed in her direction. When she finally reached the end of the passage, two huge doors and two equally large guards blocked her way. Naomi looked down at the mouse.

"My turn," Mr. Squibbles whispered.

Naomi moved closer to the guards, staying as deep in the shadows as she could. She closed her eyes to slits to make herself more invisible. She almost opened them wide, though, when Mr. Squibbles opened his mouth. As loud as he could, he shouted, "Errilol is so dumb that if he spoke his mind, he'd be speechless!"

The guards jumped at the sudden insult.

"Errilol is so stupid, he wouldn't know up from down even if you gave him three guesses!"

The guards drew their swords as they looked around for the owner of the voice taunting them.

"Errilol is so dumb, he'd try to drown a fish and throw a bird off a cliff."

The guards stepped from the doors to search for the voice in earnest.

"Ha, and his followers are just as stupid! You have to open your pants to count to twenty-one."

The guards were getting madder with each insult. They poked the shadows with their swords, looking for the voice. Naomi had to step aside once when they almost hit the shield. Mr. Squibbles scurried back down the passage to lead them away. "You all are so stupid, you tell everyone that you're 'illegitimate' because you can't read."

The guards moved further down the passage, slashing the shadows, hoping to hit the voice. Mr. Squibbles kept leading them further away.

Naomi crept along the wall to the doors.

"You guys are so stupid, you need twice as much sense to be a half-wit."

The guards disappeared around a corner, following the mouse.

She took a deep breath and prayed the doors were well oiled. She had a feeling that the guards would notice a loud creak no matter how badly Mr. Squibbles insulted them. She pushed open the door. It didn't make a sound. She opened it wide enough to slip inside and then carefully closed it. She stood pressed to the door for a few seconds, listening for an outcry from the guards, but she didn't hear any. She barely heard Mr. Squibbles' taunts anymore. He'd moved on to the size of the guards' members.

"Who's there?" asked a raspy voice.

Naomi whirled around and stared into the chamber. The room was circular, with more of the sputtering torches, only these burned green. At the center of the room was a large sarcophagus. She couldn't see the source of the voice.

"Answer me!" demanded the voice. She recognized the voice. It was Errilol. She was in his inner sanctum.

Naomi tightened her grip on the horn as she crept further into the room. Nothing moved or changed. The only thing of note was the sarcophagus. She kept her mouth shut.

The voice began to chuckle. "Naomi, is that you? I'm impressed. I didn't think you'd be this bold at all."

She stiffened at the god using her name. She wondered if he could tell it was her by the beating of her heart, because it was pounding loudly in her ears. The torches flared and lit the room brightly, giving everything a sick green hue.

"It was very clever to get a draught from Calax, but you probably didn't think of that. The unicorns are meddling, and after I made it very clear that I would not hold with any of their interference. Why don't you say something, Naomi? I'm sure we could work something out."

She ignored the offer. She had to find Errilol and stab him. The unicorns had told her that he would be in an earthly vessel. The only likely spot for this earthly vessel was the sarcophagus. She crept quickly up to it. It didn't have a lid. She peered over the edge and found a mummified body lying inside. This was it. She leaned over and raised the horn. She had to stab him in the heart. She brought the horn down with all of her strength. A crumbling hand shot out and stopped her invisible arm. The eyes in the shriveled head popped open. Green light burned inside them.

"I see you," Errilol chuckled. She wrenched her arm back, but the desiccated corpse came with her. Errilol continued to chuckle. "I see quite a lot of you. Have you come to offer yourself to me?"

The idea made Naomi sick, and puking directly onto the decayed corpse hanging off her arm might actually improve its looks. She didn't know if this body was once Errilol's, suggesting he was once mortal, or if the corpse were of a favored follower—and at the moment she didn't much care. She wanted to be free of the abomination and to kill the entity that animated it. She continued to pull away, but Errilol just came with her, his body sliding limply out of the sarcophagus. He wasn't exerting any effort to keep her still, but passively holding on like a rag doll with a claw-like grasp on her arm. She whacked the dead arm with the shield, but at the odd angle, she couldn't get any strength behind the blow to break the arm.

"Let go!" she shouted, not really expecting him to do it, but she really, really, REALLY wanted him to let go of her arm. She was going to catch something from him, she knew it. Rotted corpses were not hygienic.

Errilol chuckled. "But I could do so much for you. Just let me in."

The way he said "Just let me in," sounded dirty, and coming from the mouth of a corpse with rotted teeth made it just all sorts of wrong. She dropped the shield to pry at his fingers. She clawed at the bones, but she couldn't even pry one up. The bones were being held together with only bits of sinew, but she couldn't budge them. The god laughed at her futile efforts. It was infuriating. If she could just get him off of her, she'd be able to do what she came to do.

In a flash of clarity, she realized how stupid she was being. Her mission wasn't to get away from Errilol but to destroy him. Now that she'd dropped the shield, she had a free arm. She should use it. She switched the horn to her free hand and stabbed the corpse in the chest. Bones cracked under the force of the blow, and the horn wedged into the chest cavity. Nothing happened.

Errilol chuckled. The horn bobbed as his chest shook. "This is why women are not warriors," he said.

Naomi suddenly found herself airborne as the god tossed her aside. She skidded across the ground in shock. The horn hadn't worked. The unicorns had assured her it would. What had she done wrong?

Errilol stood now under his own power. He was no longer a rag doll but a walking abomination.

Naomi shakily picked herself up as she kept a wary eye on the god. She was now defenseless. The horn was still stuck in his chest, and the shield rested somewhere on the ground. She realized with unhappy irony that by making her weapons invisible, she couldn't find them.

Errilol grasped the horn to pull it from his chest, but searing light erupted from the object, and the god howled in pain.

Naomi crept around the god as she tried to pinpoint

where she had dropped the shield. It had to still be close to the sarcophagus.

The god tried to remove the horn again, but the light erupted once more, brighter than before. The god let out another enraged howl.

Naomi was practically blind now from the bursts of light, but considering that what she sought was invisible, the state of her vision didn't matter. She ran her hands over the floor, searching for the shield. She let out a silent sigh when her hand grazed it. She quickly slipped it onto her arm and it was a good thing, too because Errilol suddenly whipped around and grabbed her by the back of her neck. He jerked her up to his face. They were so close that if he had a nose, hers would've bumped it. She brought the shield up between them, gladly using it to keep his body from touching hers.

"Remove the horn, woman."

This close to the god, she noticed fine cracks had formed in his rib cage. The horn was harming him. She realized that he hadn't tried to grab the alicorn when he'd held onto her arm. It would've been simple for him to take it from her, but he hadn't reached for it once. When he'd tried to remove it, the alicorn had stopped him. He couldn't handle the horn himself.

"Having a little trouble?" she asked.

The god shook her by the scruff of her neck. She felt like the rag doll now, but even so, she saw more small cracks form in his bones, spider-webbing out. The horn was working, but maybe she could speed up the process.

Errilol brought back in close. When he spoke, his acrid breath coated her face, making her eyes water and nose burn. "My priests are on their way. They have killed your friends. Tavik is dead, too. He is no longer of any use to me. Give up."

She didn't believe him, but all he said could be true. She shook as she answered, "No."

"Why would I lie? They're dead. How could you think

you could destroy me? I am a god. You're only a puny woman, not even a virgin."

She knew he was doing something to her. His eyes were pulsating with green fire that made her head spin. He was trying to get into her mind, make her believe his words, influence her. She had to fight him. She thought about everyone who was depending on her: Agatha, Yula, Mr. Squibbles, the unicorns, and especially, Tavik. There were countless others. People across the lands would benefit from Errilol's demise.

"They're all gone. No one can help you now. The unicorns are powerless. They've already abandoned you. They knew this was a fool's mission. You stop me? I am a god. What hope could you have? But I could be magnanimous. I could spare you. Reunite you with Tavik. Serve me and all will be forgiven."

She needed to shut him up. Her head was feeling funny. His words were too cloying. They were beginning to distract her from her mission. She reached out, and her finger grazed the horn. "Yes, that's right. Pull it out, Naomi. It's the only thing you can do. I'll make you powerful and strong," he urged.

"I thought you said Tavik was dead," she said, the tips of her fingers just reaching the alicorn.

"Did I? I didn't mean it. He's alive and well. I'll send you back to him and together you'll be my terrible wrath manifest. Think of it: the power, the strength you'll both have in my service. There will be nothing to stop you."

"We'll be together?" she asked. Her hand closed around the alicorn.

"Yes, together. That's what you want, isn't it? To be with your husband?"

"That's what I want," she said as her grip tightened on the alicorn.

"Perfect. Now just pull out the alicorn and we will begin."

"I do want to be with Tavik," Naomi said.

"And you will be."

"But I don't want to share him," she said, and pushed the horn. It shot through the rest of Errilol's body until the point broke through to the other side.

Errilol screamed and threw her away again as bright light erupted from his chest. She hit the wall and slid down it. She woozily held the shield in front of her to block out the light. Errilol continued to scream. She thought the sound would make her ears bleed. The light was blinding her. She couldn't see Errilol or the room at all. She huddled behind the shield. She squeezed her eyes shut and threw her free arm across her face to block out as much of the light as possible, but searing whiteness still stabbed into her brain. The screaming continued. It would ring in her ears long afterward.

Finally, there was an explosion, and debris pinged off the shield. The light vanished. Naomi blinked blindly as she peeked over the shield. It took a few moments for her vision to clear. When it finally did, she saw a small blast crater had formed in the center of the room. There was no sign of Errilol. She noticed the torches no longer burned with green fire. They barely burned at all.

She crept to the crater's edge and looked into it. A broken unicorn horn lay in the center. There was no sign of Errilol. The blast must have completely destroyed his body. She hoped it had completely destroyed him as well, and he wasn't about to pop up in another corpse even worse than the last. The unicorns had assured her that this would kill the god, but if it hadn't, she was defenseless. "What are we supposed to do now?" she asked, looking down at the broken horn. Not only had it been her only weapon against the god, it had also been their ticket home. Yula, Agatha, Mr. Squibbles and she were now stranded. That was assuming that the others were alive. What if Errilol hadn't been lying?

The dim room began to fill with a golden glow. Naomi turned around and found herself once again surrounded by unicorns.

"I thought you weren't allowed in the homes of gods," she said.

They weren't, but it was no longer a home of a god. She had succeeded. Errilol was slain.

"Naomi!"

She turned to the doorway in relief at the sound of Agatha's voice. She couldn't help giggling at how the two women bounced as they ran into the room. They didn't look hurt in any way. They skidded to a halt at the sight of all the unicorns.

"Who wants to go home?" Naomi asked.

CHAPTER TWENTY

"Unicorns did not save my life. They gave me one."
—*Lord Tavik*

Naomi knew no fear as she stood in the courtyard of Tavik's castle because this time, she had her own guard to protect her, for who would be foolish enough to attack a blessing of unicorns? The castle inhabitants gathered around, slack-jawed. Naomi broke away from the unicorn she'd traveled with. Yula and Agatha had held onto a unicorn each as well to make the trip. The blessing of unicorns stood still in the courtyard, unfazed by the wonderment of the servants and guards.

Naomi entered the castle without anyone moving to stop her. Yula and Agatha followed behind her. They met Mrs. Boon at the foot of the stairs leading to the private chambers. The sour housekeeper didn't scrape her knee to Naomi, nor did she look at all pleased to see her.

Naomi gave the housekeeper a cool stare. "I would get my things in order if I were you."

"I am to be let go?"

"What do you think? You held me prisoner, lied to me, and worst of all, you enjoyed it. If you don't leave, I'll do the same to you."

Mrs. Boon's back stiffened, but she nodded. Naomi continued up the stairs and didn't pause again until she was outside Tavik's door. She stared at the wood beams. He was on the other side. She put her hands flat against the door and leaned her forehead onto it. It was almost over. Everything was almost over.

"Could you let me be alone with him for a bit first?" she asked her two friends, who had followed her up.

"Of course, dear," Yula said.

Agatha rubbed her back. "Go to him, Naomi. He's waiting."

She lifted her head and nodded. She opened the door and slipped inside. It was almost over. Errilol was dead. The unicorns were safe. All that needed to be done now was awaken Tavik. She felt a gut clenching fear at the task. It had been several months since he'd seen her. The time when he was delusional didn't count. What would he think when he opened his eyes? Would he be happy to see her or would he turn away?

She took a deep breath to steady her nerves. His reaction didn't matter, she told herself. All she truly wanted was to restore him back to health. If he turned away from her, she would go. She'd find something else to do, see if Agatha needed an apprentice maybe. His well-being was all that mattered.

She wished she really were that self-sacrificing, but she knew the truth. If he turned away from her, somebody was getting hurt in the physical sense. She'd lay odds on him. She'd just killed a god for him *naked*. What more could a guy ask for?

She marched over to the side of the bed. Someone had been in to tend him since her last visit. The burnt blankets had been replaced and repairs made to the bed. And the damn helm had been put back on his head. Why did they keeping doing that? She pulled it off roughly. Her irritation prevented her from being gentle. She turned it over in her hands to look at it. She was going to smash it. She'd find the biggest hammer possible and just destroy it. When she was done, no one would know what it had once been.

She was stalling. She was focusing on the mask because she was still worried about how Tavik would react to her return. She turned her eyes back to Tavik. Her hands went limp, and the mask slipped from her grasp to hit the floor with a dull clang. The Errilol's mark was gone from Tavik's forehead. She laid her palm across his forehead where the tattoo had been. The skin was smooth, but it was like a block of ice. She wondered what the priests and servants had made of his state.

She leaned in and laid her lips across his, which were cold and lifeless. She squeezed her eyes shut to block out thoughts of funerals and final farewell kisses. He was coming back. He would be okay. His lips remained lifeless under hers. She pressed her mouth closer, but it made no difference. Why wasn't he waking up? Tears began to leak out. She raised her head to wipe her tears off of him.

"Come on, Tavik. Wake up," she begged.

She lowered her head again to kiss him. The unicorns had assured her that this would work. She began to despair at the lack of response. If he didn't wake up, it would be her fault. She'd been the one to put him in this cold state. She'd done it to protect him, but it wouldn't matter if he didn't recover.

He still didn't stir. She rose and stumbled back. She'd call Agatha. The witch would know what to do. She turned toward the door.

"No, Naomi, come back. Don't leave me."

She whirled back to face Tavik. His eyes were still closed, but he'd spoken. She rushed back to the bed. "I'm here, Tavik. I won't leave you. I'm here to stay," she babbled. "Tavik, open your eyes. Look at me."

He didn't open his eyes, and the blue pallor had not lessened. Had she imagined it? She touched his cheeks. They were still blue and cold.

"Missed you," he breathed. She gasped with relief. But why wasn't he opening his eyes? She grabbed his shoulders and shook him.

"Wake up, Tavik. I need to know you're going to be all right."

It made her sick the way his head lolled on his neck. She jumped on the bed and straddled him. She held his head between her hands. He'd talked. He knew she was there. But she was missing something. She was determined to bring him back fully, but the only way she knew how was the way she'd been told. Kiss him, the unicorns had told her. She began to rain kisses down on him. She kissed his eyes, cheeks, forehead, mouth, ears, chin, jaw, eyebrows, and nose. She covered his face with kisses. Her lips swiftly grew numb on his cold skin. She was kissing his mouth once again when it responded and opened to her. Her cry of joy was muffled. She kissed him a few seconds longer before raising her head.

His eyes were open now. He looked up at her with wonder. "You're back," he murmured.

She dumbly nodded her head as she wiped her tears of relief away.

His brow furrowed. "I can't move my body."

She had an inkling why. She picked up his hand and brought it to her lips. She gently kissed it all over, not caring how the cold numbed her lips. His hand flexed and cupped her cheek. She laughed. Tavik looked bemused. She had just begun to kiss down his arm when the bedroom door swung open, and Yula and Agatha tumbled in. They picked themselves up and blinked at the picture of Naomi straddling Tavik on his bed.

"I don't think they've finished their hellos," Yula said, grabbing Agatha to drag her back out of the room.

Agatha brushed her off. "I think the sun will rise

before they're done." Naomi blushed and crawled off Tavik. Agatha came up to the side of the bed and looked Tavik over. "Well, how do you feel?"

He chuckled. "I'll tell you once Naomi's done with me."

Agatha raised an eyebrow and looked at her. Naomi could feel her cheeks burning brighter.

"He'll be all right," she muttered. Tavik chuckled some more. She sent him a warning look.

"But you kissed him, obviously, so he's fine," Mr. Squibbles said, sticking his head out of Agatha's pocket.

Naomi stared at her shoes.

Yula grew concerned. She came up to the bed and laid her hand on Tavik's brow. "But you must be all right. Naomi went through such peril to help you. She killed Errilol and saved the unicorns. The unicorns told her a kiss would save you."

She'd been holding onto Tavik's reawakened hand. It twitched and squeezed hers as he slanted his eyes to her. "Errilol's dead?"

"Can't you tell?" Agatha asked.

He closed his eyes and took a deep breath. They watched him tensely. She'd been sure Errilol was no more, but if Tavik could still sense him…

His eyes opened. "He's gone. I don't feel him at all," he said in wonder.

Agatha smiled and looked over at her. "Naomi did that. She saved you."

"Yes, she did." His eyes slanted back to her. She stared back.

Agatha slipped her arm around Yula's shoulders and began to lead her out. "Well, let's let these two get back to their kissing," Agatha said with a twinkle in her eye.

Once they were gone, Naomi groaned and flopped down beside Tavik.

"What's wrong?" he asked.

"Your mother knows."

"Mothers know everything."

Naomi propped her head up and looked down at him. She pulled the sheet back. "So, what would you like to get the feeling back in first?" she asked.

"You choose."

She ginned wickedly. "You're going to regret that."

"I highly doubt it."

The End.

ABOUT THE AUTHOR

S.A. Hunter lives in Virginia and works in a library.
She can be found online at www.sahunter.net.

She also writes The Scary Mary Series.

Don't miss the exciting sequel to Unicorn Bait ~
Dragon Prey.
Coming in 2014!

Made in the USA
Columbia, SC
28 March 2018